MW01601871

# THE WHITE SQUIRREL

From Northern Liberties Press a new novel...

# THE WHITE SQUIRREL

*Commercial artist Harry Pitman is a man who has a seemingly idyllic life—a good job with an advertising firm, a house in the country and an adoring child he can dote on. Pitman also is a man with a secret that could tear apart his life.*

*Hard-driving reporter Peter Gribbin lives for the hunt, whether he's chasing down the beautiful Barbara Smedley—wealthy socialite turned social worker—or the latest hot lead. Gribbin has little idea where his snooping into the mysterious Harry Pitman will lead him, but he is sure to follow his nose to its shocking conclusion.*

*Rotund lawyer Caesar Kent is the best at what he does. With a theatrical flair and mental agility that belies his large frame, Kent is a killer in the courtroom. This is a tale of the unlikely collision that sets Pitman, Gribbin and Kent crashing into each other. The stakes? A 13-year-old boy.*

# THE WHITE SQUIRREL

BY

LEE CARL

northern liberties press

**Philadelphia, Paris, London**

Published by
Northern Liberties Press
Old City Publishing Inc.
628 North 2nd Street
Philadelphia, PA 19123, USA

This book is a work of fiction. Names, characters, places and incidents either are products of the author's imagination or are used fictitiously. Any resemblance to actual events or locales or persons, living or dead, is entirely coincidental.

ISBN 0-9704143-1-5  (hardcover)

Library of Congress Cataloging-in-Publication Data

Carl, Lee, 1929-
    The white squirrel / by Lee Carl.
       p. cm.
     ISBN 0-9704143-1-5 (hardcover)
     1. Commercial artists--Fiction. 2. Journalists--Fiction. 3. Childhood--Fiction 4. Kidnapping--Fiction. I. Title.

PS3603 A75 W48 2001
813'.6--dc21

                                                        2001036366

Printed in the United States.

In memory of my wife

and

For my mother,
who started it all.

# ACKNOWLEDGEMENTS

Special thanks must go to my dear friends Fred Maher and Guy Griffiths – Fred for his conscientious editing, dedication and editorial suggestions; Guy for his publishing assistance and his wholehearted commitment to this undertaking.

# Chapter One

Her black hair separated as it lay about her shoulders and neck. Someone had combed it before Harry Pitman's arrival, turning a messy tangle into elongated ribbons that pointed in sundry directions. She sat awkwardly on the bench, her dark eyes focused far beyond the man who faced her, beyond the gardens and the evergreens, to some point of serenity in a drifting mind. Flesh was scant beneath her fair skin, sharpening her once soft features.

Harry glanced toward the late-day sun, then said, "I have to go."

Ellen failed to respond.

Clearing his throat, Harry tried to shake off discomfort, rose from his bench and repeated, "I have to go." He wanted to say more, but knew that the words would simply reverberate through space. How he had tried again and again, on this day as on others, to reach her with meaningful words and names—those that might awaken her, or even jolt her because they once bred trauma. "White Squirrel." "River." "Felix." "Freddy." "Oakford." Harry signaled a male nurse who sat beneath a tree 100 feet away, then turned and, without looking back, walked with heavy and deliberate strides across the grass toward the gate. His deep breathing gave little relief from a muggy afternoon that was much too warm for early September.

As in the past, Harry did not look back at the monstrosity of stone and bars, the old building, reminiscent of a far different time, some distant era of horror. North and south of the old building stood giant squares of brick—modern man's additions to

Northampton State Hospital—most of which were abandoned now, in the late seventies, because of up-to-date beliefs in letting loose the near normal.

A guard opened the iron gates. "Good day, Mr. Pitman."

Harry watched for cracks in the uneven sidewalk, lifted here and there by aging sycamores. His soft brown eyes were set beneath a high brow that led to dark hair streaked with silver. He was older than his 43 years, stood six feet, and wore a clean brown suit of yesterday's cut. His nose was straight, his features sharp.

When the walls gave way to shops, Harry crossed the street and entered an old brownstone station of castle turrets and cone-shaped roofs. He sat on a wooden bench and faced a barred ticket window and a wall of peeling paint. His thoughts rode a rough course, as they did after every visit, turning and twisting about yesteryear's joys and painful upheavals. In recent years, duty had replaced hope as the prime reason for his visits. That realization, long suppressed, now angered him as it troubled his conscience.

Only minutes passed before Harry boarded a two-car electric train that stopped at every hamlet on the eastern edge of Northampton County.

She didn't look much older, he thought while taking a window seat as the train moved. Almost unconscious of the movement or the sights about him, he allowed her image to return again and again to his mind's eye. She's just about the same, he thought. Sort of dormant. Suspended in a complacent agelessness. Some softness gone, but still pretty.

The recent image faded, as it did after other visits, to be replaced by the haunts of years past—Ellen, soft, shy and self-conscious on the college campus; Ellen, cuddling the white squirrel. How she loved that squirrel, Harry recalled. But then he saw her glow turn to anguish. He saw blood on white fur. And again thoughts of Freddy erased all else.

"Oakford. Next stop, Oakford."

As Harry stepped from the train his eyes fell on a smiling 13-year-old boy—blond, blue-eyed, straight-nosed, wind-blown, quick of motion, in sandlot baseball blue-and-white, minus the cap.

"You didn't have to come to the station." Harry smiled and put his hand on the boy's head and rumpled his hair. "It's a long walk."

"I got tired of waiting."

As they hurried toward a six-year-old, tarnished green sedan, one of but three cars at the small station, the boy said, "Millie fixed us some cold stuff. She went home early."

"It's her bingo night."

"How's Mom?" Freddy looked into his father's eyes.

"About the same." Harry opened the car door. "She seems happy." A frown deepened ridges in his forehead as he heard his own words. In truth, he didn't know where to place Ellen on a sad-happy continuum. And he had no wish to burden Freddy with an explanation of limbo.

"We still going to the fair?" asked the boy as if wanting to change the subject for his father's sake.

Harry had forgotten about the Woodbine street fair. But it was Friday night, and he had promised. "Okay. After we clean up and eat."

Special events came seldom to Oakford, a vacation hamlet in a valley of hemlocks. The fair in nearby Woodbine was anxiously awaited by many, especially the scattered youngsters of the small towns and surrounding farms.

Freddy slid low in his seat, and a serious expression turned down his mouth and wrinkled his brow. "There was this guy asking about you." His voice was soft and sober. "He was hanging around the ball field."

"Who?" A sick feeling moved up from Harry's stomach into his throat as he tried to hide his alarm. "From where?"

"Said he was a reporter."

"What did he want?"

"He was talking to Billy Allen. Billy pointed to me, and the guy came over and asked my name. Said he knew you from Clarkton. He was friendly, but I remembered what you said about strangers. I told him I had to go."

Harry tightened his grip on the steering wheel. Nausea weakened him and he stalled the car in front of his house, a summertime cottage almost buried by tall pines and hemlocks. The house was like many in Oakford—clapboard, wide porch with wooden railing, well separated from other dwellings, thick

3

with overgrown plants and shaggy shrubs, paint peeling slightly under the eaves.

"Put on your long pants, Freddy. The blue ones."

The boy was quickly out of the car and onto the porch. The screen door banged as Harry lowered his head, leaned on the steering wheel, and pinched his troubled brow.

Harry Pitman loved his boy with desperation. He grabbed, held and cherished each hour of that love, fearful that somehow all would be taken from him. His love for the soft and youthful Ellen of days past blended into his love for the boy. It was all one now, and his life was centered on this 13-year-old.

Slow deliberate strides took Harry to the porch and into the house where he stood amidst a strange assortment of furnishings, somewhat unified only by the artistic nature of the man—a craftsman with a keen sense of color and balance. As with his dress, he had allowed things to slip and fade a little, partly from years of preoccupation. The few Victorian leftovers from Ellen's Aunt Beatrice were not obtrusive among the Early American couches and chairs that had been trucked from Clarkton after the closing of the Logan Drive house. Braid rugs and prints fit much better in the Oakford cottage than did Beatrice's overbearing ornaments, the remainder of which were purely accents. Harry's oil paintings of winter and summer along the Logan were the eye-catchers. The room gave comfort, especially on winter nights when the brick fireplace blazed. Father and son would squat on the floor and warm themselves. Freddy would listen and try to understand his father's thoughts about life. Love would deepen.

The boy was pleased that Millie had left early, for it was special to sit alone with his dad at the kitchen table and wrap bread around lunch meat—sort of like an indoor picnic.

The Pitman kitchen was somewhat sterile—pale yellow walls trimmed with white woodwork. But it contained the latest devices to ease work for Millie, the housekeeper.

"That all you eatin', Dad?"

"I'm not hungry."

"Something's wrong, isn't it?"

"No."

Harry wanted to know more about the stranger. He would ask a few questions before bedtime, and maybe a few in the morning. Not too many at once. No big interrogation. Just casual queries, now and then. His heart was in his throat, and he couldn't get it back where it belonged. He kept trying to convince himself that a simple explanation would surface and allay his fears. Apprehension had nearly ravaged him before, but always blew into the wind as the cause evaporated.

Freddy sat on the back porch, surrounded by honeysuckle, impatiently rubbing one sneaker on the other. When the horn sounded, he was up like a springing kangaroo, sprinting, pouncing onto the car seat, and off with his dad into a still and warm evening, squinting at a low sun that edged the clouds with orange-pink. Winding roads took the green sedan through hilly farmland, broken here and there by dark clusters of trees.

Woodbine was typically small-town U.S.A. It was the hub of spokes leading to Oakford, Pineville, Shady Nook, Ageratum and Logan's Inlet. Tonight, the heart of Main Street was brightened by colored lights and balloons. The women of Trinity Church sold ice cream, the Woodbine Civic Club peddled fried chicken, the Fire Company Auxiliary displayed pies and cakes, and local businessmen steamed clams. Artists hung their oils and watercolors on clotheslines between booths of trinkets and knickknacks. But the crowds gathered at the carnival rides and games-of-chance.

Freddy ran to a bow-and-arrow booth sponsored by the Pineville Archery Club and waited impatiently for his father.

"Dad, shoot an arrow."

"Three shots for a buck," said the tall blond teenager in the booth. "Hit a feather and win a prize."

Harry reluctantly picked up a bow, but sent the arrow far above all feathers.

"Ah, Dad," said Freddy with a look of disapproval.

"Let's see what you can do," suggested Harry, who then put his arm around the boy to help him bend the bow. For a moment he held too tightly, as if wanting to engulf the youngster in the protection of his body. Freddy squirmed and Harry loosened his grip.

Together they sent a yellow feather fluttering to the ground, and

Freddy won a toy rocket that he slipped under his belt.

"You're a real champ, son." Harry rumpled the boy's hair.

Freddy sighted a fast-moving whirligig, hurried toward it, but stopped abruptly. When his father reached his side, the boy nudged him and pointed to a nearby booth where a man was tossing darts at balloons.

"That's the guy—the one who talked to me this afternoon."

Harry fixed his eyes on the stranger, who was about 35, dark, handsome, muscular but trim, and crowned with an overgrown bush of black curly hair. He wore a blue-and-white striped jersey shirt and tight white jeans. Next to him stood a woman of about the same age, but from a far different world. Her lavender pants suit was soft and flowing. Her blonde hair turned in as it touched her shoulders. She held herself in a regal manner. Even the way she tipped her head, curved her body, moved her shoulders and tossed her hair seemed to reveal her station in life. Perhaps she had escaped her blue-blood palace for the excitement of her bushy-haired friend with the bulging jeans.

Harry grasped Freddy's arm, hesitated, then said, "Go ride that... that, whatever it is. That thing over there."

"Aren't you going to ride?" Though Freddy asked, he knew the answer, having sensed his father's tense mood and interest in the stranger. He was well beyond his 13 years in reading silent messages and quietly accepting the unknown.

"Not now. Here." Harry shoved a few dollars into the youngster's hand. "Go ahead."

The boy hurried off while his father walked toward the dart booth, glancing back now and then. Apprehension was so severe in Harry that he feared it would impede his speech. But his words were sharp and clear as he spoke to the dart-thrower.

"Should I know you?"

The stranger lowered his arm, dart in hand. He looked into Harry's eyes and asked, "What's that?"

"I said, should I know you?"

"Well, I don't know. Should you?"

"You talked to my son this afternoon."

The man forced a smile. Yet he said nothing for seconds, as if toying with Harry. Turning off his sardonic grin, he said, "Oh, Pitman. Oh course. Harry Pitman. I should have known. Yes, yes, I recognize you."

The woman looked away, but continued to listen.

"Then you know me?" Harry's words were quick, his expression stern.

"To a degree."

"And what's that supposed to mean?"

"You wouldn't remember me. As for your old neighbors—I've grown to know them quite well. The Bakers? Surely you remember the Bakers."

Harry had learned control over the years, but could not fully hide the fear that flashed in his eyes. As for words, they came without hesitation: "The Bakers, yes. But not you. I don't know you. My son said you're a reporter?"

"I'm with the Examiner."

"Your name?"

"Gribbin. Pete Gribbin." The reporter kept his eyes on Harry's, as if unwilling to break the cat-on-cat stare.

"Stay away from my son."

"Hey, look man, I was just being friendly."

The woman could feel the tension. She glanced at her friend with disdain, then stepped away, but continued to listen.

"How do you know me?"

"I was there. At the drowning. Getting color from the neighbors."

Harry looked down, breaking the stare. Aware of his retreat, he spun around and looked for Freddy, then turned fiery eyes back on Gribbin and said, "I don't know what you want. But stay away from the kid. You get that? If you want to talk to me, okay, but stay away from the boy."

Harry backed off, then turned and hurried toward Freddy.

Peter Gribbin took careful aim at a balloon and threw the dart with force. The balloon quivered and squeaked.

"Getting closer," he called out to the woman.

"You can smell blood, can't you?" she said with derision. "On the hunt again. I might have know you wouldn't have driven sixty miles to take me to a small-town street-fair. You are a bastard."

"He's guilty. It's written all over him. Don't feel sorry for that son of a bitch, Barbara. And stay out of this one."

"Do I ever?" She pinched his nose, then kissed it.

"Goddamnit, I mean it! So help me, Barbara!"

"Where would you be without me to counter your aggression? Your enemy, I'm not." She ran her finger across his lips, then tickled his ear. Glancing about, she said, "I must say this is a page from a storybook of bygone days. I didn't know such fairs still existed."

# Chapter Two

Freddy closed his eyes and saw the lights of the spinning ferris wheel. Thoughts of the street fair carried him swiftly to sleep. Harry opened the door to look in on him, then stood quietly gazing at the ruffled hair on the pillow. The boy's lips were parted, and he breathed with the deepness of slumber.

Harry's smile was short-lived. The pain of fear moistened his eyes. He recalled romping with Freddy on grassy slopes in Willow Park, fishing with him at Lake Mohawk, digging for sand crabs with him on Inlet Beach. How well he remembered the boy's struggle with braveness when Ellen was first hospitalized—the tears, the tight lips.

Harry was slow to undress, and slower yet to fall asleep. A whirlpool of spinning lights and balloons rode a swift hurricane's course around a dark eye that opened to memories.

Ellen sat on a rock near a creek at the edge of campus where the trees opened to allow sunlight. Her face was smooth and youthful, fresh as the new morning, seemingly touched with the same dew that brought sparkle to the laurel leaves.

Harry hurried toward her. Youthful and agile, quickly at her side, he put his foot on the rock and rested his books on his knee. A thick outcropping of hair covered much of his high forehead. He wore a heavy sweater of white knit, for the autumn days were beginning to cool.

Twenty-two-year-old Harry had just begun his senior year at State College, where he was active and outgoing. His major was advertising with a commercial art emphasis.

Ellen was a junior, majoring in history. Shy and self-conscious, she had found her way into Harry's life simply because of his persistence, beginning when he sat next to her in Dr. Houck's anthropology class. She was thankful for his relentless intrusion into her life, because on her own she never would have reached out to him. Her dark eyes, fair skin, softness and quiet beauty attracted many a man, but she would never know or never believe. Her inner self could not recognize the Ellen of Harry's world, but she loved him for what he saw in her.

Harry kissed her, rubbed his nose on hers, looked into her eyes and asked, "Were you waiting long?"

"It's always long when I wait for you. We're late for class."

Ellen and Harry had arranged one class together—Dr. Glensheimer's course in art history. It gave her history credits while it gave him art credits.

"Let's cut class," suggested Harry with the bright-eyed urgency of lustful passion. "We'll go down by the lake."

Ellen smiled, reached out and took his hand and placed it on her cheek. "We can't afford another cut."

"Come on." Harry tossed his books to the ground and pulled her from the rock.

"No, really. We shouldn't."

"Yes we should."

"Can't you wait?"

"I don't want to." He tucked his books behind the rock and covered them with leaves.

Harry and Ellen scampered like children as they raced along the edge of campus, circling trees and rocks, grasping each other, teasing, laughing. They left campus where the maples and oaks gave way to open fields of goldenrod. Raising a cloud of pollen, they ran toward a grove of birches whose leaves had turned yellow. Not until they were among the silver-white trunks did they see the shimmering water of Birch Lake. Harry came to a sliding sit-down between two trees at the water's edge, reached for Ellen and pulled her to him.

"I love you, love you, love you," he said intensely, his neck muscles tight, his chin rigid.

"And I love you."

He rolled her over, and kissed her feverishly, almost harshly. She released herself, and he could feel her give in to him. Her abandon excited him.

In time he bared his legs and she squeezed the muscles of his firm thighs. He opened her blouse and buried his face between her breasts. For almost an hour they touched, moistened and fondled, renewing the old and exploring the new.

The sun was high by the time Harry retrieved his books. He and Ellen walked hand-in-hand toward the center of campus. They followed a zigzag route of concrete walkways, part of an elaborate system that tied together the red-brick buildings that surrounded the main quadrangle. The grass was still green, but the trees were beginning to brighten with autumn colors. Thick clusters of orange marigolds and yellow chrysanthemums lit up the garden beds. Students darted here and there, hurrying to and from classes.

Harry and Ellen stood outside of Palmer Hall, the psychology building. She looked into his eyes. "Let's have a baby boy first." Her words were whispery and warm. "Then a little girl." She twisted her fingers around his. "And after that I want a sandy-haired puppy with floppy ears."

Harry's eyes sparkled. "Okay. I'll give you all three."

Students hurried up and down the steps of Palmer Hall. Now and then one would try to catch Harry's eye. "What's the word, Pit!" called a redhead, who didn't wait for an answer.

"Hey, Pit, what's on for tonight?" asked Bill Newman, rah-rah man-about-campus. He put his hand on Harry's shoulder. "There's a party at the Sigma Pi house," said the tall broad-shouldered blond. "Why don't you join us?"

Harry looked at Bill and tried to gather his thoughts. "Tonight? Well, maybe." He turned to Ellen.

"Bring along the fox," added Bill.

Harry asked Ellen with his eyes.

"I... I don't know, Harry." Her face muscles tightened as her body tensed.

"Look, I got to move," said Bill. "If you can make it, just show

11

up. Okay?" He hurried off.

"Thanks," said Harry with subdued enthusiasm, and without turning his eyes from Ellen. "Hey, what's with you? I thought you were getting over that."

"I'm sorry."

"Don't."

"Don't what?"

"You know. It's always 'I'm sorry.' I hate that."

"But I am."

"Don't be sorry. Just come with me."

Harry had come to know Ellen's quick shifts in mood. He knew how she recoiled from the strong, the dominant, the gregarious. He was aware of her discomfort in social gatherings.

"I've embarrassed you again," said Ellen as she looked away from him.

"What the hell are you talking about?"

"I saw the way he looked at me."

"You're out of your mind!" He grabbed her arm. "How many times must I tell you that you see things that aren't there? Christ almighty." After sighing, he bit his lower lip. "Now, we're going to that party. And we're going to have a good time."

# Chapter Three

Harry was not a member of Sigma Pi, but he had friends in the fraternity who welcomed him to many a party. When he pushed his way through the doorway of the three-story white castle of stucco, pulling Ellen behind him, he found several of his friends sprawled on leather couches and chairs in the dimly lit, spacious room. The crest of the fraternity marked the wall above the stone fireplace. A dozen trophies lined the mantle. But nothing or no one kept Harry from hurrying Ellen to the back stairs, where laughter and song rose from the crowd below.

Dressing up in coat and tie for mug-swinging beer parties had just about vanished from Sigma Pi with the gray flannels and white buckskin shoes of the fifties. The sixties brought jeans, and it was still mainly jeans now. Harry knew he would find the Sigma Pi brothers and their dates elbow-to-elbow in the basement party room.

Also gone was the chaperon. He disappeared from fraternity parties years before the onset of mixed dormitories and overnight visiting privileges. No longer did a Sigma Pi man need to sneak his woman to an upstairs bedroom.

Harry and Ellen said a few hellos and knocked a few shoulders as they passed boisterous students coming and going on the stairway. They pushed their way into the crowded room—a long, dark room that flashed with colored lights. Road signs, flags, banners, restroom signs, a stop sign and a blinking traffic light decked the walls.

13

Ellen struggled to keep up with Harry as they made their way to a keg in the corner, next to a bar tended by pledges. Ignoring the pledges, Harry drew two drafts. Ellen's lips caught the foam as it overflowed her mug.

Harry joined in one conversation after another, always making an effort to include Ellen. But she was pleased when singing grew so loud that it erased small talk, even though the songs grew more and more bawdy.

When the crowd thinned enough to form a circle, the bleary-eyed beer-bloated brothers began their ritual chant. As the young men and women cheered and clapped, a petite brunette named Jane Haskins danced her own version of a fast-paced fraternity stomp, after being pushed in from the circle. The men grinned and whooped at every wiggle. Bill Newman was the second victim as the singing, laughter and mug-swinging intensified.

Suddenly Ellen pulled from the ring and hurried to the far end of the room where a purple wall held paddles dating back to 1910.

"What the hell's wrong with you?" asked Harry when he caught up with her. He didn't hide his annoyance.

"I'm not an exhibitionist." Ellen's fear was obvious.

"It's just fun. Christ almighty!"

"I'm not up to that. Can't we just talk?"

Harry bit his lip and stared into Ellen's eyes. Without much thought he barked, "It might've done you some good to be pushed in."

Ellen recoiled, her eyes showing disbelief.

Harry breathed deeply, then softened his harshness. "Jesus," he muttered. "Boy, you sure are self-conscious." His words sounded forced and foolish to himself.

Stepping back, Ellen shook her head as if to ask, You didn't know that?

Again Harry breathed heavily, sighed and said, "Okay. What do you want? Do you want to go upstairs? We can use Bill's room."

"No. Let's get out of here."

Harry forced a smile in an effort to warm his expression.

Ellen tried in return. "I've embarrassed you again."

"Hell, no. No, you haven't. Those guys are so far gone they

don't know their asses from their ... whatever."

"Please? Can we go?"

Harry kept looking into her eyes. He touched her lips with his finger. "Okay."

The night was cool. Stars splattered the sky. Harry and Ellen walked quietly, following the lamplit pathways. Classroom buildings were dark, but the library was still aglow, and scattered window lights brightened the dormitories. Harry put his arm around Ellen and drew her close.

"If you were like those other girls," he said, "maybe I wouldn't love you so much. Maybe because you seem to need me, that makes me need you. Maybe I want you because you're not always so damn sure of yourself."

Ellen simply held him more tightly. Not until they sat on a bench near a lamppost in front the women's dormitory did she speak: "Let's talk about when we're married and have a baby."

"Why do you do that?" Harry pulled his arm from her and stiffened.

"What do you mean?"

"Always talk about babies? I mean, hell, I want a kid—someday. But right now I want us. I want just you and me. Us. Together."

"It'll always be us. We'll always have each other. But I want a baby. As soon as we can have a baby, I want a baby."

# Chapter Four

Harry's ego required boosting, so Ellen met his needs almost as much as he met hers—maybe because he got little praise in his budding years. His yearnings went unanswered as Mama thrust all energy into her garden club, the hospital auxiliary and the historical society, while Daddy slipped off with the guys night after night. Not that his parents didn't buy him expensive gifts. But it was Ellen who looked up to him, clung to him, and gushed over his advertising layouts. A big hole in his psyche was filled when she praised his efforts, asked his help, squeezed his muscles, boosted his manliness. She, on the other hand, needed a dominant man who would cater to her wants, take care of her, fondle her.

Their needs led to marriage soon after college. Harry landed a job with a small advertising agency thanks to his workaholic father, a Chicago advertising executive who had contacts in the East, yet little interest in his son. The couple settled in a small house along the Logan River on the west side of Clarkton, a city within an hour's drive of Harry's workplace across the state line. The house was a perfunctory wedding gift from Harry's disinterested parents. Ellen's aunt, a frugal New England spinster, arranged for the wedding with money from Ellen's trust fund—the same fund that paid college tuition. Aunt Beatrice cared little for Ellen, but, as guardian, had seen to her schooling. Separating when Ellen was still a toddler, her parents had fled to new and unknown fates.

Harry and Ellen, therefore, were left alone to build their own, self-satisfying kind of life. Visits to his parents in Chicago would be seldom if ever. Their first year in the white house with the flagstone walk and juniper bushes brought fulfillment since each catered to the other. In particular, each enjoyed the other's body. They entertained seldom, though Ellen proved a capable hostess when Harry—with adequate warning—would bring a colleague home from the agency.

Harry turned out to be a man of surprises, often arriving home with a gift—sometimes flowers, now and then a stuffed animal. Ellen collected fuzzy, cuddly things.

Late in the second year, Harry's gift-giving became more frequent and his gifts grew larger, for he was confronted more often with the fact that he had yet to give Ellen the gift she really wanted. Checked again and again by her gynecologist, she now pointed her finger at Harry.

One evening in early summer, during their 20th month of marriage, Harry stepped from his two-door car in front of the Logan Drive house, only to hesitate and gaze at the late-day sunlight splattered on the river. He walked to the water's edge where the grass was thick from the spring rains, then turned and looked at his house as a peculiar feeling of inadequacy pervaded him. In time he followed his long shadow to the flagstone steps, glanced at the scrawny junipers, promised himself to buy more shrubbery, picked up the newspaper and pushed open the door.

"I'm home!"

Ellen was kneeling in the center of the living room—a room decorated through the helpful eye of her husband, the artist. They had chosen the burnt shades of autumn. Harry's oil paintings of Logan River sunsets and moonglows were framed in white.

"What the hell is that?" asked Harry as he stepped toward his wife and tossed the newspaper onto the couch.

A small, white animal squirmed on a orange-brown cushion on the floor at Ellen's knees.

"It's a baby squirrel."

"A white squirrel?"

"An albino, I guess. He's only a tiny baby, poor thing. I found him under the oaks, by the river. He can't see. He looks blind."

"I never heard of a white squirrel." Harry stepped toward the cushion for a closer look. He knelt near the animal and touched it with his forefinger. "Maybe he's too young to see. Or maybe he's sick."

"He wants to walk. Look."

"Probably wants his mother. He belongs outside."

"No."

"What do you mean, 'No'!"

"His mother doesn't want him."

"How do you know that?'

"Well, maybe she doesn't. Maybe because he's white."

"What are you going to do with him?"

"I want to keep him."

"Ellen, you can't." Harry looked at his wife with annoyance and frustration. "He belongs in those oak trees. He wouldn't be happy here."

"I want to keep him. He doesn't have the protective coloring of other squirrels. He wouldn't be safe outside. An owl or a hawk or something could easily spot him, swoop down and carry him away."

The tiny squirrel tried to leave the pillow, but Ellen picked it up, smiled, pursed her lips as if to kiss, returned it to the center of the cushion, and began to pet it gently with two fingers.

"Build him a box," said Ellen. "A big box. We'll fill it with leaves and twigs, and keep it in the kitchen. I'll feed him milk from an eyedropper, and later little bits of soft peanut butter."

"You have it all figured out, don't you?"

"And when he's bigger we can gather nuts and berries."

"When he's bigger he'll need to run up and down trees and leap from limb to limb. You can't keep him in a box then." Harry stood and looked down at Ellen. "What will you do then?"

"Please, Harry?"

"You'll get too attached." Harry walked around the room, toying with his hair. He was well aware of Ellen's attachment to soft, fuzzy things. "And when he's too big to keep, and we have to put him out, you'll get upset."

"Please? Let me take care of him."

Harry knew he would give in to Ellen's pleas, even as he continued to argue. Again and again he pointed out the problems of raising a squirrel in the house, but Ellen heard nothing. Before bedtime he had built a wooden box with walls two feet high, and had placed it in the kitchen near the stove. The next morning, Ellen replaced the cushion with dry grass and leaves. She spent much of the day hovering over the squirrel, attempting to feed it milk and peanut butter, and worrying about its closed eyes.

That evening Harry bounded into the house with news: "He's not blind! Look here. Read this." He found Ellen in the kitchen, stooping over the box. "Look at this." He held a booklet from the State Extension Service. "I stopped at the county agent's and got you this thing on squirrels. It say their eyes don't open until the thirty-seventh day. That little thing's not even thirty-seven days old."

This was the beginning of the season of the white squirrel. For much of the summer, life for Ellen and Harry was to revolve around the squirrel. Harry's interest was more in pleasing his wife than anything else. The animal gave him another chance to cater to Ellen and suppress any thoughts of inadequacy. He would bring home and proudly present every book or pamphlet on squirrels that he could find in libraries, bookstores and nature centers. As the squirrel grew, Harry helped his wife gather nuts and seeds. Twice he rebuilt the box, making it larger and giving it higher walls.

He became vaguely aware that doubts about himself kept pushing him into placating Ellen and gratifying her needs. His reward? She stopped taunting him, and, again, he postponed his visit to the urologist.

# Chapter Five

Harry actually grew fond of the white squirrel. And the summer became a season of happiness for him and Ellen. The project kept expanding and going off on tangents. Hunting for food in the woods, researching, studying the habits of squirrels—all this and more buoyed life overall. The intensity of the nurturing—a kind of passion that erased negatives—generated more and more excitement as it swelled. Before the Pitmans realized it they had become nature zealots who collected seed pods and pine cones, transplanted berry bushes from the woods, and learned to differentiate varieties of toadstools. One night, after feeding choice fruits and nuts to the squirrel, they cooked a pot of weeds for themselves—lamb's-quarter, plantain and pigweed.

"In February groups of male squirrels pursue a female in a noisy, energetic chase through the tree tops," Ellen read aloud one night at the kitchen table. Harry nodded and drank his coffee. It wasn't long before the books and pamphlets led to chipmunks and woodchucks.

In August Harry and Ellen joined the Clarkton Hilltoppers, a hiking group that followed winding trails up and down the slopes of the Allegheny foothills. He was pleased to see her mix, although she trailed quietly and often spurned post-hiking coffee or cocktail get-togethers.

Ellen named the white squirrel Felix soon after the veterinarian had declared him a male. Why Felix, she wasn't sure, except that it

20

seemed a cute name, fitting his pointed mouth, cat-like whiskers and twitching nose.

When Ellen was busy in the kitchen, Felix's pink eyes usually followed her, reacting to her movements and anticipating her frequent attention. He grew to know her habits and actions. At feeding time, he would scamper around his box, knowing she was on her way with acorns, beechnuts, pine seeds, or whatever. Ellen learned that hickory nuts were among his favorites, and that led to hickory hunts beyond the north bend of the Logan. It was there one day that Harry and Ellen sat on the earth, rested their backs against a hickory tree, and stretched their legs into a patch of huckleberry. They stayed later than expected.

"I love you," said Ellen. "You're so good to me." She put her head on his shoulder.

A moment later Harry turned about and settled his head in her lap. He looked up into her face with bright, sparkling eyes and smiled warmly. "You're still that soft, quiet girl that I married. Still a little shy." He reached up and touched her mouth and chin. "But I wouldn't want it any other way."

That night they arrived home long after Felix's evening snack of nuts and corn. They found the house in disarray. A lamp had been knocked over and cracked. Stuffing had been pulled from chair cushions. Candles and vases lay on the floor along with pieces of torn magazines.

"Felix!" shouted Ellen as she dashed to the kitchen. Harry was right behind her, looking over her shoulder.

"I knew it would happen!" yelled Harry. He looked into the empty box of leaves and dried grass. He hurried back through the dining area to the living room, glancing here and there at the havoc. "Son of a bitch! Look at what he's done. My God, even my college mug. It's smashed. He's too goddamn big for a box."

"Felix!" called Ellen as she looked about the living room.

"Squirrels leap from tree to tree. How the hell do you expect to keep one in a box?"

"Felix!"

Harry raced up the stairs two steps at a time. He found the bedrooms undisturbed. Then he turned on the bathroom light.

21

"Here he is."

"Where?" Ellen was halfway up the stairs.

"Here. Come looked at the little bastard."

Suddenly awakened by the light, Felix rose on his haunches atop the toilet tank and began twitching his nose. He held his silver-white plume of a tail upright.

"Aaahh, look at him," said Ellen warmly. "How's my little Felix?"

"He's got teeth sharper than a rat's, and they're going to sink into your flesh one of these days."

Ellen turned on Harry with fire in her eyes. "How can you talk like that? All of a sudden it's all my fault, right? You love Felix as much as I do. I know you do. But when something goes wrong you act like you had nothing to do with it." She went to Felix and he leaped to her shoulder. "You'd never bite your mama, would you, Felix?"

"Well, he's got to go outside. We don't have a choice. Didn't I tell you that long ago?"

Ellen held her cheek against Felix and ran her hand down his back. Continuing to pet, she cradled him in her arms and carried him from the bathroom.

"Put the pantry screen on top of his box. And put something heavy on the screen."

The night had its harsh and soft moments. Debate quieted to talk, then escalated to argument, only to slide back to talk.

"We'll build a bigger box," Ellen urged.

"Forget it." Harry was firm. He fretted over his broken mug as he maneuvered about the living room trying to put things in order. "What are we going to do about these cushions? Look at them!" He grabbed a handful of stuffing.

"Please, Harry. Let's try once more. With a bigger box. Maybe with a screen on it with a door in it, or something."

"He's going out." Harry showed extreme frustration as he stared at his wife. "Out. Understand? Out."

They finally reached an agreement. Felix would live outside, but Harry would build some sort of a home for him, perhaps on the back porch.

"Thanks," whispered Ellen that night in bed. She played with a piece of hair on Harry's chest. "I really do love you." Shifting, she pressed her breasts against him, and, moments later, fondled him. But her efforts failed to totally arouse him. Embarrassed, he turned away.

# Chapter Six

Autumn had yet to bring winds cold enough to nip the zinnias whose colorful flower-heads held themselves high on each side of the back porch and steps. Shades of red and yellow reached toward the squirrel house that rested on the north side of the small porch. Harry had painted the little house white and decorated it with Disney animals—rabbits, chipmunks and, of course, squirrels.

It was shaped like many a doll house, and even had a chimney on its slanted roof. It had two entrances, one leading from the porch, the other from the zinnias. But they were seldom used. Felix preferred a home in the trees and had found himself a deep hollow in a nearby oak. He often perched atop the little house, however, and gnawed on tidbits from Ellen.

The white squirrel had become famous in the neighborhood, for he was seldom missed as he flashed through the trees. Children sometimes sneaked into the Pitman backyard to watch him eat his dinner. Felix would stand upright on his haunches at the peak of the sloped roof of the Disney house. As if king of the perch and ruler of subservient zinnias, the princely squirrel would lift his head and tail and look about, then return to nibbling a nut.

The whole outside experiment troubled Ellen, who let little time lapse between visits to the back porch. Again and again she would open the door, or peer out through a kitchen window.

Felix often disappeared for long periods of time, especially as he grew accustomed to his outdoor environment and allowed his natural instincts to take over. It was right to chase other squirrels, and be chased; normal to scamper, climb and jump among the branches; natural to join in squirrel talk—slow warning barks, scolding and teasing chirps and squeals, and assorted playful chucks.

But Felix never forgot Ellen, and he would return to amuse her with his jerky tail-flicking. He would crawl slowly to her outstretched arms. She would hold him to her cheek, never fearing his bite. And he would accept her affection.

"You're so beautiful, Felix. Yes you are. Such a beautiful squirrel. And you're special. So special. Like no other squirrel."

Felix warmed Ellen's heart so much that her eyes would moisten. Harry knew that she gave too much attention to the squirrel, but pushed such thinking to the back of his mind, yet never admitted, even to himself, that he was trying to placate her. He loved her with a blindness that erased fault. Yet the blindness was somewhat contrived to protect. By giving in and rationalizing, he was able to accept all of her, helped by fantasies that kept alive his courting days at State College. He enjoyed watching her at toil or fun, and still became caught up in her smile and warmed by her touch. He could sit with her quietly, or run with her along the river; enjoy coffee with her at breakfast, or tickle her toes in bed. Harsh words melted as quickly as snowflakes on a warm cheek. So Ellen stayed soft and desirable because he kept her that way. His rewards were the warmth of her body and her caresses—touches that surely would never again fail to stiffen his member. Sex seldom failed to lead to a heart-pounding crescendo that was beyond anything Harry could imagine or verbalize.

September's last Saturday was warm. Yellow and red only tinged the tree leaves. Bright sunlight entered the window of Harry's upstairs study, fell on his left shoulder, and cast a bright streak on his drawing board. He pondered over an advertising layout, distracted by the noise of youngsters racing up and down the street and playing in the driveway. He went to the window and closed it, then returned to his drawing board.

Moments later he heard a muffled scream. T-square in hand, he raced down the stairs, through the kitchen, and into the pantry. He pushed open the screen door and saw Ellen standing on the grass amidst scattered, broken pieces of zinnia stems and crowns. At her feet lay Felix, still as death, his white fur smeared with blood. Next to the squirrel lay a bloodied, three-foot stick, white fur caught in its splinters.

"Oh, my God!" said Harry as he tossed his T-square. He hurried to his wife's side and put his arm around her waist. "Christ almighty, who would do such a thing?'

Ellen said nothing, but Harry could feel her body shake. She simply stared at Felix, her eyes glassy and distant, her lips parted and quivering, her complexion pallid.

"Go inside, Ellen," Harry urged. "Please."

She didn't move.

"Ellen!"

She seemed unable to move, as if immobilized by trauma.

"Oh, Ellen, please. Go into the house. Let me take care of this."

Suddenly she broke away and ran to the porch. She hesitated but an instant, then dashed into the pantry, allowing the screen door to slam.

"Son of a bitch," Harry muttered. "I'd like to kill the bastards." He kept asking himself: Why would they do this? How could any youngster do such a thing? Why? Why? Why? He kicked the bloodied stick, then kicked the zinnias. A moment later he raced to the garage and grabbed a shovel. After glancing about and circling, he dug a grave at the back of the yard, near a cluster of bushes. He returned to Felix, lifted him, carried him with care, and buried him. With an angry thrust he plunged the shovel into the earth as a marker. Later he would find an appropriate stone.

Fury raged in him. He gritted his teeth and tightened his fists as he stormed along the driveway to the front of the house. He looked up and down the street, then kicked pebbles and tripped, swearing aloud, as he hurried to the backyard. Breathing heavily like an attacked jungle beast, he stood in the middle of the yard, staring with angry eyes at the shovel. He needed to hit someone, throw bricks, smash windows.

Suddenly he wanted to be with Ellen. Again the screen door slammed, this time as he began his race through the house. He found his wife upstairs, belly down on the bed.

"Are you all right?' The question seemed inane.

Ellen didn't answer. She lay still, facing the windows, her eyes focused on infinity.

Harry sat next to her and placed his hand on the small of her back. "I'm so sorry, honey." He sought other words, but they didn't come.

Only breathing moved Ellen's body until Harry put his firm hands on her shoulders. Then she grasped his hand and squeezed it tightly. He kissed her on the neck.

"I loved Felix," she whispered. "Why would anyone want to hurt him. He was so beautiful." Only then did tears begin to well in her eyes. She turned and looked up at her husband. Harry smiled sadly as he wiped her cheeks.

That night Harry lay awake late attempting to console his wife. In the morning he rose early and made his own breakfast. He considered buying her a pet of some sort. But something pushed the idea from his mind—a fear, perhaps, that another animal would bring more heartache.

# Chapter Seven

Harry arrived home from work tired and burdened with an overloaded portfolio of dummy sheets, drawing paper and half-completed layouts on that October Friday, nearly three weeks after the slaying of Felix. His day had been tense and troublesome—a morning of displaying layouts for an important client, followed by a heavy 2 p.m. lunch entertaining that client. Too many martinis had put him nearly to sleep by late afternoon, but he pushed on until 5:30 trying to complete several sketches. It was then that he shoved his papers into his portfolio and started home with a headache.

"I'm here." Harry lowered his portfolio to the floor and leaned it against the wall. He wasn't totally happy to be home. Ever since Felix's death his anxiety had grown, increasing each time he opened the front door. Tension seemed to rise in direct proportion to Ellen's nagging—her mounting complaints about his failure to have his sperm checked. "Ellen, I'm home."

He found her in the kitchen on a stool with a sandy-haired, floppy-eared puppy on her lap.

"Where did you get that?"

"I found him. Isn't he cute?"

"What do you mean, you found him?" Harry's heavy head gave him little patience for riddles.

Ellen turned the sad-eyed puppy on his back and scratched his belly. "He likes to have his tummy rubbed."

"Where did you find him?"

"Along the river."

"What do you mean, along the river?" Harry continued to show annoyance. "That pup probably belongs to some kid who's worried sick."

"He wants so much love." Ellen lifted the puppy to her cheek. "He's so cute, so cuddly." The little roly-poly dog licked her face. "He was all alone. He doesn't even have a license."

"He doesn't need a license until he's a year old." Harry pushed hair from his forehead and sighed in exasperation. "Look, I'm tired as hell." He leaned against the sink. "I had a bitch of a day. Why don't you take that dog out of here and see if you can find its owner. Didn't you start dinner?"

"We're having tuna salad. It's in the refrigerator." She cradled the puppy in her right arm and stroked its head with her left hand. "You're a good puppy. Yes you are."

"He's a good-looking pup, all right, Ellen, but you've got to find his owner. Okay? You hear me?"

Ellen paid little attention to Harry's pleas. She smiled serenely as she continued to pet the puppy.

In a rare moment of rage, Harry yelled, "Give me that goddamn mutt!" He grabbed the dog from Ellen's lap and stomped through the house toward the front door.

"No!" Ellen cried.

"I'm taking him back where he belongs!"

"Wait, Harry!" Ellen ran after him. "Please? Just for a little while? I only want to keep him for a little while."

Before opening the door, Harry turned and faced his wife. Seething, he held back, made a deliberate effort to calm himself, then said, "Look, maybe I'll get you a dog of your own or something, okay? We'll talk about it, okay?"

Ellen didn't answer. She simply stared at him. Harry hesitated, then opened the door behind him and stepped away from Ellen.

"Two blocks up the river." Ellen's words were but a whisper.

"What?"

"I picked him up near that green house with the white trim, at Linden Avenue. Maybe he belongs there."

Harry couldn't believe Ellen's words. "You mean you picked him up way up there and carried him all the way home? You didn't ask anyone about him? A lot of kids live up that way. Did anyone see you?"

Ellen looked sheepish, then forced a smile.

"Jesus, I don't believe this." Harry backed away. "What were you doing up there? Hunting for dogs? Is that what you were doing? Were you out on some sort of a dog hunt?" He turned and hurried away, fearful of questioning her more. Without looking back he walked north on Logan Drive, his mind spinning. It was not easy this time to brush away Ellen's words and dismiss her actions. His love was not that blind. At one point he began to make excuses for her, only to be jolted by his image of her serenely petting the puppy. Her words about the green house and his thoughts about her carrying the dog for several blocks sent strange feelings through his body, frightening him.

He stroked the soft bundle in his arms, then lowered his head and let the puppy lick his chin. Depressing sadness mixed with feelings of apprehension.

The river was calm and glassy. The sun was low in the sky, and the trunks of trees cast long shadows across the grass. As Harry approached the pea green house trimmed in white, a gray squirrel scampered to an old maple and climbed to a low limb, alerting the puppy. Harry held tightly as the big-eyed pup yipped and yapped.

A tall, oval-faced woman with thick salt-and-pepper hair bounded out of the house as Harry mounted the steps. "That's Floppy!" she exclaimed. "Where on earth did you find him? We were worried sick. My son is out looking." She reached out to Harry, took the little dog, and held him to her bosom.

"Why, we found... or my wife found him," stammered Harry. "She thought maybe he came from up here. We live down the river. Name's Harry Pitman."

"I'm Elsa Bookman. Floppy's my son's dog. He tied him to that lamppost when the phone rang. He came back out in minutes, but Floppy was gone. We thought someone took him. Can't figure how he got loose." She held the puppy to her cheek.

Harry fished for words. "Maybe your boy didn't tie him tight enough."

"He's no boy. He's twenty-two. And he can tie a stevedore's knot."

"Oh."

"Where did your wife find him?"

"Along the river. Down there, somewhere." Harry pointed as he backed away. He hated his thoughts. He loathed the feeling that permeated his body.

# Chapter Eight

Although the images in his dream were still vivid, Harry began to hear the words, "Dad, Dad, Dad!" Freddy's calls mixed with the visions of sleep for seconds before they penetrated enough to bring consciousness. And they would have been slower in waking Harry if Freddy had not been kneeling on the bed shaking his father.

"Dad, get up! It's late!' You've been talking funny in your sleep."

Harry struggled to focus on time and place. His dreams had been deep and intense. It took time for him to fix his thoughts on today's reality and yesterday's anguish. Suddenly he remembered the reporter at the street fair, and the sickness of fear pervaded him. He grasped Freddy and pulled him close. Again, he held almost too tightly.

"Hey, Dad!"

Harry released the boy, looked into his eyes, and forced a smile. "Did you know that you were almost named Felix?"

"Felix?"

"Almost. Your mother wanted to name you Felix. But I picked Fred."

"I'm glad I'm Fred. I wouldn't want to be Felix. Nobody at school is named Felix. That's a stupid name."

"It's not stupid. But it's not you." Harry squeezed the boy's arms, then lifted himself and sat on the edge of the bed. He smiled and rumpled Freddy's hair. "Now, why don't you run outside and play with Billy while I get dressed? Okay?"

Billy was Freddy's after-school buddy. Together they did more than play sandlot baseball with a team sponsored by Pete's Fish Market. They explored the river bank and woods, caught frogs at Laurel Pond, collected toadstools, gathered clay from sewer digs to make pots that fell apart, and built a tree hut.

"It's Saturday." Freddy slid from the bed. "I thought we were going to do something together. You promised. Don't you remember? Besides, I haven't had breakfast yet."

Harry pushed his fingers through his hair. "Go on down and put the cereal bowls on the table. Let me get myself together. I'll be down soon, and we'll have breakfast together."

Freddy moved fast, his yellow hair flopping. Harry could hear his quick feet on the stairs.

"And pour us some orange juice." Harry words were almost too loud for his own ears. Sleep had exhausted him instead of refreshing him. He sighed, shifted, propped up a pillow, stretched his legs out on the bed, leaned back against the headboard, and stared at the ceiling.

He thought about another Saturday—the first time he had taken Freddy to the zoo—and recalled how it felt to hold the boy on his shoulders to help him see the hippos and rhinos. Then he remembered a winter night when his car had stalled in a snowbank near Beaver Valley. Help had been slow coming, the boy's mantle of bravery slipped away, and Harry worked hard telling tales of adventure and funny stories until flashing lights brought help. It was then the boy had said, "I love you, Dad."

Again Harry sat on the edge of the bed. He wanted to make things right before it was too late, but didn't know how. He could take the boy and run, but then he would always be running.

Clarkton tugged at him. It was a powerful magnet that would not stop pulling. What good would come of going there? What purpose would it serve? Yet he felt driven to walk its streets, gaze on the Logan River, climb the steps of the Examiner Building, open the door, and march into the city room. His irrational self did battle with his rational self. Plead with Gribbin? God, no. How he hated Clarkton, once the city of his love, of hickory nuts, of the white squirrel. Each building that flashed in his mind brought shivers of horror, as did the statue of John Clark in the city square. Twice his office had sent him there to woo clients, and he had prowled about like a KGB spy, fearful at every corner. Again and again he had scolded himself, telling his illogical mind that he had little to fear, but the trauma persisted.

Freddy sat proudly at the kitchen table awaiting his father. He had poured orange juice and filled bowls with cereal, topping the flakes with raisins and sliced banana. He had placed a candle on the table, not far from a pitcher of milk. Candles were for fancy dinners, he knew that, but he wanted to do something special.

The absence of Ellen had pushed man and boy into an inseparable bond. Each leaned on the other, yet supported the other. Each year had made Freddy more responsive to the void in Harry's life, and the more he gave, the more he loved. He often did the unexpected, such as shine his dad's shoes or straighten his bureau top. He had spent weeks one Father's Day polishing a river stone into a paperweight for Harry.

# Chapter Nine

The newsroom had quieted. It was 5:30 p.m., long past deadline for the late edition, and most reporters and editors had left for the day. Among the rows of computer terminals, only two units hummed and reflected blue-white light on writers' faces. In a far corner, a young sports reporter was putting finishing touches on a guts-and-tears locker room feature. And far at the other end of the rectangular room, baldheaded Jimmy Dunlap was pecking out the next day's obituaries on his computer keyboard just as he had pecked at his typewriter keys for years. Upgrading to computers had only recently taken place, as it had at numerous newspapers in the late seventies.

Peter Gribbin had pushed his chair away from his desk and positioned himself under the nose of the city editor, Clarence Day, who was flipping through the late edition. Day was another old-timer who missed the clatter of typewriters.

"I could do a story right now," said Gribbin, "if I wanted to pack it with maybes. And they'd be powerful maybes. Is the Baker kid still alive after all these years? Is he hidden away in a small town, miles from here? You know the kind of stuff."

Day, a thin, narrow-faced man with steel gray hair and a mustache, looked up from his newspaper. "We'll run it when you get the hard facts."

"That's what I want, Clarence." Gribbin was defensive. "Christ, don't get me wrong. Damn if I want to tip off the Courier. I'm just saying I could put together a piece like that, and I'd be damn sure of myself. But shit, I don't want Noski on the trail. And I don't want to spook Pitman either."

"From what you tell me, you've already done that."

"You think he'll run?"

"You tell me."

Gribbin looked at the ceiling and pondered. Day studied him for seconds, then grunted and returned to his newspaper.

"I checked the birth records here and in Northampton and Woodbine counties," Gribbin said. "And there's no Frederick Pitman. I called Stacy at the State House, and there's nothing there. I'll check across the river, but I'll bet you a fuckin' aardvark I won't find anything there either."

Day simply grunted again.

"You should have seen the bastard. Honest to God. You hear me, Clarence? I mean, holy shit, there was no question. Guilty as sin. He had it written all over his fuckin' face."

Day looked up. "So, what else do you have."

"I rechecked those dates. Nobody in the neighborhood saw Ellen Pitman after the drowning."

"It's been a long time."

"They remember others things. Some of them knew her. No, she wasn't there. But Pitman was. At least for awhile. I found a couple people who remember talking to him. The way I figure it, he joined her later, so the sudden move wouldn't look so obvious. Y'know? Hey, man, I've got him. No question. I just got to put the right pieces together and make the right moves."

Day looked up, but not at Gribbin. His eyes focused on the swinging doors beyond the shining head of Jimmy Dunlap. "You've got company. And she's storming."

Gribbin turned his head so fast that pain shot up his neck. "Uh-oh. Christ, I forgot her. Man, I've had it."

Barbara Smedley, dressed in a smart, white pants suit, stood just inside the doorway, her hands on her hips, a scowl on her face. The bright red silk scarf around her neck reflected its color on her angry chin.

Gribbin moved too fast from his chair. His ankle gave way and his elbow hit the edge of Day's desk, sending a funny-bone shock up and down his arm. "Son of a bitch!" Holding his elbow and limping slightly, he hurried toward Barbara.

"Goddamn, I'm sorry. The time just slipped away."

"Let's see," she said coolly. "You were to pick me up at five o'clock and take me to Omar Khayyam's for a drink before driving me home. And then we were to get an early start for the Journalism Society dinner. Or did I have it all wrong?"

Dunlap looked up and smiled, then glanced at Day and winked.

"Hey, Barb, I'm sorry," Gribbin whined. "The time just got ahead of me. What can I say?" He knew that her slow burns were sometimes dramatized, but usually short-lived. In truth, she had become accustomed to his forgetfulness and tardiness, especially when he was chasing a story. He glanced from Day to Dunlap to Gordy Evans, the young sports writer, then took Barbara by the elbow and quickly ushered her out of the newsroom.

"It's Pitman, isn't it?" she complained. "I can expect second billing for the duration, right? Unless, of course..."

"Unless? No, no, no you don't!"

With a quick spin, she turned away from him. "We don't have time for Khayyam's. Take me home. I want to change."

# Chapter Ten

Barbara Smedley was dressed in an expensive dress that tied about the neck and was open at the back. The color was lime—delicious, eye-catching lime. Cool and refreshing, the dress flowed softly to below the knees.

Gribbin hurried Barbara to his yellow sports car, perhaps because they were late for the dinner meeting of the Society of Professional Journalists, or more likely because he wanted to escape quickly from the stone "Castle of Smedley"—a sprawling house of many wings and porticoes. When he called at the Smedley home, the experience usually irked him, even intimidated him—and hard-nosed Pete Gribbin was seldom intimidated by anything. His late-night visits to Barbara's bedroom were exceptions, of course. Barbara's mother did not approve of Pete, and her father couldn't tolerate him. As for the residence itself, it was far from Gribbin's world. The graystone house with its many bay windows and steep slate roofs stood on a hill among thick evergreens on a 30-acre estate. It cast a frightful shadow on Pete.

The sports car sent pebbles flying into the hemlocks as Gribbin drove too fast around the curved driveway toward the gate. Barbara had strapped herself in, for she was well aware of Gribbin's frequent assaults on the family driveway—one of his "subtle" ways of telling Barbara that her father could "shove it."

Gribbin was a bright, earthy, quick-moving, hard-working reporter from a blue-collar family. He had worked his way through college, and had never expected to date a Vassar girl—especially one whose father had reaped a Wall Street fortune, and whose grandfather had made millions in the rubber industry by breaking the backs of immigrant workers. Though he hated Barbara's world, he was addicted to her—so addicted that he was willing to put up with her father's put downs.

Actually it was Barbara who had chased and captured Pete after a chance meeting. From that day on she had the guts to prance into the Examiner Building whenever she pleased.

Barbara had tired of the men in her social set. Their conversations had become as boring as their foreplay. The last of her efforts with so-called "acceptable" men had been a date with her second cousin, George Biddle Smedley, whose desire to look at her breasts, but not touch them, had prompted her to spill brandy in his lap. Barbara's decision to earn a master's degree in psychology was partly an effort to keep herself from drowning in a pool of blue blood. It had led her to the Nettleberg Clinic on Clarkton's south side, where two days a week she nursed neighborhood neuroses, much to her mother's distress. "That neighborhood! You know what those people could do to you? You could be raped! You could be murdered! My God!"

Gribbin had met Barbara while investigating misappropriations at the city's clinics.

By going outside of her circle, Barbara had made it easier for Pete to tolerate certain aspects of her life, despite his long-standing dislike for rich do-gooders. "They need something to play with, or they're feeding their freakin' guilt, or they're sucking up a tonic for their own screwball perversions."

Barbara's frequent need to champion social causes often plagued him—so much so, sometimes, that he would explode. Now and again she would interfere with his reporting, especially when she believed that some unfortunate soul was being unduly tortured by the press. And, to Pete it seemed she saw a curable sickness in every thief or murderer.

But they meshed well despite frequent arguments and the conflicting drives bred by his reportorial urges and her passion for the deprived. They relished each other's zest and energy. In fact, bedroom ardor seemed to burst from their fiery battles. Despite

Barbara's protests, she adapted well to Gribbin's stressful tension and explosive energy. She liked his forcefulness, firm body and combative lust. She found him tough and exciting in and out of the bedroom. His eyes were alive, and they gave truthful and trustworthy messages. During his gentle moments, she sensed his childhood hurts. She was among few who knew his soft side, so often hidden under his tough facade, and she had learned to draw his crazy charm out from under his protective hide. Gribbin was a born reporter who lived for the hunt. He had many enemies.

"You're preoccupied again," Barbara said. "Will you get Pitman off your mind while you're with me."

Gribbin lowered his foot on the accelerator, racing the car along Ivy Drive, a well-shaded avenue that wound through wealthy Eddington, Clarkton's northern suburb. He loosened his necktie, for the September evening was warm and humid.

"I think I'll go talk to that poor man you're harassing," said Barbara in a teasing tone to irritate Pete.

"And I'll bite off your nipples."

"Oh, Peter, Peter, pumpkin eater, you haven't learned that old lessen about honey and vinegar, have you? Some sweet talk from me might help him and you at the same time."

"Help him?"

"He seems like a nice man."

"You don't even know the bastard!"

"And you do?"

"Stay out of it, Barb, I'm warning you!"

"And if I don't?"

"I know you're just playing games with me."

"I've helped you before."

"You've gotten in my way."

"You don't like to concede that I've helped you. Macho man has to do it all himself."

"You're really irritating me, you know it?"

"I helped you with the Greybowski case, didn't I? If I hadn't collected funds for the family, you would never have found out that his wife was a cheating scoundrel."

"That was different, and you were lucky. I mean it, Barb, keep your itchy fingers out of this one. I can't afford a leak. It's not only the Courier, it's the cops."

"So you're out to get the Clarkton police, too?"

"They closed the case too fast."

Barbara slid down slightly in her seat and quieted. Within minutes she rubbed the back of his neck and toyed with his ear. "Pete, don't take me so seriously."

"I wasn't."

"You were trying not to, but you were." She massaged his neck.

"Well, sometimes it's a bit hard to trust you. Besides, I'm nervous as hell about this one."

The shaded, winding roads of suburbia gave way to Clarkton's busy downtown streets. The city was big enough to have a few high-rise office buildings, three department stores, a few fountains, a small art museum, a south-side slum, and even a short strip of porno shops. Gribbin drove around the city square and then to a layered parking garage across from the Logan House, an old brownstone front, once a private residence, but now a dining and drinking club. The Logan House board of directors leased its rooms for luncheons and dinners.

"I know we're late, but I want to grab a Scotch anyway," said Gribbin as he looked at his watch and rushed Barbara up the steps to the big oak doors. "Let's see who's left at the bar." He ushered Barbara past the leather chairs and portrait art that dressed the parlor and reception room, then into what had been a crowded barroom only minutes before. Now, only Joe Noski of the Courier leaned on the ebony bar, a massive piece of polished wood that extended the length of the room.

"They've gone down to the Paul Revere Room, Mr. Gribbin," said Jake, the bartender, a round-faced, bald man of about 60 years. "Except for Mr. Noski, of course." Jake stopped wiping the bar and glanced at the Courier reporter, a dark-skinned 29-year-old of slight build and sharp features.

Noski sucked up the last bit of bourbon from his glass, rattled the ice, then turned his bleary eyes on Pete. "Christ, if it isn't the Big Grib himself."

"What's the word, Joe?" Gribbin's greeting was devoid of any friendly spark. His long-term dislike for Noski had more than doubled since they were assigned overlapping beats. "You know Barbara, of course."

Noski nodded and Barbara forced a smile. She disliked him, too, and suddenly recalled her last encounter with him: a messy scene when he was even deeper into his bourbon.

"Gin and tonic for Barb," said Gribbin. "I'll have a short Scotch, heavy on the ice."

Noski edged closer to Pete. "I hear you've been asking questions about that old Baker drowning."

Gribbin might as well have been whacked by a bullwhip. He thanked God that he wasn't facing Noski, for the Courier reporter would have seen alarm flash in his eyes. He struggled to recover, but his mouth stayed open too long. Even Barbara felt dismay. She offered solace by tightening her fingers around his biceps.

Pete waited for his drink, poured down half of it, then turned toward Noski. "Who the hell told you something like that?"

"Oh, what do you call them? Friends? Acquaintances? Contacts? You know. The citizens who make things work for guys like you and me. Nice people, down by the river."

Pete looked into his Scotch. "I've got nothing yet, Joe. Just following a hunch that might blow into the wind."

"Let's go, Pete," urged Barbara in an effort to help him. "We'll be lucky to find a table."

That night's dinner meeting of the Society of Professional Journalists was agony for Gribbin. He and Barbara sat far from the speakers' table. But, more than anything, it was Pete's preoccupation with Noski that kept him from hearing Commissioner Leo Anastasia's lengthy explanation of the city's new urban renewal plan. On top of it all, he couldn't tolerate the small talk among four women at his table. The gregarious foursome, all from the social desks of the Examiner and Courier, occasionally felt obligated to draw him into their conversation, much to his displeasure.

Later that night, as Pete drove toward Eddington, Barbara criticized: "You could have done more than grunt. You were miserable company, do you realize that? Really miserable. Did you see Sally Grove staring at you in disgust?"

"I should worry about Sally Grove?" He raced the car, hugging the curb as he cut around corner after corner.

"Go ahead. Get us killed."

"You know where I'd like to shove Noski's little weasel face, don't you?"

"You're possessed."

"Ever notice how he snarls every time he talks?"

"Really possessed."

"He wouldn't have tipped his hand if he hadn't been drunk. You know that, don't you?"

"He wasn't that drunk. I've seen him far worse."

Pete grunted as he fretted. "He had to be drunk. No way he would have opened his mouth. For him to tell me he suspected I was into that case—come on, no way."

"I think he knew what he was doing."

"Then I don't get it."

"May he has some other agenda?"

"Weasel!"

"Now you'll push even harder, won't you?"

"That first piece has gotta be mine. After that, it'll be a free-for-all. Everybody'll be into it." He gunned the engine as Barbara tightened her seat belt. "Maybe Pitman will crumble as soon as I hit him with what I've got. Shit. I wanted just a little more time first. I need more. Noski's going to get in the way."

"An exclusive story is more important than a person's life, right?"

"Not another damn lecture, Barb. You hear me?" Gribbin tightened his grip on the steering wheel and fed the engine. "That bastard's the only guy I know who won't fill you in when you leave a meeting to take a piss. Know what he did to Sam Green at Mason Borough Council?"

"Yes, you told me a dozen times."

"Said he'd fill him in, but never told him about Schmidt's resignation."

"I know. I know."

"Just forgot. Huh! Sure, just forgot all right." Gritting his teeth,

Gribbin sped the car around the dark curves of Eddington.

"Don't forget, there's a little boy involved, and maybe lots of love."

"We call it human interest, and it's part of the story." His tone was condescending.

"Sometimes your human interest comes a little too late."

"Oh?"

"After the damage is done. Like in one of your sob-sister follow-ups."

"For Christ sake, Barb, think of the Bakers. And the stupid-ass cops. If you want to talk about justice, we can talk about justice."

"Justice? Well, that's a surprise." Barbara was well aware that fairness stirred within Pete. Otherwise she might have flushed him out of her life long ago. She also knew that he seldom exposed his deep-seeded principles or idealism for fear of sounding preachy. Her keen insight and psychological training had helped her decipher clues that slipped through his elephant's hide. She realized that, long ago, his youthful battles with his childhood peers had forced him to conceal feelings.

Barbara said nothing as Pete drove onto the Smedley pebbles and, again, sent them flying into the hemlocks. He brought his sports car to a skidding halt before the wide steps of the main portico. Both sat quietly until Barbara looked at Pete and said, "Why the hell do I want you so much when you're such an annoying itch."

"Beats me." He smiled at her.

"Come on in, damn you." She sighed. "I don't know why I should, but I'll rub some of that wicked tension out of your shoulders and back."

Pete's smile turned into a silly grin.

Barbara's parents retired early to the East Wing, and she never hesitated to take Pete to her bedroom in the West Wing. It was there that he first saw her in the froth of a blue negligee, her body temptingly silhouetted in a misty cloud of chiffon as she flowed from her powder room into a richly furnished bedroom of plush carpets and draperies and a massive four-poster bed. He was accustomed to women who presented themselves in panties or nothing.

Barbara had been dating Gribbin for more than a year. She

would have skipped the negligee months ago if not for the turn-on it provided Pete. He would lie on her bed in his jockey shorts and wait. Despite his aversion to the house and its furnishings, he couldn't help but secretly relish the lavish setting that seemed to lift his station in life. At first it had been a game of lustful luxury that boosted his ego. He had since fallen in love, but that was no reason to give up the misty turn-on. Even the bed posts excited him. All he had to do was lie on the bed to bring full arousal.

"Peter the Great!" she proclaimed on this night as she spun about and stared down on him. "You think you're king of the mattress, lying there like a sultan awaiting the first of his harem."

"Don't," he said, aware that she had altered the ritual somewhat.

She unfastened her negligee and let it fall to the soft carpet. "Relax and forget about Noski." She climbed on the bed and began to massage his thighs. "Turn over and I'll keep my promise."

Pete seized her and kissed her forcefully on the lips, then tasted her neck and ears and breasts.

"Turn over," she repeated.

Barbara rubbed the small of his back. She fingered his ribs, then leaned forward and massaged his shoulders and the muscles around his shoulder blades. "Does this help?"

Gribbin grunted. Minutes later she tugged on his arm and he turned onto his back. He grasped her shoulders and pulled her against his chest, then rolled her over.

Pete knew how to savor the pleasure. But in time he raced on, and Barbara bit the corner of her pillow.

# Chapter Eleven

Freddy was outside playing with Billy when Millie, an obese woman of middle years, finished the dinner dishes, put a few personal items into her shopping bag, waddled into the living room and opened the front door. "I'm leavin', Mr. Pitman. See you tomorrow." A full-faced woman with rosy cheeks, she wore homemade, tent-like dresses that hung smoothly over her big bosom and massive hips. Her gray hair was streaked with black and pulled back into a knot.

"Wait a minute, Millie," Harry called from upstairs. He hurried down the steps, then stood close to her as he quietly asked, "Is Freddy outside?"

"He and Billy are out collectin' wood for their tree hut." She continued to hold onto the doorknob as her broad smile puffed out her cheeks.

"Did he say when he'd be back?"

Millie's smile slipped, and her eyes showed puzzlement. "Now, Mr. Pitman. Boys that age don't do that."

"I... I guess you're right."

"You know Freddy. He never misses dinner with you. I'm sure he'll be back in time, as usual." She stepped onto the porch.

"Wait. The reason I wanted to talk with you... Look, the office is sending me to Clarkton tomorrow." Harry tried to hide his anxiety. He made a deliberate effort to modulate his words. "It's possible that something could come up, and I could get a late start home. Maybe not. I'm not sure. But just in case, I was wondering if you could plan to stay late. Or just until I get here."

"Y'mean stay after dinner?"

"If I'm late, you and Johnny could go ahead and eat. And then, perhaps you could wait until I get here. I know it's a big favor to ask, and I hate to give you such short notice. But do you think you could do that?"

"I'd be pleased, Mr. Pitman. I'll plan on it."

"Are you sure?"

"Yes, sir. I'd be pleased to stay."

"Thanks, Millie. You're a sweetheart." He squeezed her hand.

Harry couldn't quiet his nerves. He paced the room, then walked to the kitchen where Millie had set two places for dinner. The aroma of beef stew on the stove failed to arouse his hunger. Within seconds he was back in the living room gazing out the window. He stayed there until he saw Freddy and Billy. The boys slapped each other's hands in a complicated high-five ritual as they said their goodbyes. Every emotion, from fear to love, road a hurricane's course within Harry.

Freddy felt his father's tension throughout dinner. He recognized forced smiles and strained efforts at happy talk. Harry's eyes were moist and intense with messages of love, yet at times remote or detached. Now and again they seemed to plead. Freddy wanted to connect in some helpful way, but nothing appropriate would gel within his confused thought process. He couldn't very well verbalize the nebulous. So he said little as he picked on Millie's stew.

"Working on your tree hut?" Harry asked at one point.

"Yeah."

"I thought it was done."

"We're adding on."

After dinner Harry used a needle to take a splinter from Freddy's finger, insisted that the boy shower, and then took him to a park concert where a local band played Sousa's marches. Freddy mumbled something about missing his favorite show on television, but immediately bit his tongue, realizing that some purpose must lie behind this switch in schedule, this sudden urge to be drowned in loud music.

Harry figured that Freddy was less apt to notice his preoccupation amidst the rousing sounds of Sousa. And for some reason he wanted to get away from the house. He needed the blaring of horns, the crashing of cymbals, the pounding of drums. Although the stirring marches hammered his brain and erased some thoughts, they failed to engulf him. He really couldn't concentrate on the music any more than he could focus on anything else.

Long after the concert, Harry opened the door to Freddy's bedroom, allowing the hallway light to cast a glow on the boy's face. He stood there, staring down on the sleeping youth. Within seconds he stepped to the bed and lowered his head to place a kiss on his forehead.

Freddy awoke. "Oh! Dad?"

"It's okay. It's nothing. I just wanted to check on you."

Gazing up from his pillow, Freddy saw only the silhouette of his father. "You can tell me, you know. I mean, we can talk about it. You always said we could talk."

"We will."

"It's that guy, isn't it?"

"What's that?"

"You know. That reporter and his lady."

Harry hoped that Freddy couldn't see his eyes. "We'll talk about it soon, Fred. That's a promise."

The boy tensed. The last time his father had called him "Fred" was after the TV news one night. For days his father seemed distant, television was banned for a week, and newspapers were quickly trashed.

"Sleep tight. I love you."

"I love you, too, Dad."

# Chapter Twelve

The century-old, five-story, flatiron building was wedged between Market and Clayton streets—arteries that carried traffic to and from the city square. Only the narrow, rounded end of the flatiron nosed into the square, exposing the building's entrance to the fountains and the statue of John Clark. The ornately carved granite between the rows of windows had darkened over the years. Pigeons roosted on the sills and under the eaves. Martin Levenson, publisher of the Examiner, had long ago considered a modern home for his newspaper, but scrapped the idea when the electronic revolution made computers necessary. Out went typewriters, Linotype machines and the old presses. The cost of equipment and up-to-date interior renovations left the soot-covered, pigeon-stained exterior standing in stark contrast to the bright and shining newsroom and business offices.

The competing Courier, on the other hand, had built a new plant just outside the city, its facade aglow in stainless steel and glass.

Harry could faintly hear the hum of the presses as he paced back and forth along the Clayton side of the building. Time and again he walked to the Examiner's entrance, only to hesitate, turn, and buck a chilling breeze as he walked back along Clayton Street. This was September's coolest day, and by mid-afternoon the sky was overcast and the wind gusty.

Thoughts crisscrossed his brain. His head ached. Frustration tore at his nerves. He was convinced of his inability to hide the truth. His secret lived only because no one had tried to expose it. He took this as fate, thought it strange, and marveled that year after year could pass without disclosure. At times he would almost forget. But the haunting past was always there, hovering over him, filling him with anxiety, molding his nature, tightening his muscles. At those rare moments when he would hear or see something that sparked fear, he would surmise the worst. Yet such panic always was for naught. The fearful flashes had taught him, however, that he could not stop the flow if the dam ever broke. His very nature would make him powerless. Pouring from the guts and disgorging all could make him whole again, if only it would not destroy.

"You've been a fuckin' weakling," he mumbled aloud. Seconds later he was fighting the thoughts that gave him those words, trying to tell himself that he had no choice but to be protective. "Like hell you didn't. The choice came long ago, you fool."

He could have talked, way back then—maybe on the day he parked his car in front of the Baker house, packed his drawing board into the truck, and carried his big lie back to Oakford. But now? He could get drunk and tell his story to a stranger in a bar, free his mind, lift some anguish. But then where would he be?

Harry made his turn in front of the entrance just as Barbara Smedley stepped from the building. He walked on, oblivious of her. After a double take, she stood watching him, her eyes on his back as he walked along Clayton. When he turned, she reacted instantly, spinning away from him and stepping off the curb. She crossed the street, only to stop again near the Dolphin Fountains at the foot of the statue of Clark. Once again she fastened her eyes on Harry. Suddenly, with resolution, she marched back across the street as he approached the entrance. Within a few yards of him, she called, "Mr. Pitman."

Harry started. His head sprang up and his eyes flashed with the fright of a wounded deer. He did not recognize Barbara at first, having seen her only at the Woodbine street fair. His lips parted slightly, but he said nothing.

"I'm Barbara Smedley, Pete Gribbin's friend. Perhaps you remember. I saw you that night in Woodbine."

"Oh, yes." Harry wanted to turn and run.

"Could we talk?" Barbara barely believed she asked. For an

instant she wanted to swallow her words and stitch her lips. She could feel Pete's fury.

"Talk?"

"Yes. I know a little place nearby." Her thoughts rapidly laid one rationalization atop another. After all, she could help Peter with his story by gathering the softer side. She could deepen the story by cushioning the hard facts with the human touch. As to her need to satisfy her curiosity—perhaps it was there, but it wasn't really important. She was not meddling so much as helping Pete and Pitman.

"I don't know."

"Come on. We'll talk."

"About what? I don't even know you."

"Let's not play games, Mr. Pitman. Believe me, you'll find it easier to talk with me than with Gribbin. Why not give it a try? What do you have to lose?"

"Really, I don't know... I'm not sure what you're getting at. I'm here on business."

Barbara simply stared at him with knowing eyes.

"Okay. Let's talk." Harry was not giving in to Barbara as much as to a nagging need.

Minutes later, on a narrow, cobblestone alley, Barbara led Harry into a dark tavern replete with mounted fish, sharks' teeth, starfish, hanging nets and ropes looped from mast to mast and tied into stevedore's knots. Harry picked a table in a far corner, under a giant blowfish.

"What would you like?" he asked Barbara as a small, blonde waitress, dressed in a brief sailor suit, approached their table.

"A margarita."

"A margarita," he repeated to the waitress, seemingly oblivious of her squeezed-and-lifted bosom. "And I'll have a beer. Just a draft. Of anything."

Barbara leaned forward as the waitress left and said, "So help me God, I'm not conning you for Gribbin. You'll just have to believe that. Pete's his own man." She smiled disarmingly. "Look, I like people. I work with troubled people. That's my thing."

Harry searched for something to say. "You think I'm some sort of a sick dude, is that it?"

"Like you said, I don't know you." She searched his face. "Look. Gribbin knows my compulsive nature. The truth is, he told me not to talk to you—in no uncertain terms. He'll have my head when he finds out."

"So, why this?"

"Let's just say I couldn't help myself."

"Con or not, you'll feed him what you find out."

"Let's put it this way. You come off anything better than a bastard, and I'll try to turn the story around. I'm the one who turned the Appleton grave-snatcher into a bereaved father. I made a thief from Nestleton into Robin Hood."

The waitress returned, and Harry was quick to swig half a glassful of beer. His face reddened.

Barbara looked directly into his eyes and said, "This doesn't have to be combative in any sense of the word." She smiled again in an effort to assuage his anguish.

"Your name is Smedley?"

"Right."

"Miss Smedley, I'm no fool. I was defeated the very day your reporter friend began his snooping. I'm not good at deceit, even though I may have practiced it because of the default of others. Perhaps that makes little sense to you."

"So, then talk to me. I'm a good listener, and I might be in a better position to help you than anyone else. At the same time I won't get in Pete's way. I can't do that. I wouldn't."

Barbara exuded an openness and honesty that Harry could not help but feel. For years his urge to unload had frustrated him to the point of crippling his functions. Yet this craving was blocked by a love so strong that he wondered, at times, if he might kill to protect it.

"They take a baby's footprints when he's born," Harry said quietly, his head down. "I'm standing on quicksand, and I know it. I'm well aware of the outcome. I know where Gribbin's digging will lead."

"What were you doing at the Examiner? Were you looking for Pete?"

"I don't know. I went to my old neighborhood and walked along the river. Then I went to the Examiner. I'm not sure whether I would have gone inside." He finished his beer and looked for the waitress.

"You wanted to tell your side of it, didn't you?"

"What is it the PR guys say? Get in on the first story if you want your side told." Harry lifted his head and studied Barbara's face. A weak smile turned his lips. "I guess I've already confessed to you, haven't I? I wondered how it would feel. Strange, but this would have happened long ago if anyone had tried. But no one came after me." He looked down again. "Why did Gribbin suspect? What led him to me after all these years?"

"He saw the suburban sports page of the Woodbine paper. Oakford kids' league baseball results. A story about your thirteen-year-old boy. He counted the years, and just wondered. Thought there was an outside chance. He's done it before—chased down other kids. You did the rest that night at the fair. It was in your eyes."

"Humph," Harry muttered in contempt for himself. "How about another margarita?"

"This one's fine."

"How do you explain things to a little boy?"

"Explain it to me. Start from the beginning."

Harry kept staring into his glass. "This won't be easy. It'll be through my eyes, of course, but I suppose little parts and pieces will come from what the boy has shared with me—his thoughts, his deeds. Damn. I guess I should start with my wife." Pausing in thought, Harry went on: "Ellen was soft in talk and touch. Happy in her own way. She's in Northampton State Hospital now. Did you know that?" He looked up.

"Yes. Peter does his homework."

"It figures." Harry bit his lip, then took a deep breath. "It's so hard to tell a story you've never told before, even though it wants to come out."

"Take you time."

"It'll drain me dry, Miss Smedley."

"Call me Barbara. Please."

Harry nodded to the waitress, who returned quickly with another beer. Again he gulped half the glass. The swallow took away his breath. He gasped several times, then struggled to calm himself. Seconds grew to minutes. "Ellen... Ellen was sensitive and shy. She had so much love in her—for all sorts of things—animals, flowers, children. Shortly after we were married she began to fret about not having a baby. I thought she was ridiculous and impatient. When she tried to talk about it, I'd push it aside. I know that's why she heaped so much love on other things—like Felix, the white squirrel. She raised him from a baby, only to have him beaten to death by the neighborhood kids. Things changed after Felix. They were never quite right.

"One day I found her with a dog that belonged to a neighbor up the street. I took it away, and she fell into weeks of depression. Then I bought her a little tan pup with floppy ears—just like the other one. She wanted to call him Felix, but I said no, you don't name a puppy after a dead squirrel. That disturbed her something awful, far more than it should have, and she never forgave me for the remark. It was strange. I can still see the look in her eyes. Anyway, we settled on the name Harvey.

"Ellen's attachment to Harvey differed from her love for Felix. It was possessive and obsessive. Even I had to walk on eggs around that dog. Her eyes would dart and watch. There was this underlying fear in her that something might happen to Harvey. She heaped all sorts of things on him. Silly toys all the time. Christmas was unreal. She even gave him birthday parties. I put up with it all. It brought peace. I was willing to pay the price. I guess that tells you something about me.

"One day I noticed a bluish tint to Harvey's eyes. I feared the worse. A kind of dread racked my innards, not because this floppy-eared dog might be going blind, but because of what it would do to Ellen—and my life. For weeks I said nothing. When I finally broached the subject, she turned me off. It was like she didn't hear me. The dog's eyes got worse, but she seemed to pretend nothing was happening. One day I escaped with Harvey and took him to the vet. He was going blind. When I told Ellen, she became angry with me. But I began to realize that she knew, that she was coping in her own way. She mothered him more than ever, catering beyond belief until he bumped into table legs and everything else and ended up shivering and shaking in a corner of the room. Then one night she washed him and sat up late brushing his hair. The next morning I found her kneeling next to him, tying a blue ribbon on his collar. She picked him up, hugged him, handed him to me, and allowed me to take him away.

# Chapter Thirteen

"City desk."

"Clarence, this is Barbara Smedley. Pete's not picking up his line. Is he there?" She spoke into a phone at the bar in Fishermen's Tavern.

"He's tied up with Evans right now, Barbara."

"That's okay. Look, I was supposed to meet him at the Tudor Inn for dinner. But it looks like I'm not going to get there. Will you tell him something's come up and I can't make it? Tell him I'll explain later. Okay?"

"Gotcha."

"Thanks, Clarence." Barbara hung up the phone and nodded to the busy bartender. "Owe you one, Tony." She hurried back to the corner table under the blowfish. "I cleared my slate," she said while sliding onto her chair. "For the moment, anyway." Staring at Harry, she saw moist eyes and wondered about his thoughts. She looked away for seconds, then focused on his face again. "You don't remember Gribbin at the drowning?"

"In a way I do, now. A couple of reporters talked to me. He may have been one of them. But there were other things that happened to me that day—things I'll never forget. They sort of wiped out the rest." Again Harry signaled for the waitress. "It was a Monday, but I didn't go to work because I had other plans—plans I kept from my wife. So I called in sick. It was a bad day for Ellen. She was at her worst. I stood in the living room listening to her."

Harry quoted his wife: "I can see what my life is going to be. It's obvious that I'm not to have anything. Not even a dog, let alone a baby."

"Ellen, stop feeling sorry for yourself."

"How could you say that to me? How could you?" She buried her head in a pillow on the couch and sobbed.

"Look, if we don't have a baby we'll adopt one. Okay? But damn, it's too soon. Give us a little more time, for Christ's sake."

Ellen said nothing.

"I think you need a change, Ellen. You need to get away from here. Take the car and go up to Oakford. I'll join you after I finish the Westley Company drawings."

She looked up from the pillow. "What? You want me to go up there alone? Are you out of your mind? What is this, anyway? You want to get rid of me or something? Is that it?"

"Cut it out, Ellen. That's stupid and you know it."

She sat up and glowered at him.

"We've hardly used that place since we buried your Auntie Bea. If we have to pay taxes, we might as well put it to some use. The air's great up there. It'll do you good. And I'll get there as soon as I can."

She stared at him long and hard, frowning in disbelief. "Careful, Harry, I might take you up on it."

"Why not? I'm serious. Take the car. I'll use the bus to get around. Go up there and think things out."

"Harry, I don't have to think things out."

"So, go up there anyway, just for the change."

"God, you're trying awful hard."

"Besides, the utilities are still on up there—the gas, the electric, water, phone, everything. Somehow we've got to take care of that."

"So that's why you want me to go up? To turn off the gas? Harry!"

"No, no, no. Not just that. Look. I'll tell you what. I'll see if I can move up my vacation, and I'll join you within ten days or so. Three weeks at the most. What do you say? Throw some things into the car and shove off."

Ellen did not respond with words. But her expression told Harry that her thoughts were spinning. She was contemplating something, for there was a glow in her visage. But it was mixed with a strange, haunted expression. After seconds of musing, she pushed herself from the couch and walked from the room.

Puzzlement spread fleetingly across Harry's face. He started to follow her, but his resolve stopped him, and he turned toward the door. "I'm going out, Ellen. I have something to do."

The river shimmered under the bright morning sun. The heat of the August day would climb above 90 degrees by mid-afternoon. Already a few youngsters were wetting their feet at the river's edge. Shrill sounds of cicadas joined the cries of the Baker's youngest child, a one-year-old boy playing in a pen on the porch next door.

Harry walked four blocks along Logan Drive, barely conscience of the sights and sounds around him, then turned away from the river toward a small business district several blocks east. His thoughts returned again and again to the Ellen of years past. How hard it had been for him to concentrate during his classes at the University when he knew that he and Ellen would soon scamper to Birch Lake. So soft, she was. So gentle. So warm. She made him feel strong. They would lie together and stare into the trees where the sunlight flickered, and little by little they would plan the rest of their lives. How happy she was at the start of their marriage. So much hope and anticipation. And fun. Teasing, kidding, touching, loving. Then, the white squirrel.

The small business district focused Harry's mind on his mission. He stopped at a yellow brick building, sandwiched between a pastry store and drug store. The nameplate on the door read Urology Associates of Logan County. Under the title were the names of three physicians.

Harry avoided eye contact with the patients in the waiting room. "I don't have an appointment," he explained to the blonde receptionist who peered at him through her window. "But I was wondering if one of the doctors could squeeze me in."

"Is this an emergency?" asked the chubby woman.

"Well, I guess not."

"Are you in pain?"

"No, but I have a serious problem that I'd like to get off my mind."

"Oh, I see. I understand. Wait a minute, and I'll see what I can do."

Suddenly Harry realized that the woman probably thought he

had a venereal disease. After all, who else would simply walk in off the street and plead to see a urologist? Glancing quickly at the other patients, he felt like yelling, Hey, I don't have VD! Honest!

Back within minutes, the receptionist said, "Dr. Costigan will see you sometime this morning. Please take a seat."

Harry sat in one of the vinyl chairs, next to an artificial split-leaf philodendron. He joined four elderly men, probably all with prostate problems, and a worried 20-year-old, probably fretting over a tingle in his penis.

By late morning, Harry's worries about Ellen churned in his head, and he was beginning to regret his decision to visit a doctor. He hadn't figured on a three-hour wait. Fidgeting, he was chewing on a fingernail when called, at noontime, into Dr. Costigan's office.

"Now what can I do for you?" asked the broad-shouldered, square-chinned man as Harry sat opposite him across a desk in a combination office and examining room. He raised his bushy eyebrows and looked at Harry from above his reading glasses.

"I haven't been able to get my wife pregnant. So... Well... I want to find out if it's my fault."

"Oh, I thought you had an immediate problem?" Dr. Costigan removed his glasses.

"My mental anguish makes it urgent. I'm having some problems. And today? Well, let's just say it's a bad day."

The physician kept his eyes on Harry for a moment, then stood, walked to a closet, and returned with a five-inch high bottle made of brown glass. "Here, take this. One day soon bring back a specimen of your semen. We'll take a look at your sperm."

Harry stood, took the bottle, but continued to stare at the doctor.

"Have intercourse, withdraw, and drop a specimen into the bottle," Dr. Costigan explained with impatience. "Bring it back here, and we'll do a sperm count."

Harry turned to leave, but was stopped by pictures in his mind's eye. Again he started to go, but his thoughts prevented him. He took two steps, hesitated, spun around and looked at the puzzled physician.

"Yes?" the urologist asked, still showing impatience.

"No, doctor. I'm sorry. Look, I don't want to do it that way. I'll give you a specimen right here, if that's okay. I'd like to get it over with. I don't want to come back."

Dr. Costigan pulled on his lip, then said, "All right. That's fine. Go through that door." He pointed. "There's a small sink in the corner and some tissues in a box near the examination table. Take care of yourself there. When you're finished, return here with the specimen."

The room was typical of those small, clean, bright units—the kind in which a patient strips in response to a nurse's command, only to shiver for many minutes awaiting the physician. Harry unzipped near the sink, but was slow to finish. Neither the room nor his mental state was conducive to fantasizing.

He cleaned himself and the bottle with wet tissues and returned to the office and waited for Dr. Costigan.

"Oh, there you are," said the physician as he pushed into the room about 15 minutes later. "Let's take a look at that."

The doctor took the bottle and led Harry to another sterile room, this one equipped with microscopes, flasks and tubes. He dropped a small amount of Harry's semen onto a glass plate and slipped it under a microscope. He studied it briefly, then called Harry to his side. "Well, you've got some there." His tone was cautious. "Go ahead. Take a look for yourself."

Harry looked into the microscope and saw a few spermatozoa slowly moving this way and that. "I see them. So, what are you trying to tell me, doctor?"

"Frankly, they're few and far between."

"That's not good, huh?"

"But what's more significant is their speed?"

"What are you saying?"

"They're sluggish."

"Which means?"

Dr. Costigan led Harry back to his office desk. "Sit down," he said as he slid into his swivel chair. "You sperm count is low, very low. But it's the sluggishness that prevents the little buggers from getting where they have to go. I must make it clear, however, that none of this means you can't impregnate your wife."

"You're being kind, aren't you?"

"If your wife is highly fertile, and one of those rascals finds his way up..."

"But it's unlikely. Right?"

"We have things we can do today." The urologist talked on, but Harry heard only words with little meaning. His thoughts crisscrossed and ran into each other. "We can gather your sperm and implant it in your wife and hope the little buggers go to work. In other words, we'll artificially inseminate her, but with your sperm, not that of a donor. It's important to know, of course, if your wife's gynecologist has found any female problems that might..." Dr. Costigan talked on and on adnauseam.

"Doctor, please," Harry interrupted. "Thank you. I appreciate your time. But I have to go." He was sure that his tight stomach muscles had moved into his chest and were now filling his throat.

Harry left the urologists' offices not only feeling inadequate, but with visions of his supplying emission after emission in little brown bottles, of his sperm swimming in petri dishes, of clinical sexual practices that would be far from romantic, of complicated struggles with timing and techniques and temperature that were certain to complicate and frustrate.

When he stepped down to the sidewalk he was greeted by screaming sirens and racing pumper-engines and rescue trucks of the Clarkton Fire Company and the Logan Rescue Squad. They held his attention only briefly, despite their roaring sounds and vibrations. His thoughts slipped back to his predicament and he began practicing the explanations that he would offer Ellen. As he neared the river, he saw an ambulance from Logan County Memorial Hospital speeding in the direction of his house. It was followed by a jeep towing a small boat that grabbed his attention and quickened his pace. He thought of Ellen's depressed mood.

Turning the corner, Harry saw neighborhood residents hurrying to the river's edge across from his house. Children were running and cycling toward the engines and rescue trucks. Two small boats were already in the water, and firemen and police were clustered about the equipment on the grass near the bank.

As Harry neared his home he saw that his car was gone. He felt relief, for only Ellen could have driven it from the driveway.

Perhaps she had gone on an errand. Or maybe she had started for Oakford. But that seemed improbable. Despite his urging her to go, a sudden departure without a goodbye would be unlike Ellen.

Looking toward the river, Harry stretched his neck to see above the trucks and equipment that blocked Logan Drive. He watched police attempt to clear the area of all but rescue personnel. Notwithstanding the confusion, a few more boats were soon in the river. While some men paddled, others swam against the swift current and dived. It was too soon for the grappling hooks.

Harry turned his eyes from the bright orange life-jackets and the agitated water, so splattered with sunlight, and glanced about for someone he knew. He approached Helen Molinski, a neighbor who was quick to talk.

"Terrible thing, isn't it, Mr. Pitman?" said the skinny, hook-nosed woman as she stepped away from a group of women gathered at curbside. She pushed wisps of black hair from her forehead. "But I always felt that Liz Baker didn't keep a close enough watch on her kids. I've seen that baby on the porch time and time again, screaming his head off, and nobody paying a bit of attention. Now, don't get me wrong. I feel sorry for her. I mean, my God, that beautiful child. I feel very sorry. Very, very sorry, poor dear."

Harry looked at the empty playpen on the Baker porch. Saying nothing to Mrs. Molinski, he followed his compulsion to hurry home and strode quickly toward his front door. He was surprised to find it unlocked.

"Ellen!" Harry didn't expect an answer. "Ellen, are you home?" He glanced here and there, found a note on the newel, picked it up and read: "Harry, I decided to get an early start for Oakford, as you suggested. E." The briefness of the note troubled him almost as much as the unlocked door. Keeping the note in hand, he sat on the stairs and re-read the words. Looking up, he focused on nothing as his body grew limp. He knew he should return to the street, offer his help, give kind words to the Bakers, or something. But he was immobilized, stymied by his emotions, angered by Dr. Costigan's findings, vexed by Ellen's sudden departure and her impatience to become pregnant. "Fuck!" He tossed the note, squeezed his upper arms and thighs, and told himself there was nothing wrong with his muscles, flesh or bones. "So what the hell's wrong with your jism?" Angered by the messages from his brain, he called himself a fool for fretting. "Who cares, asshole!" But he couldn't convince himself that he didn't care, no matter how hard he tried. So he lashed out at his wife. "Damn you, Ellen!" he muttered aloud. "Why is a baby so freakin' important?"

Twenty minutes passed before Harry grabbed the newel and pulled himself to his feet. He stepped to the entranceway mirror, gazed at himself, studied each part of his face, and told himself that he was whole, sound, undamaged goods. After flexing his muscles he opened the door and peered through the screen at the crowd, the emergency vehicles and the river drama. Between the tree trunks and under the low limbs he could see that a half dozen small boats had gathered in formation for a sweep of the river. Grappling hooks, fastened to cross-bars at the stern of each craft, were lowered by chains into the water. The boats, some powered by outboard motors, others by men and oars, were spaced and staggered to prevent tangling of hooks. They sent V-shaped ripples into the choppy water as they bucked the current.

Harry knew that most hope was gone, that the men were unlikely to retrieve anything but water-logged debris. Dragging was almost futile in the Logan River because of the fast current and the quick carry-off.

Suddenly the flaming red hair of Elizabeth Baker turned Harry's eyes. The tall, slender woman, fair and freckled, had bounded from her house. She ran across the lawn, followed by a nurse who shouted, "Mrs. Baker, please come back!" News cameramen photographed her as she hurried toward Police Chief Clarence Kirby, who was talking to a fireman near a pumper-truck in the middle of Logan Drive. Harry watched her hands fly wildly and move in furious gestures as she spewed anguish at the chief. Then he saw George Baker, a kindly faced blond with receding hair, run to her from the river bank, grab her wrists and hold them tightly. A slight man with chiseled features, Baker quieted his wife within minutes, turning her hysteria to whimpers and tears. His sad eyes followed her as the nurse led her back to the house. Harry stepped outside and froze for a moment as he watched Baker.

Minutes after Baker had returned to the river bank, Harry began to stroll toward Kirby, but stopped when the chief was approached by a newspaper reporter. He turned his attention to the river, where the boats were making wide turns to start another sweep. As he stood on the curb, gazing between an ambulance and a fire truck, his mind traveled back to Dr. Costigan, but only briefly. He pushed the thought away.

"You're Pitman, aren't you?"

Harry was startled to suddenly find Kirby at his side. "Oh, hi, Chief. Yes—Harry—Harry Pitman."

The chief was a short, fat, bald man, who was straightforward and blunt. He was seldom without a cigar in his mouth, often an unlighted stub that he chewed for hours. "You're the one who did those posters for the Policemen's Ball," he said, chewing his stogy stump as he talked.

"Right. That's right."

"Did you see anything?"

"No. I'm afraid not. I wasn't home. Just got back. Terrible thing. Really terrible. Anything I can do?"

"We're doing all we can. It doesn't look good. In river water like this, you get 'em right away, or you don't get 'em at all. Hell, that baby could be floatin' in the ocean by now. If it had been later in the day, when the tide was in, we might've stood a chance."

"Anyone see the baby fall in?"

"No, but we found marks right down to the water, and a bootee right on the edge. The kid went in all right, I'm sure of it. The Baker woman doesn't want to believe it. But they never do. I've seen it before." The chief lit his cigar and spit into the gutter. "I'll tell you, it's a fuckin' sin—these people who don't watch their kids." He nodded toward the Baker house. "That playpen has two or three loose slats." He puffed twice, but the cigar lost its light. "That's as bad as the Skinners over at Pinewood. Their kid drank a can of spot remover while they were puttin' down shots at Carney's Bar. Died before they got 'im to the ER."

"The Bakers are good people, though. I feel for them."

"Last week a stupid jerk in Berryside left his little boy in a car with the goddamn motor running. Leakin' carbon monoxide almost did 'im in. Kid was turning green when we got to 'im."

Harry simply shook his head.

"I'm assuming Mrs. Pitman didn't see anything?"

"She's not at home. She drove up to Oakford."

"When?"

"I'm not sure."

Kirby studied Harry's face.

"Early today sometime," Harry added. "While I was at the doctor's."

Kirby kept staring at Harry, as if expecting more.

"Ellen's aunt died suddenly," Harry explained, "and left us her summer home. Surprised hell out of us. We hadn't seen the woman in years. But she had no one else. Place is overgrown with weeds." Harry was suddenly aware that he had lost Kirby's attention, but he talked on anyway. "I'm glad Ellen wasn't here. She wouldn't take well to this."

Kirby turned and walked toward the river as a reporter approached Harry.

# Chapter Fourteen

Harry sat at the kitchen table and peeled heavy, fleshy skin from a fat sausage of liverwurst. He sliced and ate the pasty meat between gulps of milk. It wasn't much of a supper, but he had little hunger and no desire to cook. As never before, the uneven hum of the refrigerator annoyed him almost as much as a recurring drip from the spigot.

Outside, a gathering of neighbors stood quietly under the maples at curbside, their somber faces turned florid by a red sun sinking behind dark clusters of trees across the river. The hour of eight neared, a few boats and men still dragged the water, and firemen readied searchlights on the remaining pumper-truck. An ambulance rested in the shadows.

Harry pushed the liverwurst aside, leaned back in his chair and reached for the wall telephone. He dialed and waited, telling himself that no purpose would be served in telling Ellen about the drowning. He had yet to speak to George or Elizabeth Baker, and the thought troubled him. In truth, he was relieved that he wasn't tied closely to the Bakers and, therefore, drawn head-on into the tragedy. Neither he nor Ellen had developed close ties to neighbors. Their relationship with George and Elizabeth was one of warm hellos and pleasant small talk.

Nervously playing with the telephone's long cord, Harry repeated "come on" again and again as he waited impatiently for an answer. His anxiety mounted as the seconds passed. He hung up and dialed again.

A warm breeze wafted through the kitchen windows, carrying the smell of honeysuckle and drying the sweat on Harry's forehead.

"Hello."

"Ellen, are you okay?"

"That you, Harry?"

"Of course it's me. Why didn't you answer?"

"Answer?"

"Yes, I've been trying to get you."

"I was busy. I couldn't get to the phone."

"Are you okay? You took off so fast. Why didn't you wait for me?"

"I'm fine." Ellen's words were quick and cool.

"Well, you could have waited. It wasn't like you to take off like that. I was worried. And your note—it was so brief."

"I didn't know where you were. I didn't know when you'd get back." Her tone was distant and unsteady. "I... I wanted to go before I changed my mind. You said I should... I mean, you told me to take right off."

"Yeah, but I guess I expected you to say goodbye."

Ellen said nothing.

"Are you there?"

"Yes."

"Did you pack enough? Do you have everything you need?"

"I'm fine, Harry."

"I'll get up there as soon as I can. Maybe I could make it even earlier than I said. I suppose I could finish the drawings up there. In fact, I could commute to work from there on the train. It's not that far. And I know there's an Oakford station."

Ellen was silent.

"Are you there?" Harry asked again.

"I want to be alone for awhile. Besides, there's a lot to do up here? This place is all dusty and musty."

"You never wanted to be alone before."

"Harry, this was your idea? Why did you want me to come up here? I want to think things out, like you said."

This time Harry said nothing.

"Harry?"

"You sound funny, Ellen."

"I'm tired, that's all."

"Are you sure you're all right?"

"Yes. I'm tired from the long drive, I guess. Look, I'll call you in a few days. Okay? Please don't hurry up here. It would be foolish for you to commute. Take your time and get your work done. Besides, I want to fix things first. Goodbye, Harry."

The "goodbye" came so suddenly that Harry sat there holding the phone in the air as if waiting for something. Sucked deeper into depression, he felt that he was losing control of things. Although he had urged Ellen to go to Oakford, he was disturbed that she had gone, yet annoyed with himself for being disturbed. As his frustration and anger grew, he heaped more and more blame on Ellen for being uncompromising. "Lot's of people don't have kids or dogs or squirrels or anything, damn it!"

Later, long after dark, Harry began to shift blame on himself. Still at the kitchen table, he placed his head on his folded arms and reflected on the years. The more excuses he made for Ellen, the more fault he turned inward. Although not new, his flogging of self was more severe because of Dr. Costigan's findings.

The kitchen's copper-kettle clock showed 11:30 before Harry rose from the table and walked slowly to the living room. He peered through the screen door and listened to the hum of motorboats. Searchlights splashed bright flashes on the leaves of low limbs as beams of light followed the boats on the swollen river. The tide was in. Harry could hear hushed voices from dark clusters of men and women.

# Chapter Fifteen

Oakford's sidewalks were uneven, lifted by the roots of old maples. Its crooked porches were draped in wisteria and honeysuckle; its gardens crowded with perennials. Weatherworn, wooden houses, built mainly for summer use, were scattered in the shady thickets to the right and left of Harry as he walked from the small, dingy railroad station on this late August evening. All about him was a rough and ragged woodsiness of untrimmed conifers and abundant laurel.

Harry's suitcase pulled on his shoulder muscles as it tugged on his right arm. His left hand held a large, square box wrapped in white tissue and a blue ribbon.

Oakford was a cool and quiet place where vacationers forgot city life. It was unlike the bright suburban spreads of green lawns, neatly trimmed evergreens and freshly painted houses. In a few months the winds would bring heavy snows, and the town's population would shrink by two-thirds. This was a summer place, off the main highways, and not far from Lake Mohawk where boats set sail in season.

The walk from the station to Aunt Beatrice's cottage was long, but Harry didn't care because his mind was busy with a mixture of thoughts. Explanations about himself and questions for Ellen kept interrupting his efforts to make plans for a short vacation—plans that would keep Ellen and him busy, generate fun, and help build bridges. He toyed with ways of whisking Ellen from hilltop to valley in hopes of peaking her interest and filling her emptiness.

Harry thought he knew his way to the house, having been there twice before. Anyway, all village roads fed into Main Street.

He saw Aunt Beatrice's hideaway more as a liability than an asset. Its weatherworn clapboard troubled him, and the Victorian leftovers that filled its rooms downright depressed him. The house had been a repository for discarded furniture, a place where Ellen's aunt had unloaded the overflow from her city brownstone. He hated its beaded lamps, flowery carvings, patterned upholstery, braided trimmings and yellowed antimacassars that clung to the arms and backs of itchy old sofas and chairs—together a dark and heavy flashback to years long gone. The massive and elaborate furnishings did not mesh well with the lightweight, cottage, vacation environment. How pleased he would be, thought Harry, to see a pile of beaded and braided junk at curbside for trash pickup. But he held out little hope, figuring Ellen was more than burdened with dust, dirt and cobwebs. As for the ornate, 19th century sideboard—a monstrosity that seemed to fill half the dining room—surely it would be there to greet him, for he knew only too well that Ellen couldn't budge it.

Harry quickened his pace as he neared the house—a squatty one-and-a-half story cottage buried in hemlocks. Its gardens of white and pink phlox were overgrown with weeds, and its fireplace chimney was missing mortar and bricks. No trash cans or bundles lined the curb—though, from what Harry saw elsewhere, it was obviously pickup day. He pushed aside low branches, mounted the wide porch, and called through the screen door: "Ellen. Surprise! I'm here!"

Ellen did not respond.

"Hey, in there! It's me." Harry relieved his shoulder by dropping his suitcase to the splintery wood of the porch. He tugged on the door, but found it latched. "Ellen! Please open the door." For a moment he thought he heard the whimper of a child. "You there, Ellen?"

Another whimper—and this time Harry was certain he heard a child or an animal just as Ellen appeared in the doorway, her somber face peering through the screen. She said nothing.

"What's the matter with you? Open the door."

"You came today."

"Yes, I'm here."

"Today."

"Yes, I came today. I said I'd come this weekend. What's with you? And what do you have in there—a puppy or a cat or something?"

"I thought you were coming tomorrow."

"I got away from work early." Harry waited for a response. "What the hell's wrong with you? Let me in."

Having an almost childlike delight in giving gifts, Harry had hoped to greet his wife with a happy grin as he thrust forth the blue-and-white package while reciting a few lines from John Keats—all part of his bridge-building plan. He had decided not to deliver Dr. Costigan's message without first laying a upbeat foundation. Instead, he found himself wary and tense. He could feel his heart pounding as his eyes asked questions.

Ellen was distant, unresponsive, nervous.

Anxious and unsure of himself, Harry shifted the gift box from hand to hand, then lifted it high. "I brought you something."

Ellen didn't move. She continued to stare through the screen. Harry could not interpret her expression. Did it show fear? Annoyance? Disinterest? He was aware that her eyes focused beyond him, as if she were looking through him. She tightened her lips, then suddenly lowered her head, flipped the door latch, and stepped back.

Harry struggled clumsily with the door, box and suitcase. He bumped his knee on the doorjamb as he entered, let the heavy bag fall to the floor with a thud, tossed the gift on a wing-back chair, stood among the beads and braids, and stared at Ellen.

A child cried before either husband or wife spoke. Harry whirled to face the fireplace at the south end of the room. There, next to a high-back rocker, was a newly purchased playpen containing two blue rattles, a yellow teddy bear, and a one-year-old, blond, blue-eyed boy.

"Christ almighty!" Harry kept staring in disbelief, his mouth open, his heart beating heavily and fast. "God help me, it can't be." He recognized the towheaded Baker child. A painful sound, like that of a strangling animal, choked up from his throat. His eyes

71

were ablaze with fear and anger when he turned to face Ellen. His mouth was open, but he couldn't speak.

Ellen's nervous tension was obvious. Her eyes darted about the room. "Don't, Harry. Please, don't."

"Don't what?' Harry's cheeks quaked. "Oh my God, what've you done? Holy shit!"

"I saved the boy. I saved him from drowning." Her quick words sputtered from quivering lips.

"Jesus help me," Harry said under his breath. "What are we going to do?" he muttered to himself. His intense eyes pleaded. "Oh, Ellen, how could you?"

"Please Harry."

"Please?"

Ellen's eyes shifted to the child, who was holding onto the slats of the playpen, bouncing up and down. The little boy fell and cried. Harry could not turn and look. He kept his intense, moist eyes on Ellen and shouted, "You kidnapped that kid!"

"No, Harry."

"You stole him!"

"I love the baby. I need him. He was at the river, and I saved him. I saved his life." Ellen rattled on, her words piling quickly on each other. "I've been so happy these past weeks. You and I—we couldn't have a baby. The Bakers had three."

"Shut up!" Harry kicked the wing-back chair, sending the gift-package flying to the floor where it ripped as it struck an old brocaded footstool. Breathing deeply, he tried to calm himself. "This is wrong, and you know it. The first thing we have to do is call the Bakers, then the police." He rubbed his temples and wiped his brow. The tendons in his neck bulged as he swallowed. He paced back and forth as Ellen stepped away from him.

"When I picked him up, I just couldn't put him down."

"Ellen, listen to me." Harry tried even harder to calm himself. "You don't like to hurt people. You're a kind person, I know that. Why would you want to hurt the Bakers? You just don't take children from their mothers, from their parents. Damn, Ellen, this is sick."

"I wasn't going to."

"So why did you?"

"He felt so soft and wonderful, and he liked me. I could tell. I carried him into the house. And I held him and rocked him. I knew I couldn't give him up. I didn't know what to do. I ran around the house grabbing things. I packed so fast, and threw things into the car. And I took off with the baby. Oh, Harry, it's done now. It's done. Maybe it's not right, but it's done, and I love the baby. He's such a good baby. I'll make a good mother. I know I will."

A shudder raced up Harry's back as he turned and reached for the telephone that rested on the peeling veneer of a round, mahogany table near the door.

"No!" shouted Ellen. She raced to him, grabbed the telephone with ferocity, and yanked the cord from its wall socket. She stood there shaking, holding the telephone in an iron grip.

"You're nuts!" yelled Harry as he backed away from her. "I mean you've really freaked out! "

"Please!"

"Please what?"

"Wait."

"Goddamnit, Ellen, you need help."

"Just wait until tomorrow. Please." Tears filled her eyes and rolled down her cheeks. "Please. Give me one day. Please."

"Do you know what I did?" Harry's voice vibrated with high-keyed emotion. "I went to a doctor and got myself checked. That's what I did. And I did it for you. Are you listening? For you! So that maybe we could have a kid." He pushed back his hair and tried to catch his breath. He took in quick, short gulps of air as if hyperventilating. After seconds of effort with deep and slower breathing, he said, "I found out that my sperm isn't worth a shit. So, it's my fault we didn't have a kid. That's not easy for me to take. Do you hear me?"

Harry could tell by the look in Ellen's eyes that his words had come too late. She paid little attention to him, and stared beyond him, toward the playpen.

"But they have things they can do today," he went on. "They have so many ways of helping people have babies. Maybe they can help us. Maybe all they have to do is juice up my sperm a little."

Ellen said nothing. A slight smile touched her lips as she watched the baby.

"Listen to me, damn it!" Harry demanded as the baby began to cry.

"I named him Felix," Ellen said softly.

"Felix!"

"Yes. Felix."

"Felix was a fuckin' white squirrel!" Harry screamed. "A dead squirrel! A bloody dead, dead, dead squirrel!"

"Stop it!"

"That kid is Georgie Baker," Harry said, giving force to each word. "Georgie Baker! He's not a squirrel, Ellen."

"I know," she whispered. "We can change his name, if you wish."

"He has a name, damn it!" Harry stepped toward his wife. "This is all wrong, Ellen, and you know it." Making a strong effort to quiet his words, he repeated, "You don't like to hurt people. You've always said that you don't like to hurt people."

Suddenly Ellen burst into sobbing cries, tossed the telephone to the floor, grabbed her husband around the waist and held him tightly. Harry wrapped his arms around her and let her cry on his shoulder. Confused, afraid, puzzled over his next move, he found it difficult to convince himself that this was reality. His hands were cold and wet. Nausea moved up from his stomach. He was angry, yet sad. But he couldn't push her aside. He couldn't turn off his need to comfort her.

The baby's cries turned to playful gurgles.

"We've got a big problem to solve," whispered Harry. "You've been under an emotional strain. I didn't realize how bad it was. We have to fix things, you know that don't you? We have to fix things."

"I don't want to think about it now. Please? Just until tomorrow?"

Harry broke his grip and stepped away. "We have to act quickly for everyone's sake, including yours."

"No one knows anything, do they?"

"They think the kid drowned."

"It's been weeks. Maybe it's fate. Maybe it was meant to be."

"Christ almighty, do you hear yourself? Don't talk that way. You give me the freakin' shivers."

"Did the police question you?"

"Routinely. So did two reporters."

"And that was weeks ago. One more day won't matter. Nothing will change by tomorrow. We'll talk about it in the morning, and if you want to call the police then, you can. But I was thinking that maybe we could get rid of some of this furniture that you hate, move in our Clarkton things, and put some of your paintings on the wall." Her words were fast and desperate in their urgency. "You could commute to work from here. It's not that far by train. You said so yourself."

"Stop it! How can you talk like that?" Harry paced back and forth, waving his arms in frantic motion. "I don't understand your mind. It's weird the way you can switch around like that." He found it strange that Ellen could move from tearful emotion to a frantic sort of deliberate plotting. He watched her walk to the playpen, pick up the little boy and hold him in her arms. She smiled as she put her cheek against the baby's cheek.

# Chapter Sixteen

Harry awoke the next morning in a small, musty room where he had slept alone on a hard mattress of a single bed. A tiny splash of sunlight had found its way between the hemlock branches and through the room's only window—a dormer that cut into the sloped ceiling. The sunlight flickered as it touched his pillow and cheek, opening his eyes to a nightmare. Disorientation gave way quickly to frightening truth as he stared at the heavy rococo trim on the footboard. His stomach tightened.

Struggling with his dilemma, Harry lay on his back, gazing at the ceiling. He dreaded any course of action, yet knew he had little choice but to contact the Bakers and the police. Puzzling over approaches, he found no answers that satisfied. Surely the police would suspect him, also. He could say that Ellen was sick. Maybe a psychiatrist could uncover her problem and explain it. But then what would happen to Ellen? And what about the publicity? The news would abound in the media. Headlines would scream about the kidnapping. He and Ellen would be pulled apart and analyzed. What would people think? How could he explain it? He might lose some clients, and they'd talk about him. He might even lose his job. His employer wouldn't like the publicity. Maybe he'd have to move to another part of the country where people wouldn't point or stare.

Nonsense, he tried to tell himself, insisting that he was letting his thoughts run amuck. But minutes later the same thoughts, and more wild ones, jolted his brain. He turned to his side and pounded his pillow. "Son of a bitch!" His eyes filled with tears.

The splash of sunlight had moved to the footboard by the time Harry lifted himself, rubbed his eyes and sat on the edge of the bed. There he stayed for seconds, looking down at his toes. "None of this is real," he mumbled. "It's not. Oh God, it's not."

Suddenly Harry moved fast. He dressed quickly, not washing, shaving or brushing. Pulling his jeans to his waist, he stiffened his jaw as he tightened his belt with an angry yank. He shoved his bare feet into his shoes, left his suitcase open on the floor, and raced to the stairs with his red plaid shirt unbuttoned.

A few steps down, and Harry stopped on the stairs. He saw his wife playing with the baby on the floor near the fireplace. The boy gibbered and Ellen answered in baby talk. Harry took another step, hesitated, then sped down and out onto the porch without looking back. He kept going—under the hemlock limbs, along the crooked path, down the broken sidewalk.

Two hours later he stopped walking at the edge of Mohawk Lake. His stomach churned and a bitter taste rose into his mouth. Nausea and dizziness staggered him. He caught himself, sat on a rock and lowered his head between his legs. Minutes later he walked among the rocks near the water, then suddenly vomited on the boulders at the very edge of the lake. Wind caught his phlegm and slapped it against his cheeks as gulls swooped overhead. The sun slipped behind a small cloud, only to peek out and set the lake ablaze with millions of dazzling flashes. Harry turned his aching head away from the glare and rested his eyes on a grove of pines. Again he sat on a rock, this time with his back to the water. He picked up pebbles and tossed then one by one at a gnarled stump as his thoughts—the same ones that had pounded his brain all morning—circled again and again in his mind, refusing to go away no matter how hard he tried to expunge them.

"You stupid-ass jellyfish!"

This was not the day that he would call the police. No matter how hard he tried, he couldn't bring himself to do it. Each time he came close, he would slip back and hate himself for his weakness.

He avoided Ellen and the baby, nibbled on fruit and lunch meat, and went to his room early only to lie awake late.

As hours passed, so did the days—days in which Harry spent

more time away from the cottage than in it. Within him was the belief that he would return the child. But each passing day made the action more difficult. He was certain, however, that every delay was truly that—just a delay.

A no-man's island grew between husband and wife, a barrier to word and touch. In the haze beyond his reach, at those unavoidable moments, Harry would see Ellen caress, feed or bathe the baby. Each such instance sent him escaping to his room, to the lake, to the woods, or into the darkness of night. The bartender at the Oakford Tavern soon learned to pour bourbon at the sight of Harry, who often sipped until closing hour.

Images haunted Harry day and night. His daydreams were even worse than his nightmares. He was tormented by visions of his wife mothering and nurturing the child in her arms. How he wanted them to end. Yet Ellen-with-child seemed so right, so much a part of what she was meant to be.

On the 12th morning of his vacation, two days before its end, Harry stood in a heavy mist at the south end of the lake. His face was moist. Wet hair streaked his forehead. He breathed deeply, turned with resolve, and started toward the cottage. The walk was long, but mental stress weakened him more than physical plodding. His determination had slipped only slightly by the time the sun had burnt away the haze. It was still there when he mounted the porch. Through the door he watched the little boy push over a pile of blocks as the day's first sunlight brightened the room. This time he did not turn his back. He watched as a broad grin puffed the baby's cheeks. The child looked up into the woman's face for approval. Ellen kneeled among the patches of sunlight and talked to him. She stacked the blocks, and again he pushed them over, gurgling as he laughed. Harry stepped inside and stood against the wall. The scene drained his energy, stymied his speech, confused his thinking.

Ellen glanced at her husband, then turned back to the baby boy and piled the blocks again. "Weeee!" she exclaimed as he knocked them down and giggled. She put her cheek against the boy's cheek, lifted him, kissed him.

Harry had rehearsed strong words on his way from the lake, but they softened, then shriveled, then slipped away. His spineless psyche weakened him physically, increasing the weight of his hands and the pull on his shoulders as he stood limply against the wall. He gazed for minute on minute, watching the blocks fall again and again.

Moments later he mounted the steps slowly and went to his room, having said nothing to Ellen. What would become of her, he asked, if he took the child away? He knew part of the answer. She would be destroyed. Without question, to sever from the bosom was to ravage, but in what manner? What devastation? What havoc with the mind, the body, the spirit? He lay on the bed, staring at the ceiling, suffering in a sweat of hate and love—despising Ellen for what she had done, but wanting to hold her flesh against his.

The setting sun was brightening the western sky with streaks of orange as Harry left the house again, mumbling something about getting drunk. "You gotta fix things somehow, you gutless asshole," he told himself.

He returned late, slightly intoxicated, with a liter of bourbon in hand, went to his room, lay on the bed with the bottle next to him, and stared into the darkness. Minutes later he sat up, opened the bottle, and began to drink, craving the throat-burn of every swig, and praying that he could drown his thoughts for moments of peace.

The moon was high and the night was quiet when he opened his jeans and masturbated angrily, as if desperate for relief, begging for any pleasure, hoping for deep sleep.

When awakened by the light of the next day, Harry found himself clothed but unzipped, aching with a head that pounded unmercifully. The stench of whiskey and sweat and stale semen, the sight of his wrinkled clothes and flaccid penis, the weakness of his body, the sickness of his stomach and the ache of his head—all of this added up to a realization that hit him hard: he was punishing himself, perhaps destroying himself.

Harry showered, rubbing his body thick with lather, then rinsing away the soapsuds with cold water. He threw back his head and let the gushing jet pelt his chest.

When dressed in his navy blue suit, he looked into the master bedroom of Victorian chests and bureaus—Ellen's room, where the baby lay in a slatted, white crib at the foot of the double bed. After staring momentarily at his sleeping wife, he walked to the crib and pulled the yellow blanket from around the neck of the little boy. The baby whimpered, and Harry touched his tiny nose and puffy cheeks.

"Quiet, boy," he whispered.

The child took Harry's big finger in his chubby, little hand. When Harry tried to pull away, the boy cried and Ellen started. Yanking himself loose, Harry reached with both hands, as if to pick up the baby.

"What is it?" Ellen asked, springing up with alarm. "Is Felix okay?"

"The baby's fine." Harry stepped back from the crib. "But Felix is dead."

"What are you doing?"

"Nothing."

"Why are you here? Why are you dressed like that?" Ellen sprang from bed and took the crying baby into her arms.

"I'm going to..." Harry hesitated. "I wanted to talk to you."

"About what?" Ellen rocked the baby in her arms, then held him tightly against her boso

"I'm going to take... I've decided... I'm driving to Clarkton. I won't be back until late."

"Why are you going there?"

"I want to check on the house," said Harry, forcing himself to sound matter-of-fact as he backed toward the door. He turned and left the room quickly.

"Harry!"

"I'll be back tonight."

"Don't do anything... Please... Don't talk to anyone... Harry! Wait!"

# Chapter Seventeen

The leaves of the oaks on Logan Drive were giving up their green for shades of russet. Wind gusts carried flutters of yellow and red from the maples into the river where the leaves spun in whirlpools, then quickly vanished in the current and the brilliant reflection of the sun. A pumpkin rested on the Bakers' porch.

Harry stayed in his car across the street, staring first at his house, then at the Bakers'. His stomach tightened and churned with each minute that passed. He hated himself for his flaws, especially the one that immobilized him. His body was sapped by fear, and no matter how badly he wanted to unload the truth on George Baker, his need to protect himself sucked strength from his legs. The guilt that racked him was not enough to nudge him.

Looking away from the houses, Harry's eyes caught sight of a gray squirrel that scampered along the curb in front of his car—a quick-darting squirrel with fur thickened by the autumn winds. He was reminded of Felix and weakened even more, knowing full well that Ellen's problems had begun long before the stealing of Georgie Baker.

Why the hell did you come here anyway? Harry asked himself. To see which way the wind would blow you? Is that it, you stupid jerk? With your ass stuck to the freakin' car seat, you'll find zilch. And what if Baker sees you sitting here like a dead toad?

Harry glanced across the street and was immediately rocked by a shockwave. The flashing eyeshot of Elizabeth Baker's flaming red hair hit him so hard that stomach acid shot up into his esophagus as a pang jolted his heart. The tall, slender woman stood on the porch looking toward the river. Harry quickly, as if by reflex action, lowered his eyes and turned his head, only to glance back a moment later. She had come and gone, like an apparition that had appeared to reproach him, only to vanish, leaving him gored. Harry agonized.

Minutes later he opened the door a crack, pushed himself, but slipped back into his seat.

Nearly a half-hour more elapsed before he stepped from the car and started to cross the street. He walked directly toward the Bakers' house, stood on the sidewalk for a moment, stared at the porch and front door, shivered in spite of the day's warmth, then turned away. He walked hurriedly toward his house, fishing for his key as he bit his lower lip.

Inside, he pushed back against the door, squeezing the knob behind him until his fingers ached. He had escaped and, although tense, he felt the safety of the haven. Fixed and rigid, he did not let go until his heavy breathing subsided.

Suddenly moving into action, Harry dashed from window to window checking locks. He opened the cellar door in the kitchen and stepped down into the dark, damp basement. In one corner he turned a valve, shutting off water to the outside faucet. In another, he shut off gas lines.

Harry spent the next half-hour moving from floor to floor, checking, locking, arranging. He unplugged the TV and kitchen appliances, telephoned the post office to discontinue mail at the Clarkton address, then disassembled his drawing board and carried it piece by piece to his car. The sun reached its apex.

Harry was burdened with a duffel bag of socks, underwear and sundry items when he ran head-on into George Baker, home for lunch with his wife. Baker had just stepped from his car at curbside and was hurrying across the lawn when Harry, in a rush and not thinking, bounded from his doorway. Harry's start and abrupt hesitancy went unnoticed by his neighbor.

"Nice to see you, Harry. How's the vacation going?" Baker's friendly attempt was forced, as were most of his efforts since the so-called drowning. "You know, you left without turning off your sprinkler. I noticed it the next morning. I took care of it for you."

"Oh. Hey, thanks." Harry quickly buried his awkwardness in condolences: "Y'know, I've been meaning to tell you again how sorry I am about... Well, you know. I'm really sorry. Terrible thing."

"Thanks."

"I'm not here to stay." Harry's switch in conversation was abrupt, his words fast. "Ellen's still up there, and I'm heading back. It's so beautiful in Oakford this time of year, with the leaves turning color and all. You should see the pumpkins in the cornfields. And the lake... the lake... it's just so beautiful. Y'know?" Harry kept his rambling message going at breakneck speed: "Anyway, I thought I'd like to stay past Halloween. Maybe even until Thanksgiving. It seems the right place to be in the fall, know what I mean? We never had a place like that before, and we want to take advantage of it." Harry dropped the duffel bag on the grass and shook George's hand. "It's not that hard to commute to work from Oakford on the train. I might try it. I just might do it. We'll see."

"I don't blame you Harry. Must be nice up there." George had thinned. His cheeks were hollow, his eyes deep.

"How's Elizabeth?" Harry asked. "I'm sorry I didn't ask right away. I don't know what's the matter with me."

"It's going to take awhile. She took it hard. I'd say she's doing okay, considering."

Harry avoided George's eyes. He lowered his head as he searched for words. "Terrible thing," he repeated.

"Hey, it's okay. Please don't feel uncomfortable. No one really likes to talk about it."

Harry tried to respond, but said nothing.

"Liz sometimes has hopes that the boy is still alive, and that's my biggest problem. Not that a tiny hope doesn't enter my mind now and then. But it's more a wish than a hope, and I try to bury it. But Liz—she's not realistic at all. She doesn't like to face the truth. I often wish the police had found little Georgie's body. Sometimes a person has to see to believe. I keep trying to help her understand, but it's hard for her to accept."

Harry glanced about, then leaned over and picked up his duffel bag.

"Come in for coffee," George suggested.

"No. I'd better not."

"Strange, isn't it. We never really got to know each other well. I'd like to change that. I think I was too busy for a lot of things. I wish I had spent more time with Baby George." He forced a smile. "Please, why don't you stop in?"

"I've got so many things to load, and I'm running late. I'm closing up the house for awhile."

"Don't be uptight about talking to Liz."

"Oh, no. I'm not. I'm not."

"She needs to talk to people. I want to keep her busy. That's why I've been coming home for lunch. The kids are in school, and I don't like her to be alone for too long a stretch."

"It's not that. It's just that I've got a lot to do, and I want to hit Oakford before sundown. I told Ellen, you know?"

"Sure."

Harry hated himself.

# Chapter Eighteen

Christmas was but a week away when a "for sale" sign was placed on the Clarkton house, unbeknown to Ellen.

On a Friday night, four days later, Harry entered the Oakford cottage with an armful of packages. Ellen stood on the stairs, gaping as her husband squatted on the living room floor and opened bags and boxes. Shiny toy cars, a red fire engine and a brown-and-white stuffed dog were among the playthings that quickened her pulse. She wanted to rush down the steps and smother Harry with kisses, but didn't move or speak, fearful of destroying the moment.

Harry had yielded little during the autumn months, although now and again Ellen had seen a warm glance at the little boy when her husband was unaware of her watchful eye. When feigning sleep, she had even seen him smile and touch the boy. Not until now, however, had she witnessed such an overt display.

"Well, it is Christmas, after all," muttered Harry. "If the kid's going to be here we can't rob him of Santa Claus." He kept his head down. "But don't take this the wrong way."

Ellen said nothing, moved only slightly, and held fast to the bannister.

"Tomorrow I'll drive to the lake and cut a tree," Harry said, still not looking at his wife. A moment later he pushed himself up, left the wrappings strewn on the floor, walked to the kitchen, and began to fix himself a light supper.

Harry still ate alone and slept alone.

That night in bed he shifted and flipped restlessly, as he did so often. Again, unruly thoughts bounced back and forth, prevented sleep. Distorted nighttime notions seemed to scream inside his head and argue with each other. After rationalizing much of his recent behavior, he lashed out at himself, angrily asking, Who the hell do you think you're kidding? You've boxed yourself in, you idiot.

Snow began to fall shortly after midnight. In the morning a thick blanket turned blinding white when the sun broke through shifting clouds that split into fleecy puffs and sped northward with the wind. Trees and shrubs, thick with snow, cast long shadows from east to west.

Harry stood on the porch in his rough-and-ready jeans and jacket, allowing the wind to strike him and toss his hair. He wanted the piercing air to cleanse and purify, and hoped exhilaration would override his affliction. Deep breaths of cold air stung his throat and pained his lungs. He was strangely aware that he was about to step into his biggest self-deception.

Turning, then opening the door, he yelled "Ellen!" and stepped inside. "Come with me, and bring the kid. We'll cut that tree."

Ellen moved faster than a hawk after prey. She dashed about upstairs, splashed water on her face, and—fearful that he might change his mind—prayed that she would be ready in time. Before Harry called again, she was fully dressed in hiking pants, sweater and boots.

"Ellen, are you coming."

"I'll be right there. I'm getting Freddy."

Harry had re-named the boy in a fit of frenzy one night to help cleanse the house of the bloody white squirrel. He had tossed his copy of Webster's Biographical Dictionary on the kitchen table, flipped it open and pointed at the first name to catch his eye— Friedrich von Hugel, baron of the Holy Roman empire. "There," he proclaimed. "Call him Friedrich, damn it!" Seeing disfavor in Ellen's eyes, he made an adjustment. "Okay, make it Frederick. Fred. Freddy."

Harry returned to the porch for more air.

After dressing Freddy, Ellen rushed him to the kitchen for milk and a hasty spooning of applesauce—a far cry from her usual hour of breakfast doting over the boy. Nearly 14 months old, Freddy was learning quickly, could munch on his own banana, and could walk several steps without falling. He could also spew a few words, including "Mama."

Harry was brushing snow from the car when Ellen and Freddy stepped down from the porch. He turned and saw the boy bundled in a blue snowsuit and knitted cap, holding Ellen's hand, and walking awkwardly through the snow. Freddy smiled, pointed to the car and said, "Ca... ca." After opening the car door, Harry reached for the boy as if to lift him, only to change his mind and walk to the driver's side.

Neither husband nor wife spoke as they sped into the countryside toward Lake Mohawk. Only Freddy made sounds— most of them unintelligible. Amidst tall evergreens near the lake, the winding roadway had not been plowed. Harry drove cautiously, following the tread marks of another car. Soon the dense woods opened to the lake, its waters shimmering in white-gold under the winter sun. Harry squinted as he parked the car on an open stretch of snow-covered pebbles at the south end of the inlet. Behind him was a dense cluster of pines and hemlocks, but he wanted a spruce or fir. He spied a few, west of the inlet, beyond naked wind-stripped maples and elms that reached for the sky.

"Over that way," he said, opening the door and pointing.

Harry took a saw from the car trunk and trudged across the snow-covered pebbles and up the western slope, kicking a trail of elongated footmarks so that Ellen and Freddy could follow more easily. He was quick to pass among the naked trees, mount a steeper incline and reach a young stand of Douglas firs. One by one the trees shed snow as Harry shook them. Suddenly he stood still, aware that he had not looked back to check on Ellen and the boy. He probed his mind and chastised himself. Was he avoiding an image already firmly fixed in his mind? Was it Freddy, so handsome and fair, almost angelic, in his snowsuit? Or was it Ellen hand-in-hand with Freddy walking through the snow—a mother-son image that he saw in his mind's eye without looking?

Grabbing a well-proportioned tree, Harry shook it and spun around to face Ellen and the toddling Freddy, who were still making their way among the maples and elms. "This one," he shouted. "Look at this one. It's perfect." Forcing himself, he kept his eyes on them as he held the narrow trunk with his right hand—a hand buried among the needled branches. He was the picture of a hunter holding his prey, the saw over his shoulder like a rifle.

Ellen smiled and nodded. "Let's gather cones in the pines before we leave." Immediately fearful that she had asked too much, she added, "Only if you want to. They make wonderful trimmings."

Gather cones. The words echoed in Harry's head. He recalled gathering cones in the woods north of Clarkton on those weekend hickory hunts in groves beyond the bend of the Logan River. Nature walks. Seed pods. Teasels and burdock. Gathering acorns and beechnuts for Felix. Transplanting May apples and berry bushes. Hiking with the Hilltoppers. Resting against a hickory tree and stretching legs into wild huckleberry. His head on her lap. His cheek on her breast. His thoughts fired by passion.

Ellen slipped on the incline and grabbed a young maple as Freddy plunged into the snow, burying his face. Harry tossed the saw and raced to the crying boy as Ellen steadied herself. He picked up Freddy, who was red faced and blubbering, and wiped snow from his nose, cheeks and chin.

"Hey, little fellow, that's nothing to bawl about," Harry said. "Come on, now. You'll be all right." He brushed the boy's snowsuit and tasseled cap. "You're a big boy. We've got to teach you to take it. Come on, now." He took Freddy by the hand and led him up the slope.

Later, after Harry had cut the tree, they gathered pine cones.

# Chapter Nineteen

Freddy was seven years old.

Harry and Ellen had begun sleeping together more than six years ago, shortly after selling their Clarkton house.

Another spring. Purple, yellow and white had faded and withered on the crocuses, leaving only tufts of green. But weeks had yet to pass before school recessed for the summer.

Freddy was on the floor of the redecorated living room—a room now more Early American than Victorian. His elbows dug into the rug, his chin rested on his fists, and his light blond hair hung toward an open book on Native Americans. The boy's legs stretched to the couch where his sneakers rubbed against a pleated ruffle. He was handsome by all standards—alert blue eyes that questioned, pleaded, thanked and warmed; smooth, fair skin that softened his even features.

The youngster was well liked at school and made friends easily—somewhat of a worry for Harry, who craved the safety of a more secluded life. Billy Allen was Freddy's best friend, partly because he lived nearby, but mainly because of affinity. Not that they looked alike, Billy being full-cheeked, pug-nosed and brown-haired. They simply enjoyed the same things: Making mud pies at age three. Constructing dirt highways and tunnels under the Pitman porch at age five. Climbing trees and digging worms at age six. Building a hut at age seven.

Harry was pleased with Freddy's tight relationship with Billy. It seemed much safer than his having a host of bosom buddies. A heavy flow of youthful traffic might have brought too much exposure and increased interplay among parents. The unavoidable lay ahead, however, and Harry knew it. Freddy and Billy were ready and anxious to breathe dust under the summer sun with a sandlot baseball team sponsored by Pete's Fish Market.

"Geronimo was smart," Freddy said. "He'd raid a ranch and then dash into the Mexican mountains where they couldn't find him."

Harry tossed aside his newspaper, lowered himself to the floor and crawled close to Freddy.

"What happened to him, Dad?"

"I think we made some promises we didn't keep, and he finally died on a reservation in Oklahoma."

"Why didn't we keep our promises?"

"I wish I could answer that, Freddy. We weren't so good to our Indians." Harry ruffled the boy's hair and squeezed his neck. He had taught Freddy much, maybe just as much as the Oakford teachers, always expanding on the youngster's lessons, adding another dimension to Columbus or Magellan or Balboa. With homework, maybe he helped a bit too much, but he couldn't seem to pass up the chance.

Ellen stood watching from the kitchen doorway as she dried a pot. Her pleasure was tamed by a touch of jealousy. She had long sensed the growing bond between father and son. "Why don't we have ice cream?" she asked. "Harry, get us some ice cream. Down at Charlie's. Maybe butter-pecan." She knew how Freddy would react. Those nights when Harry would surprise them with ice cream from Charlie's Drug Store always brought a bouncy elation to the household.

Harry looked up. "We're right in the middle of Geronimo!"

"Oh, yeah, Dad, please?" Faster than jack-in-the-box, Freddy was on his feet, his big blue eyes pleading with his father.

"I guess Geronimo will have to wait," said Harry as he rolled over.

"Oh, yeah!" Freddy exclaimed as he prepared to slap Harry with a double high-five.

Harry pushed himself awkwardly from the floor and waited for his knees to un-kink before high-fiving Freddy.

Oakford's only drugstore pretended to be a 19th Century

apothecary shop, although in truth Charlie stocked the latest in just about everything. The collection of mortars and pestles, and the bowls of ginseng root, camomile tea and licorice dressed the window for effect more than anything, as did the giant apothecary jars of red and green water.

Charlie was thin, weathered, bald and friendly—well known and liked by summer residents as well as winter residents. He no sooner smiled his greeting at Harry than he said, "I have those confounded filberts your wife ordered—all thirty pounds of them. I got 'em in sacks behind the candy counter."

Harry stared dumbfounded as his thoughts of ice cream vanished. "Filberts?"

"All thirty pounds. I had to get most of 'em from over at Hiley's place in Pineville. They're going to run you about sixty bucks."

"What are you talking about?" Harry felt a painful knot in his chest.

"Your wife was in here. Asked for thirty pounds of hazelnuts. I told her I had a few pounds of filberts. Same thing, you know. But thirty pounds, I said, 'You've got to be kidding, Mrs. Pitman.' That's what I said. 'You've got to be kidding.' Thirty pounds. I don't stock 'em like that. She didn't smile, so I put 'em on order."

"There must be some mistake."

"Better not be. Not now. Not with me having all these nuts."

"There's some sort of mixup here."

"No mistake, Mr. Pitman. No mistake at all. She said they were for Felix."

A shiver ran up Harry's spine and down his arms. He shook his head in quick, nervous jerks and stared strangely at the pharmacist.

"Are you all right, Mr. Pitman?"

Harry turned abruptly and headed for the door.

"Look here, Mr. Pitman, what about these nuts?"

Distraught to the point of uncontrollable shudders, he raced into the night and ran all the way home, not seeing or hearing, only thinking a whirlwind of frightful thoughts. He stood outside the house trying to catch his breath. "She's the hazelnut! A goddamn fuckin' hazelnut! Oh my God, Ellen, why?" He bit his lip until it bled.

Rushing to the door, he stopped again and gazed through the screen at the living room floor where Ellen was petting Freddy's blond hair. He didn't like the way she petted, and for a moment he hated her. When he saw Freddy shake off the petting as if annoyed, he burst into the room and demanded, "Freddy, take your book and go to your room."

Ellen and the boy spun their heads and stared at Harry, wide-eyed and open-mouthed.

"You heard what I said, Freddy."

"But Dad, what about the ice cream?"

"There won't be any ice cream. Please, Freddy. I'm sorry. I have to talk to your mother."

Ellen stayed on the floor. Her face turned ashen.

"What's wrong?" the boy asked.

"We'll talk later," Harry barked. "Now, do as I say."

Halfway up the stairs, Freddy turned and riveted his moist eyes on Harry. His expression—a sad, bewildered stare—could have squeezed a tear from Attila the Hun. Within seconds he whirled and raced up the steps.

Ellen pushed herself to her feet and backed away from Harry, who said nothing until he was sure Freddy had reached his room. In truth, the boy stayed at the top of the stairs and listened. Glaring at his wife, Harry kept his eyes on her in an almost merciless stare of anger.

"Why did you order thirty pounds of nuts?" he asked in a piercing whisper that was more cutting than a scream.

"Nuts?"

"Yes, nuts!" He no longer whispered. "You know damn well what I'm talking about. Nuts. N-U-T-S, nuts! Thirty pounds of freakin' filberts, or hazelnuts, or whatever the fuck you want to call them."

"Don't talk to me like that."

"You need help—serious help. I mean it, Ellen, you need help. Charlie Miller told me you ordered the nuts for Felix. Felix is dead! You hear me? Dead! Understand? Felix is dead, dead, dead!"

Ellen shuddered.

"Remember?"

"I didn't..."

"You didn't what?"

"I didn't mean it literally. I meant squirrels in general."

"Squirrels in general? You ordered thirty pounds of hazelnuts for squirrels in general?"

"I don't know. I wasn't thinking. I guess I didn't know... I mean, I didn't realize how much thirty pounds of nuts was." Ellen turned her back toward Harry.

"Look at me."

She refused. "To tell you the truth I had forgotten all about it."

"How could you forget thirty pounds of nuts. Damn it, Ellen, people don't forget things like that."

"I don't know. I'm sorry."

"Ellen." Harry softened his voice. "Please look at me."

"Leave me alone." She walked away from him, toward the kitchen.

"Felix is dead, Ellen. And Freddy isn't Felix. In fact, Freddy isn't even Freddy, or have you forgotten?"

"Stop it!" Ellen shouted. She spun around. Her eyes flamed as she yelled, "Don't you ever say that!"

# Chapter Twenty

Freddy was mature for age 11 and had learned long ago that mysteries surrounded his life. He had heard much, figured much. He scribbled notes—often at nighttime—and stuffed them under a loose board in his closet. But most of his secrets were stored in his head. Someday his father would explain everything, he was sure of that. His dad was troubled, but his dad was special.

The signs of worry in Harry became more obvious to Freddy as time passed, perhaps because of the boy's developing instincts. Increasingly insightful, Freddy picked up on little clues as well as the obvious. As for fatherly love, it was abundant and never in doubt. In fact, the boy knew he was loved by both parents. He was also aware that his mother's affection was much different.

Freddy realized that his mother was troubled, too, but in far stranger ways. She did peculiar things at odd times, and made his father sad—and that saddened him. Sharpening his wit day by day, he recognized some of her small aberrations, even when they went unnoticed by his father.

The boy was driven to learn quickly by his suspicions of impending doom. He was certain that he had to grow up fast before it was too late. Intense and curious, he listened and looked and sensed, held tightly to the pieces, and tried to put them together. The jigsaw cuts were strangely shaped. Many didn't fit. Holes abounded.

Young Fred had grown into a giver, not a taker. Maybe because of family tension. Or, in spite of it. Perhaps he wanted to comfort, especially after those puzzling and jolting episodes. Then again, maybe benevolence was simply his nature, something in his genes. It was special to help Dad plant rose bushes, or to buy Mom a geranium for Easter; to surprise Dad with a homemade beetle trap, or to cut out a Valentine heart for Mom.

Introspective, yet outgoing, Freddy played just as hard as he thought—and his thinking was mighty heavy for his age. Never did he fear smashing his handsome nose when diving head first into second base. No tree was too high to climb, no stream too rough to cross.

It wasn't until age 11 that Freddy and Billy began to ask themselves about the word FUCK cut deep into their favorite tree— a beech tree that took a slashing and cutting like other beeches because of smooth, gray bark. The four letters had grown bigger and spread wider through the years, and although Freddy and Billy had felt their texture many a time, it was not until a recent warm afternoon of tree climbing that Billy had asked, "You know what that means, don't you?"

"Yeah, Lester Ward told me."

They both giggled.

"Ever see a girl's thing?" Billy asked.

"No."

"You?"

"Not exactly."

"What do you mean, not exactly?"

"I looked up Nancy Parker's dress. In the school yard. She was above me on the bars."

"What did you see?"

"I'm not sure."

"You didn't see anything, did you?"

"Maybe," Billy said in a teasing tempo.

"You're lying!"

Billy was quick to switch tracks: "How big is yours?"

"Not too big. Not like Lester's."

"Lester show you his?"

"He shows it to everybody. He's 14. He was held back three times. He pulled it out in Miss Haskins' class. Stella Garfinkel saw him and told Miss Haskins."

"What happened to him?"

"Miss Haskins sent him to the principal."

"So then what happened to him."

"I don't know."

Billy punched his buddy in the ribs and ran, zigzagging through the woods. Freddy chased and tackled him in a thick patch of poison ivy. For weeks they itched, despite the calamine lotion that covered much of their bodies. The rash was bad, but they were more chagrined by their ghostly pink-white faces.

"Let's cut school today," Billy urged. "We can hide in the hut."

"You think we should?"

"Yeah."

A note from the school principal led to a heart-to-heart talk between Harry and his son. The punishment imposed on Freddy would have pleased many a youngster: No yard work for a week.

Harry suspected that Freddy's handsomeness would cause him trouble in years to come—too many choices, women galore. But that was the least of his worries. His daily inquietude always mounted as the hours passed, reaching its peak as he neared the house. In fact, his uneasy walk from the train station was a steady climb into serious anxiety. One Friday in July, he arrived home early and, before entering the house, strolled to the rear to check on blossoms and bugs in the sunny stretch behind the shaded cottage. He brushed Japanese beetles from the roses, then turned to find a patch of broken and twisted plants—zinnia heads, stems, leaves and scattered petals. An eerie and ominous feeling pervaded his body, tingling his fingers and tightening his gut. The scene, so remindful of the brutal and bloody death of the white squirrel, sickened and frightened him much more than 30 pounds of nuts or any other Ellenism.

Quickly conquering his fear of entering the house, Harry ran up the steps and into the kitchen where he stood for a moment and tried to convince himself that he was being irrational. But his gastric acids continued to flow, his neck muscles continued to twitch.

"Ellen! Ellen, where are you?" He walked into the living room and stood at the foot of the stairs. "Ellen! You up there? Freddy, you home?" One part of his mind kept trying to tell another that the ripped flowers meant nothing. But he couldn't convince himself. "Damn it!" He walked halfway up the stairs and called again. "Ellen!" Then, in a mumbling whisper, he asked himself, "Jesus, Ellen, where are you?"

Seconds later he was on the back porch again, looking down at the broken and twisted zinnias. His upper teeth were so tight against his lowers that his jaw ached.

"Freddy! Hey, Freddy, you around?"

The boy and his friend were in the old beech tree, deep in woods behind the garage. Freddy gave a Tarzan yell, and Billy echoed it. Minutes later they stood facing Harry, their faces almost as dirty as their T-shirts.

"What's up, Dad?" Freddy's smile faded. His expression suddenly mirrored that of his father. He glanced down at the zinnias, then back at Harry.

"Have you seen your mother?" Harry's tone was stern, his anxiety obvious.

"I think she's in the house." The boy's words were quiet, serious and questioning.

"No she isn't," Harry snapped.

Freddy looked down. Billy stepped back, picked up a twig and fiddled with it. Suddenly it occurred to Harry that perhaps Ellen was upstairs and simply hadn't answered his calls.

"Go back where you were," Harry ordered.

Billy started toward the woods, but Freddy refused to move, lifted his head and looked at his dad with beseeching eyes.

Harry softened his words. "Please, Freddy, we'll talk later."

"But I want to..."

"I know you want to help. But we don't know what's up. There's nothing to help with, right now. Go with Billy, okay?"

Freddy backed away slowly. He could read Harry's eyes, and he knew when not to push. He had learned that long ago. Turning, he ran after his friend, moving his legs fast in hopes that they would outrace the sense of foreboding that again plagued him. So often that feeling permeated his body at night. But in the morning he always stood strong against it because of the messages in his dad's eyes.

Harry found Ellen upstairs in their bedroom. She was sitting on a padded window seat, looking out through a dormer that offered little view of the street because of thick hemlocks.

There among the peach-colored curtains she turned her head halfway and became a quiescent cameo in a quiet room of peach and apricot. The room was Ellen, and Ellen was the room, for one was born of the other, and nothing of Aunt Beatrice remained between the walls. Ellen had fashioned the frills of the apricot bedspread on the white four-poster bed. She had placed the little pieces of orange-pink glassware on the sills of the dormers. She had arranged the fluffy white puppies and bears on the corner shelf. And more and more she had escaped to the room while Harry worked and Freddy played.

Standing in the doorway, Harry asked, "Are you okay?"

"Yes." She had yet to face him.

"Why didn't you answer when I called?"

"Did you call?"

"You must of heard me?"

"I don't know. I'm not sure."

"It's almost dinner time."

She looked at him, somewhat bewildered.

"It's almost time to eat," he said.

"Oh, the time went, I guess. I hadn't realized."

"The flowers in the backyard—what happened to them? Who ripped them up like that?"

Ellen turned away and stared out through the window again.

"Ellen?"

She didn't answer, and Harry made a quick decision to talk later about the zinnias. He backed off, stood quietly in the hall, then said, "Come on. Let's get something going for supper." She stirred, and he started down the stairs, hoping that she would follow.

Moments later he stood again on the back porch looking at the zinnias. He caught movement in the periphery of his vision and turned to see Alice Gardner, his next-door neighbor, moving with apprehension or uncertainty toward the hedgerow that separated their properties. The squatty, white-haired woman of 60, somewhat frog-like with popping eyes and a broad mouth, until now had always greeted him with a smile. But this time she was grim and nervous. She motioned him toward her. In seconds, they stood facing each other across a low clump of laurel.

Alice and her husband Wayne, a gray little man, had been good neighbors even though they found the Pitmans aloof. Wayne, who was nearing retirement after two decades as county traffic engineer, had refused to stop offering garden tools, even during Harry's early years in Oakford when he was more than reclusive, almost in hiding. And Alice had always shared cherry pies in season. Their houses were so separated that a walk from one to the other was enough to cool a freshly baked pie. Though far from intimate, their friendship had grown in recent years, especially after Harry realized that he couldn't avoid the Gardners anymore than he could fight off the PTA or the sandlot league.

"I know this isn't any of my business," Alice said in hushed tones. "And maybe I shouldn't say anything."

"What is it?" Harry questioned.

"Like I say, it isn't any of my business, and I hesitate to say anything. But I don't think Ellen is well."

"What do you mean?"

"I was over here loosening earth around that holly bush when I heard something—something odd, like whispering. But a funny kind of whispering. I looked up and saw Ellen ripping up those flowers. It wasn't natural-like. She seemed so intense, so driven. It scared me something awful. At first I just watched, sort of stunned. I was really too afraid to... well, you know, get close and try to do anything. Then I got myself together, cut through the bushes and hurried to her." Alice looked away, then back at Harry. "I know I'm rattling on something terrible."

"Please."

"Well, I talked to her. 'Ellen,' I asked, 'are you okay?' But she didn't seem to realize I was there. The look on her face—it was like she was horrified by something. Like she saw something evil or shocking. I wanted to grab her arm, but her elbows kept swinging and jabbing. I just kept talking. I'm not sure what I said. But I just kept talking. When she seemed to realize that I was there, she quieted. She looked at her hands, then at the broken flowers." Alice glanced toward the Pitman house, then looked down as if gathering her thoughts. "I'll never forget that look on her face." Again she hesitated.

"Is there more?"

"She cried."

"And?"

"She cried from deep down here." Alice pressed her belly. Her eyes moistened. "Like she was brokenhearted. And then she ran into the house. I didn't know what to do. I just stood there for a minute. Then I knew... I knew I had to follow her. So I did. I ran after her. She was sitting at the table, staring toward the window, her cheeks wet with tears. I made a pot of coffee."

"Did she say anything?"

"Not then. She took the coffee, but her hands... they were shaking. I steadied her cup."

"She drank it?" Harry's mouth was dry. He tried to swallow.

"Some of it. I sat with her, but we didn't talk. Her thoughts seemed way off somewhere. I didn't really know how to help her. I stayed, partly because I was afraid to leave her. It wasn't until later, when I stood up to go, that she started to talk. About Freddy, and how big she swelled during pregnancy. About her labor pains, and how she almost lost him. About how she loved breast-feeding him."

A shudder ran through Harry's body as he turned white and tasted vomit. He stepped back from the laurel bush, opened his mouth as if to speak, but said nothing. He spun toward his house, only to turn again and face his neighbor. "Thank you." His thoughts rampaged. He kept looking at the woman, trying to say something more. Finally he asked, "If for any reason I need to send Freddy to you, would you keep him for a few hours, a night, or even a day?"

"Of course," she said with kindness. "Anytime."

Minutes later Harry was again standing in the bedroom doorway, staring at the back of Ellen's head, silhouetted in the window and framed by the peach-colored curtains. He had made up his mind. But his words had to be direct and clear, his tone deep and forceful. He could not shift into high pitch or choke off. And no matter what her reaction, he would proceed. In fact, he would try to interpret her reaction. He practiced silently, one word after another.

"You did not give birth to Freddy." The words did not

reverberate. Each one seemed to stand alone and then die in a hush, snuffed out by the stillness of the peach and apricot room.

Ellen turned, glared and shouted: "Don't you say that! Don't you ever say that!" Her face reddened. She raced to Harry and beat his chest with her fists.

"Snap out of it, Ellen!" He grabbed her arms, shook her, and forced her up against the wall.

Outside, Freddy had not climbed the beech after returning to the woods. Introspective and almost sullen, he had stayed on the ground among the protruding roots of the big tree and cut into the bark with his penknife, carving every bad word he had learned from the boys at school, reddening his hand and ripping open blisters. Billy had become annoyed to the point of frustration. From high among the limbs he had yelled again and again, "Come on up!" With impatience he had asked, "What's wrong with you, anyway? You sure are acting funny."

About the time that Harry had left Alice Gardner and returned to Ellen, Freddy had said "So long" to Billy, leaving him in the tree. From a thicket of shrubs, he had watched his father enter the house before he walked into the yard where he dawdled, picked up the crown of a yellow zinnia and pulled it apart petal by petal. By the time Harry had spoken to Ellen, Freddy had entered the house and was standing in the living room at the foot of the stairs. Minutes later he began to tiptoe up the steps.

After forcing his wife against the wall, Harry said, "You've got me worried sick by the way you're acting. Maybe you need some help, huh? Maybe I should take you to a doctor?" He lowered her arms, but still held them firmly. "Tell me you don't believe what you said about Freddy." As he stared into her eyes, a feeling of compassion mixed with his anger, pity and love mixed with his bitterness. He stood helpless, staring into her face. But within seconds, a strange look in her eyes obliterated any affection or empathy, wiping out brief feelings that somehow this freakish horror could be buried in an embrace. A floating flicker of childish teasing broke Ellen's distant stare now and then. Harry felt fear. Something was terribly wrong.

Suddenly Ellen's eyes cleared and focused. She pulled away

from Harry and ran to the hallway where Freddy stood, sadly gaping. Embracing him, she petted his head and kissed him about the neck. She spoke over-sweet sentiment: "I love my baby. And you love me too, don't you Freddy? Don't you love your mama?" The boy didn't respond. His arms hung at his sides.

Harry could not tolerate the display, yet failed to intrude for fear of a damaging flare-up. He had witnessed too many of Ellen's saccharine exhibits of drooling over the boy, and had come to realize that Freddy disliked them. Momentarily stymied, Harry stood immobilized, though he found her smothering embrace particularly loathsome. Suddenly he pushed past Ellen and Freddy, mumbled "son of a bitch," and started down the steps with his teeth and fists clenched, only to reverse himself, step up and rip Freddy from Ellen's grasp. He pushed the boy down the steps as a loud, guttural gasp erupted from Ellen.

"You go over to Mrs. Gardner's and you stay there for awhile," said Harry as he kept pushing Freddy. "You hear me? Please, go on, get out of here. Wait until I come over or call."

"Dad, I want to stay with you." At the front door, Freddy turned and looked at his father. Tears filled his eyes. "Please, Dad. I understand more than you think."

"I can handle things better alone right now, Freddy. Please. I'm sure you know more than I realize, and we'll talk about it. I promise."

Ellen stood at the top of the stairs, her eyes wild, her lips drawn.

Harry opened the door and shoved the boy onto the porch. "Now, get over there! I'm telling you, get over there!"

Tears rolled down Freddy cheeks as he said, "I don't care if I'm not really your kid."

The words hit Harry hard. His throat filled and his eyes welled. The sudden knowledge that Freddy knew that part of the puzzle shocked him.

"It's okay, Dad."

Harry's protective instinct was pulling at him as he pushed the youngster off the porch and into the hemlocks. "For my sake, Freddy, go to the Gardners. Mrs. Gardner knows. She understands. Please. Go on." He put his hands on the boy's shoulders and looked into his wet and puffy eyes. "I love you. I love you very much."

Perhaps it was the words of love. Whatever, the boy ran toward the Gardner's house. Harry watched him disappear among the evergreens.

A warm evening breeze mussed Harry's hair as he turned toward his porch. The sun was low, and only the roof of the cottage was touched by speckles of yellow-orange light, moving, sometimes darting as the wind tossed the tree limbs. Harry was slow to mount the steps, impeded by thoughts of the secrets that must have hurt Freddy. On the porch he gazed through the door window and could see the blurred image of Ellen standing next to a beaded Victorian lamp, an Aunt Beatrice leftover. He wondered if her eyes were focused near or far, wondered if her thoughts drifted to bygone days, to havens of escape, or to horrors.

A feeling of deep sadness came over Harry as he thought of the good things about Ellen—the soft and beautiful things. But he knew now that she needed help that he couldn't give. Disturbing thoughts troubled him. A probing psychiatrist would dig into her past and learn the truth about Freddy. A doctor would question him about her history. How could he explain it? Yet if he protected her, did not get her help, she might get worse. Then he'd have no choice; he'd have to take her somewhere. He couldn't hide her in the attic. Besides, the cottage had no attic.

Harry backed away from the door. His thoughts went on a rampage: You fuckin' weakling. Freddy thinks you're bright and wise and strong and honest. But you're a fuckin' weakling.

Fiercely angry at himself, Harry opened the door and stepped inside, momentarily sharpening Ellen's wits. But she slipped away quickly, staring into infinity. He took her by the hand and led her to the couch. She sat quietly, tilted forward and slightly to the side.

"Ellen, listen to me." He stood in front of her, studying her face. "Ellen!"

Again her expression changed as her muscles tightened. Suddenly alert but agitated, she straightened up and focused on Harry. "You... you want to take him from me."

"That's nonsense." Harry could feel the beating of his heart, the churning of his stomach.

For the next hour, Ellen's periods of escape lasted far longer than her short outbursts. Both were unnerving to Harry. Realizing that he had no choice, he went upstairs and packed a few of her things. He knew that neither Oakford nor the surrounding communities had a psychiatrist, so he decided to take her to Northampton State Hospital—a 30-mile drive.

Carrying a small overnight bag, Harry guided Ellen toward the door.

"Where's Felix?" she asked.

# Chapter Twenty-One

Barbara Smedley glanced at her watch, then looked around the dining room of Fisherman's Tavern. Among the hanging ropes and nets, sponges and starfish, sat the late diners, especially the after-theater patrons. Pete crossed her mind. She pictured his annoyance and wondered if he had tried to reach her, despite her message.

Harry was gulping a fresh and frothy beer. He swallowed too fast, then struggled to catch his breath. His face flushed and his eyes teared. Barbara looked down at her third margarita—only half gone. She had nursed it for 40 minutes. Keeping her eyes on her glass, she ran her finger around its edge to feel the salt crystals and to give Harry time to recover. After another glance at her watch, she looked up at him.

"So you drove to Northampton State Hospital," she said, finally prompting him to go on. As long as he would talk, she would listen.

"That drive was a nightmare. I can hardly handle it today, when I think of it. Ellen sat there, mumbling about spilt jam and her Aunt Beatrice, about being locked in her room, and I don't know what all. I was edgy as hell, mainly because I didn't know what to expect from her. Every sound made me jump. There's something about twilight time that distorts. And it kept getting darker as I drove on. Everything seemed out-of-shape, malformed, or something. Remember in the movies, when Snow White ran through the dark woods, and all the trees and branches became monsters that frightened her and grabbed at her. That scene gave me dreams when

I was a kid. It stayed with me. And that's how it was that night with Ellen. Dark, distorted images seemed to loom at me around every turn. The roads up there—they're so narrow and shadowy, and they snake through such thick growth. I was scared. Very scared. I'm not ashamed to say I was terrified. A grown man—and terrified. My heart jumped every time a car came around a curve. Everything seemed wrong, or in my way. On the open stretches I guess I pushed my foot to the floor, not realizing it. Even when I saw the flashing lights in the mirror I didn't slow down. I just wasn't with it. The siren jolted me, and I stopped the car halfway in a ditch. The cops found me shaking like hell. I got out and rattled on like some nut. This cop—he tossed me his handkerchief and told me to wipe off the sweat. They looked me up and down, looked at each other, and then looked at Ellen. She was mumbling something about teddy bears. Finally, they bought my story, I think. Anyway, they let me go. Followed me to the township line."

Harry gulped beer again. "You know this is crazy. Really crazy. The way I'm babbling on like this."

"It's okay." Barbara offered an assuring smile.

"Like I said, I've never told any of this to anyone."

"That's why it's pouring out."

"Maybe I've had too many beers."

"So, maybe the beers help. Please. Don't stop."

"Where was I?"

"On the way to the hospital."

"Oh, the hospital. Well, I really wasn't prepared for the hospital. The walls were so ominous, and my emotions got the best of me. Little light was left in the sky when I drove through the gate and up that winding road. The main building looked like a black monster against a dark sky—some creature with angles and points. I remember that globe light hanging high and reflecting on those tall doors. I kept staring at it from the car, unable to move. A guard come toward us, and that got me going. I led Ellen up the steps. She clung to me. It was better that she clung to me. If she had fought— well, I don't know. Anyway, when we got inside, I was really upset by the look of the place. These high ceilings. Everything painted white. All those pictures of grim looking doctors. Big round lights hanging from the ceiling. But it was me, my mood, as much as anything else. The place was clean, after all. Just old. They told me that the new buildings were closed down, what with policy changes. You know, putting people back on the street.

"I remember the night nurse, though I never saw her again. A huge woman with a cap on this big bush of frizzy hair. She was matter-of-fact with an automatic smile and a built-in routine. When she took Ellen by the arm, I flinched. I had this terrible feeling, like I was deserting my wife. But Ellen didn't resist when they led her away. For a moment I felt like running after her, but I just stood there and waited, and then filled out all sorts of forms that frustrated me all to hell. I was told to see Dr. Nevins in the morning.

"I went to a motel—cheap place for taking cheap women, I guess. Small cabins with big beds. I didn't sleep at first. Didn't even get undressed. I just lay on the bed thinking. Good and bad thoughts. I kept seeing Ellen as she was years ago. At school, down by the lake, the wind tossing her hair. I guess I cried."

Barbara looked away and fiddled with her watch.

"Fear and pain hit me where it hurts that night," Harry said. "The feeling was sharp. Real pain. Here, and down here. In the chest and stomach. Funny about those wee hours, they wiped out any good thoughts. I hated myself. I even hated myself for loving Freddy. I felt guilty for loving him so much. I was so scared for him. So frightened for him. I tried to convince myself that I couldn't undo what was done. I couldn't undo what I had allowed to happen. He was my son, now, and I needed him. Oh my God how I needed him.

"Sometime in the morning, before dawn I guess, I fell asleep. I woke up with a headache. The sun was bright. It was nine o'clock. I threw water on my face and went back to the hospital in wrinkled clothes and a full day's stubble on my face. Everything looked different. Bright and green. Patients were walking on the grass and sitting near flower gardens. A flock of goldfinches flew up from the driveway as I drove in. My grandmother used to call them salad birds. I'm not sure why." Harry tried to smile. "I told myself it didn't look so bad. I've often told myself that. But that old building—it haunts me. It always will."

# Chapter Twenty-Two

How do you lie to a psychiatrist? Harry asked himself again and again as he wandered the grounds of Northampton State Hospital on that sunny Saturday, that bright morning after that restless night in that cheap motel. His mind's voice talked to the statue of Carl Gustav Jung, the noted Swiss psychiatrist, who stood among bright flowers in a circular garden bed: Yes, Ellen had bad experiences, but they're hard to explain. Children? Yes, we have a son.

"Shit!" He'll see it in my eyes. And I'll have to keep my eyes glued to his, or he'll know I'm lying. He'll know anyway. Shrinks know when you lie.

Harry told himself that he had lost control of the moment, the day, perhaps his life. He stared into the statue's eyes and lied— twice.

Three times that morning he had been curtly informed that Dr. Nevins was busy and would see him later. Three times he wandered the grounds, trying to ease the anxiety that increased after each rebuff. The delays were torture.

Don't think, he told himself. Just let things take their course. If you can't control things, you can't control things.

Harry couldn't convince himself.

He walked among tall cedars that gave way to sunlight and a huge, square, brick building with barred windows. Startled, he looked up for a moment, then hurried down a grassy slope.

A splash of pink caught his eye. It was the loose garb of a

woman who was picking toadstools under a maple and stuffing them into her dress at the bosom. Unkempt gray hair fell over her eyes each time she plucked one.

Harry hurried off again, back toward Dracula's castle. His irritating inner voice replayed Miss Greenwald's broken record: Sorry, the doctor's busy with a patient. Sorry, the doctor's busy with a patient.

Miss Greenwald—fiftyish, tall, black hair pulled into a knot, a hook nose—was an overpowering woman who guarded the portals of the inner-sanctum. This time she stood and smiled at Harry as she leaned across her tidy desk in the outer office of Dr. Nevins. The room's white walls held three framed certificates, a portrait of Sigmund Freud and an oil painting of the institution's main building and grounds. A large metal scale stood in a corner next to a door marked Philip T. Nevins, M.D.

"Dr. Nevins will see you now, Mr. Pitman. He's been with your wife for the past hour. I'll buzz him." She pushed a button on her intercom. "Doctor, Mr. Pitman is here. Shall I send him in?"

"Please do," returned a deep voice. Harry pictured a bearded Freudian type, wearing heavy eyeglasses.

Dr. Nevins was not at all what Harry had expected—no beard, no glasses. He was a skinny, sharp-nosed, pasty-faced man who looked undernourished and stood only five feet four. Sparse hair was pulled into ribbons across his balding crown.

"Please sit down, Mr. Pitman." Standing, Nevins reached across his desk and squeezed Harry's hand, then seemed to shrink as he fell back into his swivel chair. "I'm not going to kid you and try to diagnose your wife's illness after seeing her only once. But I will give you a few impressions."

Harry glanced about the walnut-paneled office but once, then focused on Nevins and tried to keep eye contact while feeling suspended in a disturbing limbo.

Nevins was not dispassionate. He was sensitive and highly intuitive. "Are you all right, Mr. Pitman?"

"Yes. Please go on." Harry kept telling himself that he wanted to help Ellen, yet kept asking himself if he could disguise the truth, or perhaps tell enough to help her, yet hold back.

"My first impression is that your wife is repressing something, maybe an entire period of her life. Some individuals react to conflict situations by escaping. They completely repress traumatic experiences." Nevins studied Harry expression. "Now please remember what I said about initial observations. This is not a diagnosis."

"I understand."

"Your wife seems childlike in her behavior—that is, when she's not completely passive. Some individuals regress as a means of repressing. This is possible in Mrs. Pitman's case."

Harry simply nodded. His steady eye contact with the psychiatrist was unnerving him.

"Perhaps you know something that might help us. Something disturbing or painful in her life. Something traumatic—at least to her."

Harry lowered his eyes, as a guilty child might do. "I'll... I'll give it some thought."

"Yes, give it some thought. We'll set up a time when we can get together again." Dr. Nevins leaned back in his chair. "You're wondering, I suppose, how long she must remain with us. Frankly, I can't say."

Harry forced eye contact. "We have a boy. He's eleven years old."

"All the more reason she should be with us. The effect of a mental patient on a family can be quite damaging. And today's thinking has resulted in too many harmful family situations, too many sick people out there wandering around somewhere. We care for too few of them in our mental institutions today." Nevins stood and smiled warmly. "In time, Mrs. Pitman will probably become an outpatient. But, frankly, I hesitate to predict anything right now."

Harry stood and shook Nevins hand. He felt an urge to open up, but flashing images of Freddy prevented it. How good it would feel to free his mind, to be honest and forthright. But he had no intention of losing Freddy.

"Comfort yourself in that Mrs. Pitman isn't aware of much," Nevins said. "Right now she's not the woman you've known."

Early afternoon temperatures had risen to nearly 90 degrees by the time Harry drove through the gates of Northampton State Hospital. He didn't look back, setting a habit that was never to be broken.

Harry couldn't help but play psychiatrist on his drive to Oakford, talking to himself in harsh tones and drawing one conclusion after another. "Hell yeah," he blurted at one point, "by repressing the goddamn kidnapping, she could turn Freddy into her own freakin' offspring."

# Chapter Twenty-Three

Alice Gardner opened her door to find a tired, red-eyed Harry, his clothes wrinkled and his jaw dark with stubble.

"Come in," she said quickly, wiping her hands on a dishtowel. She reeked of onions. "Forgive me, I'm in the middle of a meatloaf." But her eyes showed that her thoughts were far from the kitchen. They asked questions.

Harry stepped into the small but attractive living room—a room nearly half filled by a baby grand piano and decorated with flowers from the Gardner backyard. Alice had been a music teacher. She was a graduate of Julliard who had never concertized, settling down early to grow everything from marigolds to holly trees.

"Thanks," said Harry, glancing around the room and toward the kitchen. "I hope he wasn't much trouble. He was so dirty when I sent him over."

Alice frowned and tipped her head. Her bewilderment was so obvious that Harry caught the message instantly. "Freddy is here, isn't he?" Panic raced through him. "My God, he isn't, is he?"

"No. I haven't seen him."

"I sent him over last night. I took Ellen to Northampton State."

"Oh, my." Alice lifted fingers to her lips.

Fear again wiped out Harry's rational thinking. His body chemicals overflowed, doing strange things to his mind and muscles. Although not thinking straight, he was quickly rescued by Alice.

"Maybe he went back to your house after you left," she suggested.

"Jesus, why the hell didn't I think of that." He fled, leaping from the porch and racing through the thick hemlocks. Tripping, he grabbed the railing as he mounted his porch.

"Freddy!" he yelled upon entering the house. "Freddy, are you here?" He stood quietly, listening, his heart racing. Moments of silence sent him running up the stairs. He hurried from room to room, then stood still at Freddy's door, exhausted and frustrated. Sadness slowed the flow of adrenaline. A subdued Harry stepped back into the boy's room, gazed at the mussed bed and wondered whether his son had slept there last night.

This was the room that Harry had slept in, alone, during those agonizing days after he first arrived in Oakford. Now it was Freddy's, and its wall held pennants, banners and photos of sports heroes. Harry reached to a shelf and touched Freddy's baseball cap and glove.

"Goddamnit!"

Downstairs, Harry clung to the newel post and tried to gather his wits. Any other father would call the police, but he couldn't. Not yet, anyway. He could hear and see the words—Missing, a blond, blue-eyed, 11-year-old youngster. The thought scared him. But he told himself that fear of disclosure wouldn't stop him, if there were no other way.

Glancing about, Harry thought of the garage and the woods. He hurried toward the back door, but was stopped short by scattered glass on the kitchen floor. Lifting his head, he saw that a small pane of glass in the upper half of the south window had been cracked and pushed in. The window was unlocked, and dirty smudges soiled the sill.

"God almighty, maybe he did sleep in that bed," Harry muttered. He raced into the yard, checked the garage, then ran into the woods where he zigzagged among maples, oaks and tuliptrees, following a path to the giant, old beech. There, on a low limb sat Freddy, still wearing yesterday's soiled T-shirt, still smeared with dirt on cheeks and forehead. The boy stared at Harry, but didn't speak. Fear and sadness shaped his features.

Harry forced a smile while sighing in relief. He held back the scolding that almost blurted from his lips—a scolding that would have carried the wrong message. Where the hell have you been?

would have meant, Thank God you're safe. Damn you! would have meant, I love you.

Not wanting to plunge into serious talk, Harry asked, "Is that your hut way up there?"

Freddy nodded.

"It looks great!" Harry kept staring at the strange collection of wood.

"It's not finished." Freddy's hurtful expression remained. "We're adding to it."

"Wow. That is going to be some hut, I can tell."

Freddy started to swing his legs nervosuly, but said nothing.

"Don't worry about the window."

"I didn't want to stay at the Gardners."

"I know."

"You mad?"

"Hell no. But you worried me."

"Sorry."

Harry's smile was real—and warm. "Why don't you come on down?"

"How's Mom?"

"She's in a hospital. They can help her there."

Still swinging his legs, Freddy asked, "Will she be there a long time? You can tell me, you know."

Harry looked down, tried to compose himself, and quickly looked up again. "Well, I'm not sure, Fred. Come on down, and we'll talk." Harry seated himself on the hard ground among the exposed roots of the old beech. He locked his arms around his knees, linked hands, leaned back against the blue-gray trunk, and waited.

Freddy stayed in the tree.

"Hey, boy, I know your eyes are wet and swollen. So are mine. It's all right for a man to cry, when he has something to cry about. Last night I cried like a baby. Come on down."

Freddy stirred, but remained on the limb.

"I thought maybe tomorrow we might dust off our fishing rods," Harry said. "We'll go up the north end of the lake and see if we can catch some perch or sunnies. Would you like that? Maybe in the afternoon we can hike along Mohawk Gorge and check out those rocks you're always talking about."

Freddy lowered himself to another limb, swung under it, hung by his hands and pushed his sneakers against the trunk to brace himself. Seconds later he let go and fell to the ground, landing on his feet. He sat cross-legged, next to his dad, and looked down at the beech roots as he toyed with a leaf.

"In fact, I'll take a few days off from work," said Harry. "It'll give us some time together." He bit his lip and cleared his throat.

"You don't have to."

"What do you mean, I don't have to?"

"You don't have to do all that stuff."

"Why not? We need some time together."

"I know why you're doing it. 'Cause of Mom, and all."

"Not just because of Mom, although that's part of it. We always did do things together, didn't we? Sure, we have to work things out now—because there's just the two of us. So?"

"We'll pack a lunch and all? And dig some worms?"

"Sure." Harry bit his lip again as his eyes reflected indecisive thinking on a touchy subject. "You know, Fred, we've got to figure out what we're going to do with you while I'm at work."

"What do you mean?"

Taking another stab at the sensitive issue, Harry said, "Well, somebody has to take care of you while I'm away. Maybe we'll have to find you a place to stay. At least until school starts."

"I can take care of myself." Freddy continued to stare at the ground.

"You probably can, I know that. I'm sure you can. But I'd get in trouble for leaving you alone all day. You wouldn't want that, would you?"

Freddy didn't answer. He pulled apart the leaf, tossed the pieces into the air, then studied the roots a bit closer.

Unsure of himself, but determined, Harry tossed out a suggestion: "Maybe we could work out something with Millie. You and Millie get along just great. And you like her farm. I know you like her farm."

"You mean, I wouldn't be with you?"

"No, no, I don't mean that." Harry put his arm around the boy and pulled him close. "I'd rush right to you every day after work. And weekends would be ours—yours and mine together."

"Will we see Mom?"

"I don't know. Maybe not right away. She has good doctors. They'll try to make her better."

"What's wrong with her?" Freddy blurted the words as if they had been long stored and ready to burst forth.

"I don't know for sure. Sometimes people get all messed up in the head because of things that happened to them."

"Bad things happened to Mom, huh?" Freddy finally lifted his head and looked up at Harry with moist eyes.

"She went through some rough times."

"Because of me?"

"Now what made you say a thing like that?" Harry recalled Freddy's words of the past evening: "...not really your kid." They reverberated in his head: "...not really your kid."

"I know things."

"Oh?"

"I've heard things when you and Mom didn't know I was listening." Freddy shifted his buttocks and pulled away from Harry. He unfolded his legs, stretched them into a patch of ferns and wiggled his feet nervously. "But it's okay."

Harry fought for the right words, but they didn't come.

"You don't have to tell me if I was adopted or something."

Harry stared straight ahead into the trees, unable to look at Freddy as he spoke. "You weren't adopted." He rubbed his forehead as he struggled to find his next words. "You were sort of found."

"I don't care."

"I want to explain it to you. I've always wanted to. I guess I was afraid I'd lose you somehow if I did." With those words out of his mouth, Harry told himself to relax, but to little avail. "You see, your mother wanted to believe you were really her kid. I didn't want to upset her. Truth is, I never wanted to face the fact that she was sick." Harry's gut churned. "God almighty, I don't know how to explain it to you. I've really made a mess of things."

Freddy spun around and buried his face in his dad's lap. Harry could feel the heaving of the boy's chest. And he wondered what emotions the boy could feel emanating from him.

"I love you so much, Freddy. I couldn't love you more if you were my own flesh and blood. I don't know what I'd do without you. It would just about kill me." Harry put his left hand on Freddy's back and rubbed it gently, then placed his right hand on the youngster's head. Breathing deeply, he pushed his fingers into the boy's hair. A moment later he was shaken by his own words: "I know where your parents are. I could return you to them."

Freddy sprang to his feet and yelled, "No!" He glared at Harry, his face red and wet, his nose running. "No! I want to stay with you! I don't want them!" His body surged and pulsated as he stood facing Harry, glowering at him. He turned and ran toward the house, not following the winding path, but pushing and thrashing through the underbrush.

Harry questioned his motives. Was he testing Freddy? Was he testing himself in some way? Did the words simply pop out because of some unknown impulse, some reason buried in his subconscious? He shivered as he heard them replayed in his mind: I could return you to them.

That night at bedtime, Harry whispered to Freddy: "I'll always be your dad, no matter what. Okay? Now, you sleep tight—and dream about all the fish we'll catch tomorrow."

The next morning, Harry and Freddy caught six little sunfish and one catfish in Mohawk Lake. At noon they pan-fried them over an open fire near Big Oak Falls at the lower end of Mohawk Gorge. Wearing backpacks, they followed the gorge as it cut through East Hill, rock formations hanging high above them, water low to their left. They rested on a large, flat rock in midstream, dangling their bare feet in the gushing water.

Freddy struggled to say something.

"What is it, son?"

"I love you, Dad."

# Chapter Twenty-Four

Barbara Smedley refused a fourth margarita. She leaned forward, studied Harry's expression, and asked, "Does Freddy know the whole truth?"

"I don't think he wants to know." Harry pushed his beer aside. "He doesn't ask, and I don't offer. I wouldn't lie to him. I couldn't. I've just been waiting. Allowing the days to grow into weeks, the weeks into months, the months into years. Now Freddy's thirteen years old. I don't know what his imagination has told him. All I know is that he wants to be my son, and I love him."

"Do you want him to know?"

"Oh, yes. I want him to know everything. But I've always thought it was up to him."

"And now?'

"Now? Now, I'm not so sure. I may not have that option anymore. In fact, I may not have the luxury of waiting one more day."

Awkward silence spanned nearly a minute, then Barbara asked, "And what about your wife?"

"It's been two years since she was committed. There's been no real improvement. I see her when I can. Sometimes on Fridays I take the train from work, spend a half hour, then ride on to Oakford. Freddy often meets me at the station. He asks about her, but I've never taken him to see her. I don't want to."

"May I suggest something?"

"Why not?"

"Go to the police. Tell them your story before they have a chance to come after you." Barbara squirmed at her own suggestion, knowing that Pete would be furious if he knew. "It might work in your favor."

That strange malady hit Harry again. That weak, sick-in-the-gut, feverish feeling. The one that always came over him when he thought of losing Freddy.

"Are you okay?" Barbara asked.

"Not really."

"Stupid question, eh?"

"Sorry. When it comes to the kid, sometimes it's a nasty belly-blow." Harry looked down at his tightly linked hands. "Go to the cops, y'say. I've thought of it. I've thought of it a hundred times. There'd be a trial. And, believe me, it's far from the first time I've thought of that. In fact, it's been a recurring nightmare. Ever since Ellen took the baby I've seen myself on the witness stand." He watched his thumbs toy with each other. "I've rehearsed the lines over and over. Know how that is? Over and over again until you drive yourself nuts. Sometimes late into the night."

Barbara tried to comfort Harry with a slight smile.

"You know, Miss Smedley, I wouldn't mind going to jail if I knew Freddy wouldn't be hurt. If I could say 'Mirror, mirror on the wall, send me to jail, but keep Freddy happy'—and by magic it would happen. Hell, I'd go for it!"

Barbara saw but two possibilities. Pete gets his story first. Or the police get Harry first. She changed the subject: "This Millie— she watches after the boy when you can't?"

"She's a great gal in her mid-fifties. Daughter of an old farmer. When I need her, she cleans, cooks, looks after Freddy. In the summer he stays on the farm until I pick him up after work. Sometimes I just visit him there, especially when I'm late. We walk along the tractor roads, follow the pasture fences, or sit in the barn and talk. The farm's been good for him. He helps with the chores. Even scrubbed down a newborn calf. And Millie fills him up with enough vegetable soup to drown a dozen hippos. Freddy and I do all sorts of things together. We go to ball games. I take him boating. We build things with wood, even metal. You should see the rock garden he made."

Barbara could feel rare upbeat vibes coming from Harry. She looked at her watch as the hour hand edged past 10. Feeling pushed to end the conversation, she regretted that she had to leave when Harry was on a father-son roll.

Harry was suddenly aware of Barbara's restlessness when he saw her glance at her watch two more times. "I'm sorry. I'm going on like an idiot."

"I have to go. I really do." Pete Gribbin's face was well fixed in her mind's eye. Besides, she had heard enough.

Although annoyed by his compulsive talking, Harry wanted to say so much more about his relationship with Freddy. He felt an almost desperate need to explain that he had taught Freddy about birds and their nesting habits, planets and stars, color and perspective in art, Indian lore, good bugs and bad bugs, Greek architecture, snow crystals, and different kinds of love.

"I told Freddy that the worst of sins was an unkindness to another human being," Harry said hastily as Barbara rose from her chair. He stood, then added, "So, damn it, ask me—a hypocrite of the first order—ask me. How could someone like me teach something like that?"

"I think I understand, Mr. Pitman." Barbara frowned as she mused. "Look, Pete's going to write his story one way or another—hard or soft."

"Hard or soft?"

"A scathing attack on a pitiless kidnapper, with no compassion for the dastardly culprit. Or a more balanced piece. Look, I'll do whatever I can do to soften Pete's story. That's all I can promise. It's late. We've talked long. Or rather, you've talked long."

"Yes, it's late. I have a long drive. Poor Millie. She's waiting." As Harry spurted his words in short blurts, he searched Barbara's face for something more.

"I must go."

Harry sank into his chair as Barbara walked away. She looked back once and smiled. He stayed there, hunched, his elbows on the table. Pissing out the poison was supposed to give relief, he thought as the beer pressured his bladder. He felt more like he had dumped in his pants and still carried the load. His beer-befuddled thoughts skipped about: A compassionate stranger? Is that what she was? Or a con artist? A seductive supplier of information? Gribbin's secret weapon? A flaming liberal do-gooder who gets her kicks comforting poor souls?

Later, as he drove his six-year-old sedan over winding roads through the dark of night, his heavily burdened mind continued to weaken his body and trigger the sickness of expected loss.

# Chapter Twenty-Five

Barbara carried four telephone numbers for reaching Pete. First on the list was 555-9787, his black and white apartment, with bold accents of red, a wild collection of modern paintings in bright colors, several odd-shaped cacti, a cluttered desk, and a bed neatened only before parties. Second was 555-5000, the Clarkton Examiner. Third was 555-2323, Larry's Diner, a lunch and coffee-break hangout across the street from the Examiner. And the fourth was 555-1198, Cooper's Tavern, two city blocks from the diner.

Pete was at Cooper's, drinking ale from a bottle and bemoaning his fate: "First time she ever stood me up like this."

Clarence Cooper catered to a newspaper crowd. Reporters from the Examiner and the Courier, as well as many from across the river and beyond, gathered nightly in his tavern to drink, swap tales, throw darts and chew on salty strips of dried herring. Marked by a red neon sign, the tavern was actually a dimly lit cellar bar below the Charlene Hotel. Behind the oak door stretched a narrow barroom, its long bar often packed three-deep. The food menu was limited, but Cooper's sizzling steaks with mushrooms, served at tables in the rear, were a favorite among the in-crowd.

Balding and unmarried, George Winston leaned on the bar and bitched about life. The undernourished, bespectacled gnome had been a copy editor at the Examiner for the past 20 years. He sat on a stool in Cooper's every night but Sunday, grumbling about whatever. Next to him was Peter Gribbin, who did his own share of snarling, but had learned years ago how to deaden Winston's discord. He leaned the other way, toward young Rudy Cox, blond and handsome cub at the Courier, a recent journalism graduate. Cox had drunk too much Scotch and was mushing his words as he talked about the investigative stories he should be handling. "But th... they keep givin' me Girl Scou' cookie sales an' churs... church news."

"Hell, I still write stuff like that," Pete said, "between other stories."

"But I don't get th'others."

"Fear not, my friend. It'll come. Give it time."

Turning from Pete, Winston leaned the other way and bitched to baldheaded Jimmy Dunlap, the Examiner obit editor: "So I gotta make Parson's look good, 'cause he's dead, the bastard, and his agency's a big advertiser. Hutchinson's worse than those horseshit preachers who wave lilies and luster over dead thieves."

"It's a bitch, all right," said Dunlap, barely aware of Winston's words.

"Noski ges th' good assignmens," said Cox, a muscle-toned gymnast who had learned his drinking habits at college. He distorted his handsomeness by displaying the brooding mood of a sad-eyed hound dog.

The name Noski sent a shockwave up Pete's backbone. Thankful for every ounce of Scotch in Cox's blood, Pete urged him on: "Yeah, they give Noski the good ones, all right. Real good, like the one he's into right now."

"Yeah."

Suddenly Pete wondered why Joe Noski wasn't in Cooper's sucking up bourbon as usual. He put his arm around the intoxicated cub. "I thought he'd be here tonight. I had something for him."

"He's a... he's outatown. He went..." Cox lifted his head and turned his bleary eyes on Pete. "Ahhh, no y' don't."

Pete backed off, realizing that Cox hadn't lost all his senses. "Let's not talk shop." Images of Noski snooping around Oakford plagued Pete as he squeezed the 23-year-old at the back of his neck. "Let me get you another Scotch."

Clarence Cooper, a jolly fatman, poured Scotch and uncapped ale, then waddled to the ringing telephone at the end of the bar. "It's for you, Pete," he yelled in a voice too high for his size. "It's you-know-who."

Pete slid from his stool, then squeezed a few shoulders as he walked along the bar. "Bill, how are you? How's it going, Tom? Barney, I'll call you tomorrow about the rotten-egg stink blowing on the Melrose project." Barney was a PR flack for Union Chemical.

As usual, Pete pulled the telephone cord as far as possible and turned toward the wall near the men's restroom. He spoke in hushed anger: "Damn it, Barb, what the hell happened?"

"Sorry, Pete," Barbara said. "I got tied up. Really tied up. I couldn't help it. Look, I'll explain when I see you. Okay?"

"Where the hell are you?"

"At a booth on Locust."

"For Christ sake, why?"

"Walked up from Fishermen's."

"What were you doing there? Who's with you?"

"No one, now. Look, I said I'd spell it out later. Give me a break."

"Like you gave me?"

"Sew it shut, Pete! Look, I want you to come to the house. In about an hour. Okay?"

"What's with you, anyway? You stand a guy up, then want him to rush to your whim. I think I'd rather hit the city room and put together some takes of the Pitman piece."

"Don't give me that, Pete. Come on. I'll see you at the house in about an hour. Give me time to get home and put Daddy to bed first."

Pete envisioned Barbara in a frothy negligee and felt an erection coming on. "Okay. I'll be there."

Minutes later Barbara's shiny blue Toyota was bouncing above the speed limit on its way from downtown Clarkton to the wealthy suburb of Eddington. Barbara's father had bought her a Mercedes that was gathering dust in the Smedley garage. She refused to drive it to the south-side Nettleberg Clinic.

Alfred Smedley was resting comfortably in his big, high-back, leather chair when Barbara arrived home. She knew he would be in his study, reading a book and puffing on his meerschaum pipe, filling the air with sweet-smelling tobacco smoke. She also knew that her mother would have already retired to the East Wing. Evelyn Smedley always went upstairs an hour before her husband.

Barbara struggled to catch her breath as she entered the study, having just run up the steps of the South Portico and through the spacious entrance hall. She waved away tobacco smoke, then said, "Pete's on his way over, Daddy. Why don't you clear out and let me have this room?"

Alfred Smedley didn't need to be asked to "clear out." He needed only one quick mention of Pete's impending visit to encourage him to flee.

"At this hour?" grumbled Smedley, a portly gentleman of 68 who had tasted the good life. Dressed in his maroon robe of silk, and sitting before his huge fireplace, he looked like a man who had just stepped out of an English novel of the 19th century. His bulldog face was topped with thick white hair, and a lion-and-serpent crest was embroidered on the left breast of his robe. Surrounding him were dark paneled walls and thousands of books on shelves of deep mahogany.

"I'm going to fix him a midnight supper," said Barbara as she reached for a large beer stein that rested on the mantel. "I want to use your stein," she said after grasping the ornate earthenware mug. It was one of those capped steins, a prized possession of her father, given to him in Bavaria by a dear friend.

Smedley's grunt turned into a choking spasm. He took his pipe from his mouth, put his book aside, stood and glared at her.

"Just this once," she said. "He likes beer and ale, and I want this to be special—very special—right there, on a table for two, before the fireplace, with candlelight."

"We have a dining room."

"Oh, that big old thing. That's for the king and his stuffy court. Can you see Pete at one end of his majesty's table, and then me, miles away at the other? No, no, Daddy." She pranced around the study, holding the stein with one hand and waving away smoke with the other.

"Wilhelm Schmidt gave me that mug."

"I'll take good care of it, Daddy."

"And that bushy-haired ape is going to drink from it."

"Oh, go to bed." She hurried to him and kissed him quickly on the cheek.

By the time Pete arrived, Barbara was dressed in a light-hued yellow negligee of flowing silk. She had combed her hair to a full, soft flow that picked up luster from the candlelight. After careful consideration, she had set a small table near the stone fireplace, not far from her father's leather chair, and had topped it with a short, fat candle in a massive stick of brass. Raw clams floated in juice on half-shells that clustered on each dish. Next to her plate, capturing the candlelight, stood a narrow-stemmed crystal wine glass half filled with Chablis. Next to his platter of clams was the Bavarian stein. The two chairs were tall, handsomely carved ladder-backs, moved from alcoves in the west wall of the study. At the last moment, she had added another touch—an incense burner that seldom saw the light of day or candle, a small brass frog given to her by Pete. It rested near Pete's fork, giving him the opportunity to light it if he so wished. She really didn't care for the scent of burning incense, but suspected it was some sort of a turn-on for him, perhaps associated with a Gypsy fortuneteller or Oriental brothel.

Barbara hurried Pete into the study where she stopped suddenly in the middle of the Persian rug and pulled him close. She kissed him sensually as she pushed her fingers through his hair.

"Hey, what is this?" he asked, after breaking from her. He enjoyed her moves, but questioned her purpose. "What do you want, anyway? And where were you earlier tonight?"

Barbara simply turned him toward the clams and said, "Look, one of your favorites."

"Maybe I want you first." Pete nibbled on her ear.

"Get over there." Barbara pushed him toward the table. "You'll find bottles of ale on the hearth."

There they were, next to a owl-shaped andiron of polished brass—bottles of ale projecting from a silver bucket of ice.

"You're crazy," said Pete as he took a closer look. "What is all this? You're up to something big. Whatever it is, it's really big."

"Don't fret about it now." Barbara snuggled up to him, kissed his cheek, and ran her fingers up and down the nape of his neck. "Sit down and enjoy all the rewards and profits first."

"I'm not that easily had, and you know it."

"So, take what you can get. Take it all, and if I don't get what I want, that's my loss."

"You don't lose that easily." Excitement put teasing twinkles in his eyes. "I'll tell you what. I'll play your game, but with caution— vigilant caution." Yet while he spoke of caution and tried to mount his defense, the lure of her candlelit face and hair was undercutting his efforts. Again and again she melted away the icy crystals of suspicion in his eyes. Focusing his thoughts, he asked, "How strict are the rules. Are we permitted to change the order of events?"

"No."

"No? Just like that—no."

"Desserts come last. They always have. Sit down."

Pleasure and wariness mixed in his expression, and a half-smile spread his lips slightly as he sat and tasted his first clam. He kept his eyes on Barbara, even when horseradish shot piercing fumes up his nose. "You fixed this yourself, didn't you?" He dipped another clam into the cocktail sauce. "You know I like it pungent."

"I wanted to heat you up," she said coquettishly, giving him a come-hither look that made him sweat almost as much as the horseradish.

"You wench," he said fondly, just before the brass frog caught his eye. A curious expression spread fleetingly across his face, followed by nervous laughter that choked off suddenly. Then he stroked the frog and uttered, "Burrrp," in a bad effort to imitate a croak. A moment later he leaned toward the hearth and grasped a bottle of ale. "I think I need this," he said while popping the cap with a carved rosewood opener that Barbara had placed conveniently near the stein. "You didn't miss a trick, did you?"

Barbara deliberately wet her lips and parted them slightly, then slowly lifted her wine glass to an alluring mouth. She sipped sensually, then said, "Someone told me raw clams are an aphrodisiac."

"I think you mean oysters. Anyway, I don't need an aphrodisiac. In fact, right now I'm having the opposite problem." He drank from the bottle.

"Daddy's stein." She nodded toward the Bavarian mug.

"A little too fancy for me, Barb."

Although annoyed, Barbara didn't show it. She smiled teasingly, ate a clam, and stabbed another with her fork. "By the way, how's the Baker case developing?"

He almost showered the table with a mouthful of ale, covered his lips, and forced a swallow. After wiping off the foam, he bellowed, "You ask that? Now?"

"Simply to make conversation."

"It doesn't fit the mood, and you know it. I don't need that kind of conversation, believe me."

"Appease me, and you'll get what you want."

"What is this? You're interfering again, aren't you?"

"Test me by telling me."

"You're prostituting yourself. You want facts instead of money, but you're whoring just the same."

"Blackmail is a better choice. Or extortion, maybe?"

"Hey, I'll buy that. Either word fits."

"Play the game, Pete. You said you'd go for it."

"What's the big deal? I have no qualms about telling you that we're rolling tomorrow with whatever I have so far. Can't wait any longer. Noski's crawling up my ass."

"You're not running the story with only half the equation?"

"Hell. no. I'll confront Pitman in the morning with what I have. If he opens up, I've got myself a new lead to hang everything on." Pete squinted his eyes at Barbara. "I don't get it. You're bleeding for a guy you don't even know. A baby-snatcher, no less."

"Don't sell short my bleeding heart. I know you dig a good sob-sister piece. Without me your Macaulay story would have had no soul. So there." She stuck out her tongue and wrinkled her nose "Now, let me get this straight. You're telling me that Noski's got the story, is that it?"

"He's damn close."

Barbara had planned more sensual sipping and misty mood-building. But she had already acquired, with ease, some of what she sought. Now came the dangerous part—revealing her audacious plunge into Pete's investigation, and presenting her transgression as a noble effort of great benefit to him.

Suddenly Barbara couldn't down another clam—let alone the second course—as she groped for the next step in what she had thought was a well-engineered plan. News that the Baker-story deadline was imminent added to her conflict. "I'm warm," she said, opening her negligee to reveal cleavage. Still floundering and trying to catch an elusive idea, she parted her lips again and stared at him with innocent wickedness. "Maybe we can change the order of events." After lifting her napkin to her lips, she stood and hurried from the study.

Pete was quick to follow, catching up with Barbara in her richly furnished bedroom of sea green and off-white—a room with soft, thick carpeting that aroused Pete as much as the massive four-poster bed with canopy. She fled into her powder room—not an unusual move—so Pete proceeded to ready himself, undressing quickly and stumbling as he pulled off his trousers. In jockey shorts only, he threw himself on the bed and stretched out to await Barbara, expecting her to follow the usual ritual and appear soon in her misty chiffon, her body temptingly silhouetted in the doorway. His briefs bulged as he envisioned her slowly unfastening her negligee and letting it fall to the soft carpet.

But Barbara didn't come out of the powder room.

In time he mumbled, "Holy shit," as hormonal frustration fired up his impatience. When his anguish reached a level of low tolerance, he yelled, "Yo, Barb, what's the holdup?"

Again, no response.

"What's going on?" Still aroused, Pete slid from the big bed, stepped on the soft carpet, wiggled his toes, and walked toward the powder room. "Barb? You okay?"

Barbara's scheme wasn't progressing as projected. Her efforts at seduction had weakened her own restraint, and only the closed door protected her from herself. She wanted Pete and pictured him lying on the bed. But she had not yet confessed and maneuvered as planned. Clever, astute, quick-witted Barbara was suddenly unsure of herself.

"I'm okay," she said.

"So come on."

"About this game I'm playing..."

"Enough's enough. I can't stand the stress."

"Actually, I was going to get your motor running full speed, then pull the plug."

"No way, Barb. We never play that game. Hear me? So what did you expect to bargain for?"

"I love you."

"Okay, that's it. Level with me. Right now." Pete's bulge began to soften.

"I really do love you."

"So, you love me. And I love you. That's agreed."

"I talked to Harry Pitman after you told me not to."

Pete might as well have been punched in the gonads, the way his deflating member suddenly shriveled. "Son of a bitch." His face reddened with anger. "You've gotta be kidding!"

"Listen to me. I've got your story. And it's a good one. He told me everything."

"I told you to keep out of it! My God, how could you?"

"I met him on the street. It just happened. We went to Fishermen's. Look, he knows I'm going to tell you. All I promised was that I'd try to get you to soften the story by telling his side of it. You need his point of view; you said so. Don't be an ass, Pete. I may have done you the biggest favor of your life."

"Come out here, damnit. I don't want to keep talking through this goddamn door."

"Not until you promise not to shout or curse or touch me."

"Son of a bitch!"

"Go lie on the bed. Way over on the other side. Then I'll open the door."

"I'm not going to hit you. I've never hit a woman. Have I ever hit you?" He sat on the bed. "Not that you don't deserve a good slap. Goddamn, you deserve it."

Barbara slowly opened the door. She stood still, staring at him.

His chin stiff with anger, Pete shook his head in disgust. "You were going to tease me until I almost shot off, then leave me there panting on the bed until I agreed to write the story your way. Right? I can't believe you'd do anything like that. Christ almighty!" He stood and kicked his shoes with his bare feet as Barbara stepped back. Glaring at her, he said, "It wouldn't have worked, you know. No way! I have more pride than that. I would've walked right out of here. Maybe for good. I still might."

Now it was Barbara's turn to simmer. Her eyes flared as she toughened her resolve. "Damn it, Pete. Sit down and listen. Maybe I was wrong to try to soften you up, but..."

"Soften me up? Is that what you call it? You mean turn me into a goddamn frustrated animal."

"Please Pete. Listen. I really wanted you tonight. That's why I stopped the game. I couldn't go on with it. When I was behind that door, I knew you were on the bed waiting, and I was a complete wreck, totally thwarted."

Pete paced in circles, sat on the bed, clenched his fists, and stared between his legs. Gaining composure, he looked up and said, "This story is important to me, Barbara. Mess it up and I won't forgive you like I did the last time—that scandal at Rosemont Hospital. You pranced in there asking questions. Everyone ran for cover. And I lost the scoop."

With hesitance and a sheepish look, she said, "Pitman might go to the police."

"What the hell do you mean?"

"I think he might go to the police. After all, he knows your screaming headlines will hit him in the face any day now. It's to his advantage to go to the police first, isn't it?

"You told him that?"

"It was mentioned. What the hell, Pete, it doesn't matter now. You said you're running the story tomorrow, and your deadline comes long before Noski's. You'll be on the streets before the Courier."

"You're forgetting their early edition."

"They wouldn't use it in that, and you know it. It doesn't have the circulation. And even if that happened, Noski's story would be hollow. It wouldn't have what I'm giving you. Look at the time. It's after midnight. I just left Pitman a couple hours ago. The Courier story would have been written hours ago, even laid out and pasted up by now."

"Your head's not on straight, Barbara. If Pitman goes to the cops, the story will be on the wire in no time. Everybody'll have it. For your sake, I hope to hell I'm lucky. Even if I'm first with the story, if it comes from the cop shop, it's not my investigation breaking it open. Any shithead can report that some bastard surrendered to police."

"All you care about is your big investigation, your big exclusive. What about a basically good guy who messes up? What about the kid?" Barbara turned her back to Pete and leaned on her dressing table. "You know, Peter, you'll have your big story, and you'll probably have it first, and it'll be a damn good one, too, if you'll just listen to me."

Pete stood and stepped toward her. She turned and eyed his body up and down, wishing the night could have been different.

"And to think I was all ready to go—ready to confront Pitman tomorrow morning, give him my angles, show him what I'd dug up, tell him I was going to run with the story, and see if he'd open up."

"So that's it. Your pride is hurt because he opened up to me first."

"Barbara, I don't have to take this."

"Get to him in the morning like you planned. Nobody's stopping you. And if he goes to the cops, so what? You can show how your investigation pushed him into it."

Pete breathed more slowly. Lowering his voice, he said, "What was he doing in Clarkton anyway?"

"Sit down and I'll explain."

Pete sat on the bed again and looked down at his naked legs. Barbara stepped close and he lifted his head and looked directly at her firm breasts, thinly covered in soft chiffon. He wished the night could have been different.

# Chapter Twenty-Six

Surrounded by hanging pots of Swedish ivy and wandering Jew, Elizabeth Baker sat alone in the large, family-size, built-in breakfast nook along the back wall and window glass of her yellow-and-green kitchen. Light from outside, filtered by feathery fronds of potted ferns on the backyard deck, splashed here and there on the table and across her face. She sipped coffee as a slice of bread toasted nearby, and stared into an empty bowl that she had intended to fill with cereal.

Dressed for the office, George stepped into the room, with a newspaper under his arm, and took a close look at his wife. "You're still in your robe."

"I couldn't seem to get going this morning."

"What did you eat?"

"I was going to have cereal." She pushed away the bowl. "But decided on a piece of toast."

"Which is burning!" George tossed the newspaper aside, leaped to the toaster and popped up the charred bread as smoke spread the smell of burnt toast through the kitchen. "This damn thing doesn't pop when it should. You can't eat this." He threw the blackened slice into the sink and turned to Elizabeth. "You've got to eat more than toast."

"If I could I would," she snapped. "I've got absolutely no appetite." Sighing, she pushed strands of her red hair from her face. Tall, slender, long-faced and freckled, she had lost the sparkle that had made her so attractive as a young woman. The years had blanched her face and hollowed her cheeks.

"You know, Liz, I feel like I'm in a time warp. Like I'm moving back a dozen years. It's deja vu—that's what it is. I don't think I can handle it again—your desperate kind of hope that paralyzes this family. Those years were hell because of your refusal to accept that he was gone. What you did to yourself, and me, and the kids..."

"But I was right, wasn't I," she interrupted.

"We don't know that. And in the meantime we have to go on living. We have to think of Teddy and Chuck. Teddy wouldn't have that goddamn twitch or tick if it weren't for..."

"Don't do that," she interrupted again. "Don't lay that on me."

"Look at me, Liz. You're doing it all over again. Just like before. You can't. It'll destroy us."

"Those reporters know. They do, George—they know."

"They have you all worked up."

"They wouldn't be doing all that snooping and asking all those questions if they didn't know."

"Maybe. But let's not take a fast ride to a sudden fall."

"It's like you don't care. It's like before—all those years when you didn't understand how I felt."

"I did understand."

"You never showed any hope."

George sat opposite his wife and rested his hands on his balding crown. His hairline had receded several inches in a dozen years. Skin was taut over his sharp features. "I had my hopes, but they were buried deep inside me. I guess I was protecting myself." His tone was soft and serious. "If I had filled the air with the kind of noise that you spewed, we would have destroyed ourselves and the kids."

"But we could have shared hope."

"No. As it was you built your hope into some sort of frenzy. I can't imagine us building on each other."

"But you never said anything. You always walked away. It was so hard. I would wake in the middle of the night and hear little Georgie crying. I would see his face in my dreams. I would try to picture what he looked like as the years past."

"Don't you think I did? I'd glance at kids in the ball field, in the school yard, on roller skates and skate boards, in the malls and I'd wonder—would he look like that, or that."

"Why didn't you tell me?"

"I couldn't." He reached for her hand and squeezed it.

"I've got to have hope, George. And I guess you do too, or you wouldn't have bought that early edition of the Courier."

"There's nothing in it."

George and his wife started when the telephone rang. But Elizabeth leaped first and grabbed it.

"Yes, this is Liz Baker. Oh, yes, Mr. Gribbin. Yes, he's here. Do you want to talk to him or me? Okay. I'll get on afterwards."

# Chapter Twenty-Seven

"Yes, that's right. But I really don't want to talk about it." Pacing in the kitchen as he talked, Harry gripped the telephone tightly as he listened to Pete make one point after another. "Yes, you're right. Okay? No, I don't want to talk about it anymore. I assume Miss Smedley told you everything." Harry sharpened his tone: "No, don't come here. I won't be here anyway. I'm going to the police this morning. No, not Clarkton. Local. Whenever I get there. Mr. Gribbin, I really can't worry about your deadline."

Harry's hand shook as he returned the handset to the wall. "Jesus!" Still in his pajamas, he sat at the table, picked up his cup and found his coffee cold. The 8 o'clock call had not awakened him, for he had been hanging his head over coffee since 6 a.m.

Minutes later he stepped onto the back porch where sunlight flashed and flickered as breezes tossed the tree limbs. Although it would be weeks before the maples reached their peak of brilliance, already the first leaves of autumn speckled the yard, sent twirling to the ground by cool winds that stirred the September flowers. He looked at the tall and straggly dahlias, their colorful heads too heavy for their stems, their lower leaves brown, crumpled and curled. They saddened him, probably because he was already disheartened. Maybe because they replaced the zinnias that he could no longer tolerate. The start of fall was always a poignant time for Harry. But this year it was deeply sorrowful.

Harry walked toward the woods at the far end of the yard and pushed through knee-high weeds behind the garage where thorns and nettles scratched and stung his bare ankles. He lost a slipper in a tangle of brier, retrieved it, and stumbled on. Unknowingly he carried burs into the underbrush and the dense woods where a woodpecker stopped its tap-tap-tap on a sycamore and flew skyward through limbs of tall trees. The path to the beech tree had been narrowed by summer growth despite the trampling sneakers of Freddy and Billy.

Finding his way to the old beech, Harry looked up at the tree hut that the boys had completed with such diligent work. There it was, a strange mixture of woods, dark and light, crudely assembled into a six-by-six foot room, complete with open door and windows, and topped with a flat, overhanging roof. It was cradled by three giant fingers that reached out from the center of the tree—three limbs that seemed to hold the hut protectively, turning up and snuggling it against the trunk.

Harry knew it was the sacred ground of boys and not a place for fathers. He knew that its secrets were sacrosanct, bound by the blood-on-blood ritual of young males. But he wanted to touch its parts, inhale its scent, feel its texture, capture its aura. He wanted to experience it, if only for a brief moment. So, in pajamas only, he climbed the tree, huffing, grunting, pushing, pulling, losing both slippers, awakening stiff muscles.

Cramped inside, he bent his neck and squatted as his eyes focused on a Playboy centerfold next to a colorful drawing of a fierce dinosaur. Harry wanted to open the many small boxes that were stacked against the back wall, but there was a limit to his intrusion. Instead, he fingered the walls as if to seek messages or feel vibes. He glanced at a large tin can attached to a hose and reflected on its purpose, then touched a piece of pink quartz among a collection of rocks next to a jar of acorns. A trap door in the roof caught his eye, and he considered its use. Perhaps it opened to the stars on cool evenings when the tree was bare, or gave a look at nesting birds or squirrels seeking beechnuts.

The barefoot struggle to climb down the tree was worsened by a splinter in Harry's big toe. But he cared little about splinters or scratches. He did grimace, however, when he landed feet-first on the roots of the old tree. Hopping about, he succeeded awkwardly in putting on his slippers.

Harry stopped in the backyard, along the hedgerow of laurel, and gazed down on Freddy's rock garden where an assortment of succulent plants grew among smooth and jagged rocks. He was well aware that each rock had meaning for Freddy—reddish brown chunks from Minnow Creek, salt-and-pepper granite from Quarry Gorge, fieldstone from Millie's farm. His throat filling, Harry bit his lip as he recalled the boy's efforts—the hunting, the hauling, the arranging. How proud Freddy was that day when he first showed his garden to his dad, and prouder yet that spring when his tulips bloomed.

Harry picked up Freddy's baseball glove from the top step of the porch, held it against his chest and did not fight the feelings. His eyes moist, he allowed his mind to flash an array of images— Freddy at bat, Freddy on first base, Freddy catching a fly ball, Freddy stealing home.

Feeling the splinter as he walked, Harry angrily told himself he didn't care if his toe fell off. Or his foot. Or his leg. Yet as he climbed the stairs toward Freddy's room bittersweet emotion erased his momentary anger. Awake but lying still, Freddy watched his dad quietly place the fielder's glove on the baseball shelf.

"Hi," Harry greeted as he sat on the bed and placed his hand on Freddy's leg, squeezing it affectionately. He smiled at the boy. "You're usually up by now. You don't have much vacation left. School starts in a couple days."

"Why didn't you wake me? And why are you still in your pajamas? Aren't you going to work?"

"No. I'm not going to work. And Millie's not coming."

"And I'm not going to the farm?" His eyes wide, Freddy sprang up excitedly, a smile spreading his cheeks. His hair, bleached almost white by the summer sun, spun in all directions, whirling from his cowlick like a pinwheel, and flopping down over his forehead.

"I thought you liked the farm?"

"I do. I do. But you and me doing something together is funner."

"More fun," Harry corrected.

Freddy sat staring at his dad, waiting for an explanation—perhaps mention of a hike, a fishing trip, an amusement park, or some coming adventure-of-the-day. He would have settled for a few hours in the yard and man-talk. But his elation was short-lived. His smile faded as he sensed adversity. The intuitive youngster had become more and more astute at perceiving Harry's mood. And the many loose pieces of fact that bounced about in his head prompted quick response to signs of misfortune. Now wide awake, he remembered Harry's late return from Clarkton, his pained expression, his forced smiles, the telephone call early this morning, the hushed words.

"What are all those stickers on your pajamas?" Although curious about the burs, Freddy asked the question primarily to fill a void.

"From out back. I looked at your hut. It's a great hut. The best I've ever seen. You've got what it takes, Freddy. I'm proud of you."

Freddy offered no verbal response. But his expression revealed fleeting pleasure, then weighty thoughts.

Harry lowered his eyes, remained silent for a moment, then said, "I'm in trouble, Fred. Serious trouble. And I'm going to need your help." Forcing resolve, he looked up and searched Freddy's face.

Freddy parted his lips as if to speak.

"Now wait," said Harry, fearful that Freddy's words would impede his course. "Let me talk." He followed a deep breath with a lengthy sigh. "When you were about a year old, Mom found you crawling near the river in Clarkton. She picked you up and took you away. It was wrong, because you belonged to someone else. But she was sick because she didn't have a baby of her own." Harry felt a pain in his chest as he watched the boy's jaw grow rigid and saw his expression become stoic as if he were preparing for blow after blow. Turning in pain and shame, Harry glanced at the floor, only to look back again and explain, "I didn't know about it until weeks later when I got vacation time and came up here. Every day I was going to return you, but for some reason I just couldn't. I was wrong. It was a terrible thing to do. But, you see, I blamed myself because I couldn't get your mother pregnant. And I felt sorry for her. She loved you so much. But there was really something more to it. I guess I was afraid of destroying everything—my life, her life, our lives together. Oh, hell, Freddy, I don't know. Let's face it, I was weak."

"I'm glad you kept me."

The words wounded Harry and sent a shiver through his body. He wanted to grab Freddy and hold him tightly against his bosom.

"Anyway, I grew to love you." Harry's eyes filled.

"I don't care about all that stuff about Mom taking me and everything. I just want to stay with you."

"You had a lot of it figured out, didn't you?"

"I guess. Some of it."

"The trouble is, Freddy, people know now."

"That reporter?"

"Not just him. I have no choice but to go to the police."

"Can't we go away some place? You and me? We'll go some place where nobody'll find us. Please?"

"That's not right. Besides, we'd be running for the rest of our lives."

"Will they take me away from you?" Freddy's stoicism slipped away. His eyes filled and tears ran down his cheeks.

"Hey, there," said Harry as he put his hands on the boy's shoulders. He tried to smile as he looked at Freddy and allowed him to see a grown man's tears. "We have to face this together. Remember, I said I'm going to need your help."

"Will you have to go to jail?"

"I don't know."

"But it wasn't your fault." The boy buried his face in Harry's lap.

"Oh, yes it was, Fred. It was more my fault than your mother's. She was sick. I don't have that excuse."

Freddy's words were muffled as he said, "I don't care if you're not my real father." Harry could feel the heaving of the boy's body.

"I know. And I love you for it. But you have a real mother and a real father—and they're nice people."

Freddy pushed himself away from Harry, exposing his red, wet face. Anger and frustration mixed with sobbing grief as he distorted his expression and yelled, "I don't want them." He ran from the room, fled to the bathroom, and locked the door.

Harry was quick to follow, but didn't try to force the bathroom door. "Come on, now." He sought the right words, but couldn't find them. Ashamed, he thought of himself as a pitiful example of a man. Finally, he simply said, "I'm sorry. Freddy, I'm sorry."

"I don't want those stinking, rotten people!"

"They're not stinking or rotten."

"I don't care. I don't want them."

"Listen to me, Fred. I can't handle this without you. Remember what I told you about problems? Remember how we used to talk in front of the fireplace, and along the lake? About the things that might go wrong? And how we'd face them together? Let's take this thing hour by hour and day by day—you and me, together. Okay?"

Harry's words stirred up a host of images in Freddy's mind— images of the man who had taught him about plants and rocks, had taken him fishing and hiking, had encouraged him to seek and learn and open his mind to diverse thinking, had patched his cuts with bandages, had soothed his hurts with talk. A view of Harry as strong, never gutless, was paramount in the whirlwind of thoughts that pushed Freddy to open the door. He stood there in his blue shorty pajamas, his chin up, his lips taut, his eyes red. "I'll help you, Dad."

The boy was tense and quiet as he dressed. So was Harry. They made breakfast together, but ate little. They argued with restraint when Harry insisted that Freddy stay at Millie's farm while he went to Westhampton Police. "Damn it, Freddy, you said you'd help me. It's best that I go alone. Show me some guts, now. Go pitch some hay. Feed the calves."

\* \* \*

The farmhouse sat on the crest of a hill, silhouetted against a bright morning sky, its details obliterated by the sun. A stiff breeze tossed tall tufts of grass along the plank fence. Dust from the dirt roadway filled the air and tickled nostrils. Father and son embraced at the crossroads amidst the smell of cattle. Harry drove away.

## Chapter Twenty-Eight

# Kidnapped Baker Youngster Held Secretly for 12 Years
## Former Clarktonian Confesses to Police
### Clarkton Youth Found Secluded 70 Miles Away

**By Peter Gribbin**

OAKFORD -- A golden-haired boy from Clarkton, thought drowned in the Logan River 12 years ago, is believed to be alive in this secluded village.

Ever since the so-called drowning of little Georgie Baker, Clarkton Police have insisted that the son of Mr. and Mrs. George T. Baker, 707 Logan Drive, had been swallowed by the river and carried out to sea. Only the boy's mother, Elizabeth, believed her son still lived. She wept today when told of the boy's possible whereabouts.

Late this morning, Harry Pitman, former neighbor of the Bakers, walked into Westhampton Township Police headquarters and confessed that he and his mentally ill wife had kept the boy hidden here in Hemlock Valley, about 70 miles north of Clarkton, for the last 12 years. Pitman, who lived at 709 Logan Drive until about 12 years ago, is expected to be charged with kidnapping.

The Baker child disappeared at the age of one year in the most publicized Logan River "drowning" in Clarkton history. On that warm summer night 12 years ago the river was dragged for hours, until Chief Clarence Kirby of Clarkton Police called a halt to efforts. The case was closed quickly and never reopened.

An investigation by the Examiner led to Pitman's confession today. Pushed by Mrs. Baker's gnawing belief that her son still lived, this reporter learned the whereabouts of Georgie Baker after discovering that a 13-year-old boy, called Frederick Pitman, was living in Oakford with the Bakers' former neighbor. The first clue was a description of the boy in a story about the Oakford Youth League baseball team in the Woodbine Journal.

In an interview yesterday with Barbara Smedley, clinical psychologist at Clarkton's Nettleberg Clinic, Pitman contended that he knew nothing of the kidnapping on that fateful summer day of the "drowning."

He said his wife Ellen, now a patient at Northampton State Hospital, had whisked the child away to Oakford unbeknown to him. According to Pitman, he found the baby with his wife several weeks later. Unexplained is why his wife left Oakford without him, or why he stayed behind and chatted with police, reporters and neighbors at the scene of the drowning. Pitman denies a kidnap plot, and contends that his "weakness" and fear for his wife's health were among the reasons he failed to return the child or notify police.

George Baker, the boy's father, reported that he had talked to the alleged kidnapper more than a month after the baby's disappearance and about two weeks after Pitman left Clarkton to join his wife for a so-called "vacation" in Oakford. According to Baker, Pitman behaved as if nothing had happened, continued to load his car with clothing and furnishings, and even asked about Mrs. Baker's health. Sometime later the Pitman house on Logan Drive was put up for sale.

During the years that followed, only the child's brokenhearted mother argued that her son might be alive. Clarkton Police ignored her, and only the Examiner took up her cause. An attractive redhead, Elizabeth Baker has grown thin with grief. She and her husband have two other sons, ages 17 and 15.

Yesterday, in his interview with Smedley, Pitman confessed feelings of guilt because of his inability to impregnate his wife. He spoke openly about his wife's desire to mother a child, and of her emotional breakdown and withdrawal that rendered her almost mute. She was committed to Northampton State Hospital more than two years ago.

Since then, it was reported, the handsome blue-eyed boy has been shifted back and forth between Pitman and a back-country woman named Millie Barnes, daughter of a small-time dairy farmer, who, it is believed, has used the boy to scrub cattle and shovel feces from bull pens. The alleged kidnapper contends, however, that he has given the boy a "good life."

Pitman is a graphic artist with an advertising firm. If he is brought to trial in Clarkton, it would be that city's first kidnap trial.

\* \* \*

143

Pete's story didn't make the deadline for the noon edition, so it missed early newsstand sale. But it was delivered to Clarkton and suburban homes in the two-star final, its front page headline screaming the kidnap news. Barbara threw the newspaper from the vestibule into the spacious entrance hall where it bounced off a teakwood plant-stand that held a bronze urn of Chinese fan palm. She looked down at it as it lay on the blue-and-white tile, grunted, sighed twice, then picked it up again, folded it and tossed it high against an upper bend in the bannister that curved toward the second floor. It fell apart and floated down piece by piece as Barbara kicked the leg of a marble-top table. A small Rodin nude turned and skidded to the table's edge, hesitated, tipped, and nose-dived to the floor. Barbara's next sigh turned into a growl, and her lips moved silently to a string of profane words as she ran up the stairs.

Dinner was served at 7:15 in the Smedley home. Barbara seldom arrived for the five-course affair, usually eating with Pete, sometimes with a Nettleberg colleague, occasionally with a female friend. When she did join her parents she normally dressed for dinner to please her mother. But not this night. Her mood was neither soft nor flowing. She entered the long, burgundy-carpeted dining room unexpectedly at 7:25, still in navy slacks and a man-tailored shirt. Barbara liked good clothes and wore expensive things, but knew when and how to play roles. For the Nettleberg clinic she tied her hair into a tail and tempered her makeup.

"Have Hattie set another place," said Barbara as she pecked her mother's cheek. Hattie was the Smedley's first white maid. Blacks had become too expensive.

"Barbara!" exclaimed her mother softly. "We thought you'd be eating with what's-his-name." Evelyn Smedley sat at one end of the long table, her husband at the other. She was a tall, handsome woman with pronounced cheekbones and slightly rounded shoulders—an aging Vogue-model type, obviously once a youthful beauty. Her hair was blue-white, teased and shaped weekly by her stylist. Draped in lavender silk, she wore a single strand of pearls. Without question, Evelyn befit the ambience of the richly appointed room.

"I'm not eating with what's-his-name," said Barbara with deliberate disdain. "I may never again eat with what's-his-name." She waved at her father, then seated herself midway between her parents, under a chandelier of several thousand prisms. Using her hands as a megaphone, she called to her father: "Hello down there."

"You didn't change for dinner," Evelyn said disapprovingly.

"Sorry, Mother, but I simply didn't feel up to it," Barbara said with her usual directness.

"Well, you'll have to settle for a fruit appetizer with your sherry," said Evelyn as she spooned a cherry from her cup. "Hattie said the clams were depleted last night."

"I fed some of them to what's-his-name. I wish he had choked on them." Turning toward her father, she said, "Oh, Daddy, did you read his story on Harry Pitman and the Baker boy?"

"Can't say I have. Couldn't find the evening paper."

"Oh—well, I tossed it about, then later picked up the pieces and shoved them into that palm plant. I'll put it together for you after dinner."

Alfred choked on a piece of pineapple, cleared his throat and frowned at his daughter. He pulled his gold pocket watch from his satin vest and looked at it. Barbara wasn't sure why. Perhaps he wanted dinner to end quickly, or felt Hattie was slow with the second course. Or maybe he simply sought diversion.

"Why you might think they kept the boy tied up and locked in a closet, the way Pete tells it," grumbled Barbara as her fiery eyes burned holes in the embossed mural of Scottish countryside that decorated the wall. "He used what I gave him without expressing Pitman's emotions, his pain, his compassion, his fatherly instincts, his love for the boy."

Hattie, a small Scandinavian in pale blue and crisp white, silently appeared and arranged a place setting before Barbara, then vanished.

Barbara glanced at her mother, then glared at her father. "And he makes Pitman seem callous as hell—chatting at the drowning, asking about Mrs. Baker, and all that..." She finished the sentence silently. "Worst of all, he implies a plot. There was no plot! It just happened! And he makes that Millie woman out to be some sort of country bumpkin. What's this 'back-country' stuff? If that isn't editorializing I don't know what is. Back country? She's a farm woman—a kind, lovable woman who happens to live on a farm."

Evelyn finished her fruit, touched her lips with the corner of her napkin, looked at her daughter and said, "You won't digest your food, Barbara—not when you're so irritated."

Alfred followed his wife and lifted his napkin to his lips, then asked, "How angry are you, dear?"

"Very." Barbara clenched her teeth and stared hard at her father.

"Good," he said softly, nodding his head and taking pleasure in his daughter's displeasure with Pete.

"Oh, Daddy!" Toying with her cocktail fork, she kept glaring at him and shaking her head. "You aren't even listening to me."

"Oh, yes. You're taking the side of the criminal again."

"Don't do that! Don't say that! You know how I hate that!"

"But your father's right, dear," Evelyn said.

"Ohhh, damn. You people are infuriating!"

"But we've told you so many times, Barbara," Evelyn commented. "He isn't really for you."

Barbara looked dazed, totally perplexed by her mother's remark. "Who? What are you talking about?"

"Your reporter friend."

"We're not discussing my relationship with Pete. You're not listening. You're not getting my point. All you two care about is my feelings for Pete. We're talking about Harry Pitman and what Pete is doing to him. I mean, that story—it's... it's... It's just so... The way he says the boy was shifted back and forth. It's despicable. It's the worst kind of slanting. It's contemptible."

"Well, I haven't read it," Alfred said.

"And that bit about scrubbing cows and cleaning bull pens— well, forgive me Mother, but it's pure bullshit."

# Chapter Twenty-Nine

Westhampton Township's three-man police force had never before handled a kidnapping case. Harry's visit had flustered the chief, a short, stocky, thick-necked man with a pushed-in face. Chief Henry Knapfoot, once a fish-bait salesman in Logan's Inlet, knew little about law. He had immediately consulted with the township secretary, Mabel Tillman, a squatty blonde who ran just about all municipal affairs: "Should I call Clarkton Police? It happened in Clarkton."

"No. I think kidnappings are federal. Besides, we're right on the state line."

"So you think we should call the FBI?"

"I think so. Or the state police, maybe?"

"Probably the FBI. I'd better talk to someone first. I'll keep him locked up for the night."

"What about the kid? He's on that farm, I guess."

"I'll check on him. I suppose I should."

"Aren't you gonna pick him up?"

"No, no, no. Let the proper authorities do that."

"You want to talk to that reporter if he calls again?"

"Put him off, if you can."

Not until the next day did Knapfoot and Tillman consult with two members of the Township Board of Supervisors. Then they called the FBI.

Hours later, when the September sun cast a late-day glow on the Barnes farm, a black sedan turned between fence posts and followed the dirt road toward the farmhouse, raising a cloud of dust. Two Muscovy ducks wheezed, fluttered, and scurried out of the way, bending their necks as they waddled under the plank fence.

Harry sat in the back of the car with a federal agent named Johnson—a middle-aged, broad-shouldered man with an aquiline nose and heavy tortoise-shell glasses. The driver, a lanky agent named Koop, was a fair 30-year-old with sandy hair cropped close. Koop stopped the car in front of the wide porch of the old farmhouse—a three-story, clapboard house, its white paint washed gray by storms and peeled by the summer sun. Battered shutters, once a deep Prussian blue, hung at the many windows of the sagging structure—a house that seemed to have settled itself comfortably on the crest of a slight hill. Weather-worn barns, silos and a milk house clustered east and north of the house. Pastureland sloped in all directions from the summit.

"How long do I have?" Harry asked. He tried but couldn't hide his anguish, so evident in his eyes and inflections.

Koop put his arm atop the seat, leaned back, looked directly at Harry and said, "We won't rush you. Johnson will go along."

"I want to talk to Millie Barnes first," Harry said. "I have things to explain."

Freddy was in the calf barn with Alan Barnes, Millie's 30-year-old, dark, curly-haired brother, the baby of the family, conceived unexpectedly and born when his mother was 41 and his father 43. Unmarried and somewhat reclusive, Alan had worked on his father's farm since he was old enough to feed calves and toss straw for bedding. He had little or no interest in women, and spent his spare time collecting and polishing pebbles and hunting fossils in a nearby limestone quarry. Freddy was helping Alan toss straw into stalls, but his mind was on Robinson Crusoe's island, a place where he and Harry might live alone in safety, finding ingenious ways to survive. Again and again his mind saw sandy beaches, palm trees and coconuts, fish-fries over open fires, wild animal hunts, and a friendly, broad-grinned native wearing a loincloth and carrying a spear.

"It's time to milk," said Alan, a thin but sturdy specimen, unlike his overweight sisters. His chubby mother had bled to death years ago after a baling machine crushed her foot. Although Alan's features were small, almost feminine, his biceps were well developed from hoisting bales and loading feed grain. But his sad eyes said he belonged elsewhere, not on a farm.

Freddy started. "What?"

"It's milking time. We'd better finish up here and go help the old man. You feed pellets. I'll get the hay."

The "old man" was William Barnes, tall, lean, strong for 73, and weathered like his house. His skin was well-tanned hide. Though he sired three sons, he was the worst of mules, swearing to run his farm until the day he died.

"I'll finish up here," said Freddy, who had fed the calves and heifers often, finding it a fun-time adventure. "You go on." Although work had never been demanded of Freddy, he had pitched hay, straw and feed on nearly every visit to the farm. With Alan gone, he talked to the young animals as he scooped pellets from burlap sacks and tossed them into feeding troughs.

Instead of opening a bale of hay, Freddy sat on it and pondered his fate and that of his father. He and Harry could go south to Mexico and, like Poncho Villa or Geronimo, live in the hills. They could hunt jack rabbits and armadillos, and grow their own corn and beans. Or they could change their names and live in a big city. Or, like Toby Tyler, they could join the circus. Being on the run would surely be better than living with strangers.

Freddy conjectured about "those people" again and again. The Bakers. How would they treat him? What were they like? Did he look like them? Blond? Blue-eyed? He didn't really want to know. In fact, he didn't really want to think about them. His stomach muscles tightened.

The door at the far end of the barn opened, and Harry stood silhouetted against the fading orange sunlight. Behind him, but not in Freddy's view, was Johnson, leaning against a rusty manure spreader.

"Fred?"

The boy looked toward the silhouetted figure, but didn't speak.

"You there, Fred?"

Freddy pushed himself to his feet and, with a burst of energy, ran to Harry and wrapped his arms around him.

"You okay, boy?"

Freddy shrugged his shoulders, held tightly, and pushed his cheek against Harry's chest.

"We have to have another man-to-man talk." The triteness of his words disturbed Harry, for surely there was a more meaningful way to describe the talk he was about to have with Freddy. "Come on." Harry led his son back to the bale of hay where they sat next to each other. He put his arm around the boy. The feeling that permeated his body sapped his energy and froze his larynx.

Fear reigned in Freddy as he looked up at his dad. When words came, they were choppy and quick: "How come you're here? The cops? What did the cops say? What's gonna... What's gonna happen? What are they gonna do?"

Harry struggled to speak.

"Dad?"

"I... I have to go back," Harry said.

"Back where? Why?"

"No bail has been set yet."

"Can we go home?"

"No. Now listen to me. I said I have to go back."

"Can't we go away?"

"Fred, please. Look—there are some men here with me, and they're going to take me back."

The boy's body quaked. "What's going to happen to me?"

Harry was slow to answer as he fought for words. "They tell me you might be a ward of the court for a little while." Again, inner turmoil closed his throat. But within seconds he said, "Chances are you'll go back to your real parents early on, because there's no question about custody."

"What do you mean?"

Harry's next words were his most difficult. Emotionally, he could not accept them. "The Baker's are your flesh and blood."

"No!"

"You were born to them. You belong to them. A custody hearing would be cut and dry."

"I belong to you, Dad. Please don't let them take me." Freddy's wet eyes pleaded as Harry had never before seen them plead.

"Look, Freddy—you've got lots of years ahead—a whole lifetime. In not many years you'll be of age. You'll be able to come and go as you please. And we'll see each other."

"You told me you'd never leave me." The boy stood and glared at Harry. "When Mom got sick, you said we'd always be together." His color reddened and tears wet his face—a face whose muscles were shaped by anger and frustration.

"You know I can't help it, Freddy."

"We could run away. Please?"

Harry answered without words. His eye's told the boy that running was not possible. "When your mother went away, I said I'd try to keep us together. And I meant it. But I always told you that something could go wrong. And I knew deep inside that it might. I want you very much. More than anything in the world, I want us to stay together. You're my son. You'll always be my son." Harry's paramount need was to have Freddy believe him. Without that, his hurt would cut far deeper than anguish.

"No, no." Freddy backed away, but kept glaring. "Then why did you go to the cops? If you wanted me, you wouldn't have. We could've gone away." Unable to cope with the destruction of his world, he became irrationally defiant and felt the need to lash out at something, anything. "You don't really want me!" he yelled. He cried openly, his face distorted by heaving sobs.

Harry stood and reached out to him, but Freddy turned and ran toward the open door.

"Freddy! Wait!"

The boy kept running—out the door, past Johnson and the manure spreader, around the silo, through an opening in the fence, and across pastureland that sloped down, then rose toward the red-orange horizon.

Harry raced after the boy. His desperation pumped adrenaline, fueling his body and powering his legs. Johnson was several steps behind him, struggling to keep pace.

Freddy's legs carried him so fast that he almost overran himself, catching himself twice as he plunged forward. His chest ached as he ran across the soft, sloping earth, a spongy cushion of grass that sucked at his feet. He dodged clumps of thistle as he ran toward the bright evening sky. To Harry he was a blurred silhouette in a brilliant halo.

Freddy fell belly down on a mound of red earth. Throbbing as he wept, he heaved with each breath, the side of his head pushing into the mound. He dug his hands into the earth and squeezed fistfuls of soil.

Harry stopped running about 100 feet from Freddy, spun and faced Johnson. "Please, back off, will you?" he yelled. "Goddamnit, leave us alone!"

Johnson stopped and waited as Harry turned back toward the disappearing sun. Half running, half walking, Harry pushed toward the mound of earth where the boy lay in the dim light of the red sky. When he reached Freddy, he fell to his knees and put his hands of the youth's shoulders. Tears moistened his eyes as he stayed there, hovering over his son, keeping his hands on the boy as if to comfort him. He said nothing as the warm glow of evening faded. In time, Freddy turned his head and looked into Harry's eyes. And a moment later he grabbed his father and held tightly.

# Chapter Thirty

Still in his blue pajamas, Freddy stood at the bedroom window, facing the river that supposedly had carried his body to sea. Through the trees he could see the water, set aglow by the morning sun. The maples, tinged with yellow and red, had just begun to feel the crisp nights of autumn.

George and Elizabeth Baker had decorated the room in all-boy red, white and blue. They had decked the walls with Yankees, Red Sox and Phillies pennants, knowing that Freddy played baseball. Built-in, rock maple bunk-beds had been installed against the north wall only days before Freddy's arrival. And the Bakers had purchased baseball, football and soccer gear of all sorts. They had bought sets of oil paints and watercolors, a chest of drawers, a footlocker, a well-stocked toolbox, and a set of encyclopedia. The books were on shelves that George had worked hard and fast to finish in time for their son's return.

Theodore and Charles now shared one bedroom to make way for their younger brother. Teddy had to give up his room, and Chuck had to suffer intrusion into his space. They had yielded unhappily after a lengthy talk with their father about unselfishness and sibling relationships. George and Elizabeth were determined to give Freddy his own room because of what they perceived as adjustment problems. Despite their efforts, Teddy and Chuck showed resentment.

Freddy hurt inside. Each morning he stared out the window, through the trees, at the river, while his mind filled with daydreams and troubled thoughts. Harry had pleaded with him to accept the Bakers, but the boy could not counter his emotions. He wanted to be with Harry in that familiar Oakford cottage. He wanted to dig in his backyard, run through his woods, climb his beech tree, play with his friend Billy, swap secrets in his hut. He knew the feel of the driveway pebbles on his feet, the broken curbstone on his buttocks. He knew the cracks in his sidewalk, the oil spots in his garage, the carvings on his beech tree, the number of rope knots on his school flagpole. Hemlock Valley had been his only home. He loved its trails, for they were the arteries that fed his heart and nurtured his mind.

Alert and keen, Freddy realized that the Bakers kept trying to please him. But he resented their efforts. He didn't want their gifts, and he rebuffed their affection. Again and again he read a line of Harry's departing letter: "Keep reminding yourself that the Bakers are your parents, and that they love you." He tried. But his efforts failed. Harry was his father, and Oakford was his home. And each recollection tugged at him, wounding body and spirit.

Tears no longer filled his eyes at night. But morning fears remained. And despondency grew.

Under the hanging plants at the kitchen window, George sipped coffee and finished a cinnamon Pop-Tart in the breakfast nook. Elizabeth forced down her last spoonful of oatmeal. Chuck and Teddy had taken the school bus to Clarkton High, leaving behind sticky bowls and half-empty glasses of milk.

"Well, he can't stay in his room forever," George said, nervously pulling on his ear. "I mean, he can't just live his life there. I don't know what else I can do. Hell, I'm a patient guy," he said, thinking of the storms he had weathered with his wife. "It's crisis on top of crisis in this family." His flesh was drawn, and his kindly blue eyes seemed deep set.

Elizabeth lifted her head and looked at her husband. "He can't miss any more school." She stared sadly, asking questions with her eyes, seeking George's help. "I can't really talk to him. Every time I try, he closes me out. I can see it in his expression, even when he doesn't walk away. And he won't accept George as his name. It's gotten to the point where I don't call him anything. I'm afraid to."

"That's not important, Liz."

"What's not important?"

"If he wants to be called Fred, then call him Fred. That should be the least of our worries." George gulped his cooling coffee, then carried his cup to the sink. "All we can do is be patient and give him more time."

"But you're losing your patience. I can see it. You just about said so yourself, only seconds ago."

"I go up and down. I'll be all right." Knowing his wife's temperament, George was well aware that he had to be the leveling force.

"He's extremely defensive toward Pitman, and that's hard to take." The wan, hollow-cheeked woman saw Harry only as a despicable kidnapper who had plotted to steal her baby. "I can't handle that part of it."

"What do you mean?"

"I want to tell him what I think. In my heart, I want to convince him. I want to condemn Pitman for what he is. But I can't. If I even tried, I'd lose him. I know that."

"If he feels some sort of love and loyalty, or whatever—then Pitman must have some decent side to him." George's effort to temper his wife's ill will and hide his own spite was typical of him. He was almost afraid to express his bitterness, his vengefulness—feelings he had never before felt for another human being.

Elizabeth failed to respond in words. She lowered her eyes again and toyed with her spoon. A nervous woman, she had worked hard through the years rearing two sons, despite her gnawing heartache. In her weaknesses—a depleting unrest, a fitful determination, a punishing remorse—she had great strength, a kind of strength that surpassed that of her husband, the pretender and peacemaker. And she usually got her way.

"I'll talk with him again before I leave, if that's what you want." George was overdue at Logan Mutual, where he worked as an insurance adjuster.

Grasping at the suggestion, Elizabeth focused firmly on her husband and nodded yes.

Minutes later George stood in the doorway to Freddy's room, annoyed with himself for feeling intimidated by a 13-year-old. The boy was still in his pajamas, still looking out the window.

"You've missed a lot of school. Really, we're worried about you."

"No need to worry about me."

"That's good. But I think you should get your mind on other things."

"How do you know what I'm thinking about?"

"I'm sure Harry Pitman would want you to go to school."

"You don't know anything about him." Freddy refused to turn from the window.

George felt helpless. "Well, I have to go to work now. Why don't you surprise me and get yourself out of here before I come home. How about that? What do you say?"

Freddy didn't answer.

Feeling thwarted again, George stood quietly for an uncomfortable moment, then backed off slowly and turned away.

Severe anxiety plagued Elizabeth hours later when she climbed the stairs and asked Freddy to join her for lunch. He refused. Again she was shattered. But despite the hurt—or maybe because of it— she didn't push, but simply walked away.

Back in the kitchen, she set to work fixing soup and a ham sandwich, with no waning in her determination. She arranged the food on a tray and carried it up to Freddy's room. Quietly, without a word, she placed the tray on the dresser, and walked away.

Freddy turned from the window and stared at the food. Minutes later, he spooned some soup, bit into the sandwich, but ate little. He dressed himself in a faded pair of well-worn blue jeans and a yellow polo shirt, deliberately avoiding an array of new clothing purchased by the Bakers and neatly arranged for him by Elizabeth. After hesitating at the top of the steps, he raced down and out through the front door. He leaped steps and dashed across the street.

"Wait!" Elizabeth called from the doorway. "Please! Where are you going?" Her alarm was obvious. It sharpened every word.

"Just out!" he yelled, not looking back. Pricked by conscience, he immediately regretted his terse answer and added, "Along the river." Suddenly aware that the word "river" might painfully distress her, he stopped abruptly, spun around, looked at the anguished woman, and said, "Don't worry. I'll be back."

Elizabeth did worry. But there was little she could do except watch him hurry north along the river. She tried to convince herself that this was good, for he had finally left his room. Yet her apprehension grew with each painful thought: He'll run away. He won't comeback. He'll try to find Harry Pitman.

Freddy looked back only once, not to see Elizabeth, but to glance at the house next door. It was just as Harry had described it, except that the blue shutters had been painted green. Freddy tripped on a maple root, then hurried on toward white water and the bend in the Logan. Hickory trees—that's what he wanted to find. How sharp the pictures were in his mind—pictures from late-night discussions by the fireplace, from long talks at the lake's edge. How clearly those weekend hickory hunts had been described to him. In woods beyond the north turn of the Logan—that's where Harry and Ellen had sought acorns and nuts for the white squirrel. It was there that they had rested their backs against a hickory tree, and stretched their legs into a patch of wild huckleberry. It was there that the chipmunks scurried and tumbled, the squirrels climbed and leaped, and the yellow-bellied sapsuckers drilled wells in the trees. Freddy wanted to find that place. He wanted to jump for hickories, run through the underbrush, feel the bark of trees that Harry had touched, sit on the earth, stretch his legs, and listen for the fluting of the hermit thrush.

Elizabeth was still on her porch when Freddy vanished amidst the trees. She ached to know the thoughts, troubles and fantasies of this 13-year-old boy—her son, yet not her son. She wanted to share, feel and understand. And she argued with God, reproaching Him for giving and taking, then giving back, but barely. Why, God, should it be this way? No, she would not condemn herself for self-pity—not a woman who had known death, labor, birth, nursing, spoon-feeding, bouts of chicken pox, bed wetting, the stretching of paychecks, the fear of cancer, and incalculable trauma—all entwined with a thread that twisted and strangled for a dozen years, an umbilical cord that stretched and pulled far and beyond.

Deep in the woods, but within the sound of white water, Freddy put his hands on the gray trunk of a shagbark hickory and fingered the loose, rough texture. He breathed heavily, for he had zigzagged in and out of thickets, dashing among the trees. When his breathing quieted, he looked up at the branches and let his eyes float from limb to limb, freeing them on a whirlwind trip of a leaping white squirrel—an imaginary squirrel, the embodiment of himself in a free-spirited attempt to elude reality.

On this day, for a brief while, Freddy escaped.

# Chapter Thirty-One

The maintenance man in the Clarkton Trust Building realized that Barbara Smedley was a woman with a mission when he asked, "How's the weather?" and she answered, "Sixth floor, please." Although the days of elevator boys had long gone, he kindly reached in front of her and pushed the button.

"Watch your step."

Barbara didn't look down. She hurried along the corridor and opened a door marked, Caesar Kent, Attorney-at-Law.

"Tell Mr. Kent I'm here to see him," she said to a thin, spoon-nosed, bespectacled brunette. Barbara was dressed in an expensive tweed suit, a blending of aqua and tan. She radiated a sense of importance.

The secretary responded. "Miss Smedley to see you, Mr. Kent."

"Have her come in." The voice was deep.

Head up, shoulders back, Barbara pushed her way through a swinging gate and an office door—with conviction and self-assurance.

Fifty-seven-year-old Caesar Kent sat behind a massive desk in an oak-paneled room that was well polished and appointed, furnished with heavy ebony chairs and glass-enclosed cabinets of law books. He stood—all 300 pounds of him. His 60-inch belt cut deep into his waist, just above bulbous flesh that expanded his pinstriped trousers into the shape of a giant Spanish onion. His large, round head was topped with thin, black hair, parted in the middle and slicked to his scalp. His tie was loose, his collar unbuttoned, his pinstriped coat hanging on a brass clothes tree at the side of his desk.

"Well, what do you say?" asked Barbara.

"He doesn't stand a chance."

"That's not the question. It boils down to the degree of guilt. You know, guilt that's so smothered by a blanket of emotion that it's almost snuffed out. And you can lower the degree and smother it." Barbara leaned over the desk and kissed him on the cheek. "Sit down."

Kent slowly lowered his big body. "I don't think so, Barb."

Barbara put her hand on her hip, glared at the attorney, and said, "Daddy's done a lot for you." Caesar Kent had been Alfred Smedley's lawyer for 20 years.

Kent pulled in his chin and gave a knowing and sardonic smile. "And I've done a lot for your daddy, and that doesn't have a goddamn thing to do with this." His eyes twinkled. He was used to Barbara's cat-and-mouse games. "I've done more than I should for you, too, baby. Chasing here and there on a dozen rat races, while you crusade for some poor bastard who sliced up his wife and kids."

"Caesar, listen to me." Barbara paced back and forth before the massive desk. "Guilty or not guilty isn't the question. Hell, I'm smart enough to know he aided and abetted—for his own peculiar reasons. But it's the judge and jury who determine the degree of guilt and punishment."

"Don't talk down to me, honey."

"I want to bring them to their knees in tears. I want to stop a crucifixion, that's all."

"What got to you this time?"

"A nice guy and a 13-year-old kid."

"You're hopeless." Kent took a pinch of snuff from a gold snuffbox and pushed it under his lip. "You want me to take on a losing case."

"But you're so good, Caesar."

"Don't try that. Flattery, I don't need."

"Pretty please."

"Sit down, and I'll tell you what I think."

"No. I'd rather stand. I want to look down on you."

"There's a strong possibility they conspired—this Harry Pitman and his wife. You say he's a good guy. Maybe he's a slippery dude who conned you."

Barbara leaned on his desk. "No way. It didn't happen that way. Now stop testing me. Wait till you get a taste of this one. It's got goodies that'll make you salivate."

"I've told you before, I don't go after cases, they come to me."

"I hate your pomposity." She pulled back from his desk, kept her eyes fixed on his, and presented a sudden smile. "Do it for me."

Kent's jelly-like flesh shook as he spewed a hiss, followed by a grunt.

"Caesar, I won't give up. I'll go to Daddy, and I'll punish him until he slices some of that blubber off your belly."

"You're a bitch, you know it?"

Barbara smiled again—wryly at first, but then allowing her grin to warm. "I knew you'd do it."

"Not because of your daddy or the whole board of directors of Smedley and Smedley. Just for you, darling, because you're so sweet." Kent had suspected he would take the case, long before Barbara entered his office. He couldn't recall ever saying no to her.

Barbara kissed him again, well aware that he reveled in their bristling relationship. She had intensified her flippant charm through the years, always underpinning it with affection.

"I've been reading Pete's stories," said Kent. His smiling eyes toyed with her.

She stuck out her tongue and trumpeted a loud, juicy raspberry.

Kent laughed. "I figured you two were at it again. Tossing balls-of-fire maybe? Remind me to stay out of your way."

"There's no 'way' to stay out of. I'm keeping my distance—for now." Spinning around, Barbara waved goodbye over her shoulder. She had known Kent since her teenage days. On his second visit to the Smedley house, he had brought her a potted rubber plant.

Kent had never married, and Barbara suspected it was because of his corpulence. He often joked about his sexual frustrations, even to her—but always in light and humorous ways, which Barbara saw as a cover-up for deeper anxiety. But when drunk one night at the

Clarkton Press Club, he had grimly and pathetically confessed to Pete, in earshot of Barbara, that his "little red plaything was buried under rolls of fat." His compensations were in the courtroom, where he was eloquent. Fluent, forceful and persuasive, he knew how to lift his booming voice to vibrant heights, then lower it to a whisper that could be heard in the last row of a hypnotized courtroom. His mother had been an actress of some talent who had given up the stage to rear her fat son.

Shaking his head in amusement, Kent smiled broadly as he buzzed for his secretary. Eleanor Brett arrived with her steno-pad.

"Start a file on Pitman," he said. "Harry Pitman. Get every newspaper article available on the disappearance of George Baker's son. Also, have LaMont get copies of all police records on the case. He might also check with the Feds. And have him run a personal-history trace on Pitman." Kent leaned back, putting a strain on his oversized swivel chair. His fat fingers pinched his lip and pulled at his chin. Suddenly he lunged forward, his chair screeching. He put his hands on his desk and pushed himself to his feet. "Sift out all names and places from Examiner and Courier stories, and make me a list. And tell LaMont to look into the medical and psychiatric history of Mrs. Pitman. I think she's at Northampton State Hospital. Get me a school record on the boy, Fred Pitman. And I want to know if he goes to church." Kent pinched his lip again. "And, oh, have Mason start a background check on the Bakers."

# Chapter Thirty-Two

The courtroom smelled of Lemon Pledge. Charlie Hastings, a 60-year-old wisp of a man, tossed his rags and spray cans into a bucket at the rear of the room, pushed strands of gray hair from his bony face, and took one last look. He was satisfied. The rows of wooden seats, the judge's bench, the witness stand, the jury box—all shone with satin-like luster. The courtroom of Judge Victor B. Long was silent but ready for the hammering of the gavel and the charge to the jury. Charlie wiped his oily hands on his overalls, lifted his bucket, and opened the doors to the courtroom— just as he had done nearly every weekday morning for 35 years. He stepped into the corridor as the court stenographer arrived.

"Morning Charlie," said the dark-haired, pale-faced little man, who was neatly packaged in a gray pinstriped suit.

Outside, the first snow of December clung to trees and shrubs, but melted on the city streets.

Five blocks across town, in the Clarkton Trust Building, Caesar Kent was still in his office stuffing papers into his briefcase. By now he knew more about Harry than Harry knew about himself. The two men had done all but sleep together during the past two months, and Kent had grown to know the defendant's hobbies, favorite foods, dreams, early hero worships, childhood diseases and toilet habits. The constant probing had frustrated Harry again and again. His head was seldom free of ache. But he welcomed the dependency. He needed to lean on someone, and Kent was surely big enough.

Barbara was never far away. And somewhere deep in Harry's dazed mind he had begun to welcome her "interference," even before she posted the bulk of his bail – with her daddy's money, of course. While in her debt for securing Kent, he was not fully aware of how great the favor, simply because he moved from day to day in a foggy nightmare, suffering heartaches from endless images of Freddy.

Mid-morning arrived before Barbara. She brushed snow from her fur collar and took a seat in the rear, just inside the double doors of the nearly filled courtroom. Clarence Kirby, the squatty and bald chief of Clarkton Police, was on the witness stand, devoid of his dead cigar.

"There's no question in your mind, then, that the defendant, Harry Pitman, knew that his wife had driven to Oakford on the day of the so-called drowning?" asked Karl Harpence, the lean, sandy-haired prosecuting attorney, a 35-year-old Harvard graduate whose youthful exuberance had not waned since his days in moot court. He pushed his fingers through his curly locks and paced before the witness stand. Highly animated, Harpence irritated Kent with his perpetual motion.

"He told me so," answered Kirby.

"Who told you so?"

"Pitman told me. That day at the river. He told me." The chief cleaned a fingernail with his eyetooth. "He said his wife had gone up to this place that was overgrown with weeds."

"Chief Kirby, doesn't it seem strange to you that this woman would take off alone for a vacation spot like Hemlock Valley?"

"Objection," said Kent, who took a deep breath, expanding his massive chest. "We're not interested in opinions here."

"Sustained," said Judge Long, a white-haired, stocky man with no chin, puffy cheeks and a macaw's beak for a nose. He appeared alert, thanks to protruding ears. And, in all truth, his keen, dark eyes watched all.

"Let me put it this way," Harpence said as he lifted his finger to his lips and faced the witness. "The defendant told you that his wife had left for Oakford, indicating that the trip was planned and that he knew about it. Right?"

"Objection, your honor." Kent leaned forward, looked at the judge, but pointed to the prosecutor. "Mr. Harpence is leading the witness. His question calls for a conclusion."

"Objection sustained." The judge aimed his beak at Harpence. "The prosecutor will confine his questions to those seeking facts."

"No further questions." Harpence had made his point. He looked at Kent. "Your witness."

"No questions."

Harry leaned toward Kent and nervously whispered, "I told her to go, but I didn't know she would. She picked up the baby and ran off."

"I know, I know," Kent said in an effort to hush his client. "We'll make our points later."

Harry was dressed in a navy blue suit, white shirt and burgundy tie. His hair was neatly trimmed. He had followed all the rules set by Kent. But the facade did nothing for his shattered innards. His self image was pitiful. He saw himself as a tainted and shrinking weakling, made smaller every minute by the staring eyes of the court.

Joe Hammond of the Clarkton Rescue Squad testified next, elaborating on Kirby's description of the river dragging. Then Chief Knapfoot and federal agents Johnson and Koop relayed statements made by Harry on the day of his "confession." But Harry heard only bits and pieces. When not thinking of Freddy, he escaped into protective reverie, only to be jolted back to devastating reality time and again.

Alert to every word was Pete Gribbin, who sat up front on the jury side, taking notes on a wad of folded paper. He was separated from Joe Noski by several out-of-town reporters. During lulls in the testimony, he would scan the jury. He recognized only an old shoemaker named Vincent Martucci, a wrinkled man with bushy gray hair.

The jury had been difficult to select because of interest in the case among Clarktonians and other Logan County residents. One who hadn't read news accounts was a well-weathered, Pentecostal dairy farmer named Ernest Wilcox, a deeply religious man who shunned the media. He sat next to Rebecca Greenberg, a 29-year-old, unmarried, long-haired beanpole whose newspaper reading consisted of Your Horoscope and Ann Landers. Next to her was a chunky, square-jawed, blond laborer from the Logan latex mills, a 32-year-old father of four named Stephen Karczewski. Between him and the jury foreman was 21-year-old Mary Smith, a round-faced china doll with tiny bow lips and big blue eyes, an escapee from a religious cult who lived with her wealthy parents in the suburb of Eddington.

Harry glanced at the jury only twice, and felt uneasy both times. He couldn't turn toward the panel without seeing George and Elizabeth Baker, who sat behind the prosecuting attorney. Their solemn profiles tightened his gut. Beyond them, at the head of the jury, sat the foreman, a laundromat operator named Shant Narkissian, a dark, bull-faced, bearded man. On both glances, Harry felt the foreman's penetrating eyes piercing him.

Surely the jurors are decent and reasonable men and women, Harry told himself again and again. But with each effort to convince himself, he slipped back to the foreboding illusion of vultures perched on high, each ready to feast on his flesh. Clear your head, Harry. Take your thoughts to crows—and Freddy, racing toward them, pointing, laughing. Mid-autumn. Sunny. A crisp day of yellows and blues. Freddy running through the field. Toward a naked sassafras. Alone against the sky. Six crows on a limb. One by one they flew. And Freddy kept pointing, laughing.

"Your honor, I'd like to call Alice Gardner to the witness stand," said Harpence as he stood facing the judge.

"Alice Gardner," called the court clerk, a small, bookish man wearing wire-framed glasses.

Again pulled from reverie, Harry watched his Oakford neighbor walk to the stand. She was dressed in a yellow-and-green print, more summer than winter. Alice likes me, he thought. At least it always seemed so. He was certain that she would not testify for the prosecution unless subpoenaed—perhaps as a hostile witness.

"Raise your right hand," said the clerk. "Do you swear the testimony you're about to give is the truth, the whole truth, and nothing but the truth, so help you God?"

"I... I do." Alice's voice cracked. Her frog eyes bulged more than ever.

Pete Gribbin watched her carefully as she seated herself and moistened her broad lips. He had interviewed her twice, uncovering little of consequence.

Harpence moved close to the white-haired woman, looked into her eyes, and asked, "Mrs. Gardner, will you please tell the jury where you live?"

"Why, in Oakford."

"And who has been your next-door neighbor for the past dozen years?"

"Why, Mr. Pitman."

"Harry Pitman, the defendant?"

"Yes—and his little boy. And his wife, until recent years."

"His wife. That's Ellen Pitman?"

"Yes."

"Do you remember when Ellen Pitman first arrived in Oakford?"

"Yes."

"Was she a friendly neighbor?" Harpence kept his eyes on the witness.

"Well, maybe not so much at first, but later she..."

The prosecutor was quick to interrupt. "At first, Mrs. Gardner. Just describe how she was at first."

Alice hesitated. "Truth is, I didn't see much of her."

Harpence paced toward the jury, then back toward the witness. "But you knew she had a baby with her?" His voice was deliberately intense, dramatic.

"Yes."

He posed, lifting his chin as he looked at her. Hesitating for effect, he went on: "How did you know this, Mrs. Gardner?"

"I saw her arrive with the baby."

"And when did you first see the defendant, Harry Pitman?"

"On the day he arrived. From my window. He was carrying a big box. A gift. It was gift-wrapped."

"A baby gift?"

Anger reddened Kent's face. "Your honor!" He struggled out of his seat. "I strenuously object! Mr. Harpence is deliberately trying to plant..."

"Withdrawn, withdrawn," interrupted the prosecutor.

Judge Long hammered twice with his gavel. "The recorder will strike the prosecutor's last remark, and the jury will disregard it. Mr. Harpence, I'm warning you."

"Sorry, your honor." Harpence walked away from the witness, then turned back. He rubbed his chin and squinted, as if in deep thought. "When was it that you saw the defendant arrive with that gift? I mean, in relation to Ellen Pitman's arrival?"

Alice shifted her buttocks. "A few weeks later. I'm not sure."

"Did you hear anything?" Harpence almost whispered the question, as if some significant secret were about to be revealed.

"What do you mean?"

Louder, almost booming: "Did you hear Pitman accuse his wife of anything? Did he shout at her?"

Kent stirred his massive body. "Your honor, I object to this line of questioning. Not only is it irrelevant, but Mr. Harpence is again leading the witness."

"Your honor," returned Harpence. "This line of questioning is essential if I'm to substantiate my contention that Harry Pitman knew all along that his wife had little Georgie Baker in her possession, and that he plotted the kidnapping with her. I'm trying to show that he greeted his wife without rancor, and with a gift."

"Objection overruled." Judge Long kept his sharp eyes on Harpence as he said, "You may proceed."

The prosecutor turned to the witness. "As far as you could determine, Mrs. Gardner, the meeting between the defendant and his wife was an amiable one, perhaps even a happy one?"

"Objection." Kent sucked in air and let it out slowly.

Judge Long stared at Kent, then leaned forward and pointed his beak at the prosecutor. "You are leading the witness, Mr. Harpence. Rephrase your question." He tapped lightly with his gavel. "Objection sustained."

Frustrated, Harpence frowned, then forced a smile. "Mrs. Gardner, would you please describe the meeting between Harry and Ellen Pitman on the day in question?"

"Well, I didn't hear any violence, if that's what you mean."

"Did you hear anything?"

"No."

"Thank you. Your witness, counselor."

Kent rose slowly and lumbered toward the stand. He smiled and nodded hello to the witness. "Mrs. Garner, you have pretty good walls in your house?" Kent's deep and resonant voice perked all ears in the courtroom.

"Yes, I believe so."

"And the Pitman house—as far as you know, it's well constructed?"

"Well, they're all cottages in Oakford. But they're sturdy."

"How far separated is your cottage from the Pitman's?"

"Oh, several hundred feet."

"Several hundred?"

"Oh, yes."

"And what lies in this stretch of land between houses?"

"Trees and shrubs. Lots of them. It's thick with hemlocks and laurel."

"Then I presume little sound would travel between the cottages, unless it was, let's say, a gas explosion?"

"I'd say that's true."

Harry drifted where thoughts arose and spun, where flashes came and went in no sane order. Ellen—drawn inward, staring distantly, unaware, her thoughts in a secret vault. Ellen—scampering on campus, circling trees. Grasping, teasing, laughing. He took her—rebounding from a hollow in his childhood—and held her, never to let her go. Never. Ellen—soft, gentle, naive. Beyond the goldenrod, among the birches—touching, squeezing, fondling at the shimmering lake.

"Your honor, I'd like to call Dr. Abraham I. Levinthal," said Harpence.

Harry recalled that big drain pipe of his youth, the one that carried a trickle of water to the duck pond in the park. He and his boyhood friends would crawl far into it. But they always knew how to get out. Now he was being pulled through a dark tunnel, and was no master of his own course. He was living some strange hell that, in his perception of himself, really had nothing to do with him. How had he lost control? He slowly curled his fingers, pushed his nails into his palms, and tightened his fists. Suddenly aware, he looked down at his hands—hands locked in vice-like grips—and released his fingers.

Dr. Levinthal had finished rattling off his credentials, including directorships of two psychiatric clinics and one state hospital, and a list of scholarly articles published in various medical journals.

"Doctor, in the case of a woman with an unusual desire to mother—if she were to kidnap a baby, would she run and hide from everyone, or would she go to a country house and wait there to meet her husband?"

The tall, dark psychiatrist with steel-gray curls opened his mouth as if to speak, his deep-set eyes focused on Harpence. He was left with his jawbone hanging as Kent interjected.

"I object," shouted the defense attorney, who rose to his feet too fast for a man of his size, causing his seat to grunt, shaking the table, and knocking Harry with his elbow. "My worthy opponent is again leading." His booming voice was up a pitch. "I'm surprised at this childish effort to gain an answer to his liking."

"Objection sustained," the judge recited with a weary inflection. His ears reddened. "I don't want to remind you again, Mr. Harpence."

The courtroom was silent as the prosecutor struck another pose. All seemed suspended as the court awaited the prosecutor's next pronouncement. He lifted his chin and grimaced. The occasion hardly called for such high drama. "I'll rephrase." He closed his eyes, frowned, then popped his lids suddenly. "Doctor, will you please explain the usual reactions when a woman of the nature described kidnaps a child?"

Kent mimicked Harpence's dramatics with a grimace of his own.

Dr. Levinthal's expression was somber as he answered in a raspy monotone: "Usually she disappears, runs away. She has a great desire to protect the baby, and thinks of little but that. She goes into seclusion, but soon finds she needs supplies. Her efforts to get them sometimes lead to her apprehension."

Kent pushed himself to his feet. "Your honor, this is outrageous. This... this doctor, or whatever, is talking in generalities. I think we all know that many individuals act contrary to expected norms. We cannot say that every mouse likes cheese. Beyond that, I protest the very presence of this man on the stand. He has no relationship to this case, and knows nothing of the illness of Ellen Pitman."

"Dr. Levinthal has been called as an expert witness, your honor," Harpence said. "He is the state's most noted psychiatrist, and he's more than qualified to explain the behavior of women with maternal complexes. His generalities are conclusions based on years of study. Surely we must be permitted to judge Ellen Pitman's purported actions against some norm. Besides, the jury knows generalities from specifics, and can determine how much weight to place on the doctor's testimony."

"You make your point, Mr. Harpence," Judge Long said. "I overrule the objection. You may proceed."

Harry took another look at the jurors—this time giving them more than a glance while Kent shuffled back to his seat. Since Narkissian's eyes and all others were focused on the witness, Harry allowed himself a full 30-second stare. Humpty Dumpty in the second row, a butterball of a man with an egg-shaped head, reminded him of an obnoxious boy in high school, a perpetual tease who laughed fiendishly when he farted. Harry had no doubt that this man disliked him.

Next to butterball was a black woman that Harry fashioned as a church-going type, ready to sway to any spiritual. She was most unlike the tall Watusi next to her—a slender black male with princely features and a militant bearing, surely a front-line protester wary of the system. Harry's paranoid thoughts pleaded: But I like everybody—black, yellow, brown, red. I've always liked everybody. Honest. And I'm not a despicable child-snatcher.

His paranoid trip was extended by the big-boned brunette next to Watusi—a small-breasted amazon with harsh features and short hair, surely a man-hating dyke who would gladly butcher his genitalia. In truth, the woman was a hard-working mother of two who flipped fries in a hash house. The two remaining jurors were skinny secretaries—one, a black-haired spook with kabuki makeup to deepen her purple-painted eye-pits; the other, a square-chinned redhead with wisps of hair uncurling from a carelessly spun knot. Harry figured they were both stupid.

His jury-stare ended when Elizabeth Baker leaned toward her husband. Harry caught the movement on the edge of his vision. He was quick to focus on his fingernails.

Harpence wrinkled his brow in thought, then asked, "Dr. Levinthal, if a woman is truly mentally ill, does she feel guilt?"

"There are all degrees of mental illness, of course. When guilt plays a role, it usually precedes the illness. What I mean is, guilt may lead to psychosis, but a really psychotic person no longer experiences guilt as we know it."

Harry continued to look at his hands, but he saw Ellen, gazing beyond the hospital gardens to some point of serenity in her shrouded mind.

Kent remained seated as he said, "I object to this entire line of questioning, your honor. It's not in the scope of direct testimony in this case. I don't see what Mr. Harpence is getting at."

"Your honor," Harpence began. "Medical records from Northampton State Hospital, where Mrs. Pitman is a patient, show that feelings of guilt may have contributed to her mental state. It is my contention that if she experienced such guilt in the years preceding her commitment, she was not then seriously ill at the time of the alleged kidnapping of the Baker baby. Isn't it important that we understand her mental state if we are going to understand the defendant's actions at that time? My worthy opponent will undoubtedly allude to Mr. Pitman's protection of his ill wife in debating his client's failure to report the child's whereabouts. On the other hand, I will argue that the defendant deliberately plotted with his wife." Harpence presented a knowing smile to the jury.

Again Judge Long overruled Kent's objection, and Harpence continued with his line of questioning.

"You were saying, Dr. Levinthal?"

"Why—about guilt—it plays a more serious role before a true psychotic state."

Harry leaned toward Kent. "What's the purpose of this?" he whispered. "What's he getting at?"

"Shush," Kent said. Continuing with hushed words: "He's trying to show that Ellen was stable at the time of the kidnapping."

Hearing Kent, Harpence protested harshly: "Your honor!"

"But she's not on trial," Harry whispered. " I am."

Kent spoke directly into Harry's ear: "If you and she were both stable... Well, maybe he hopes that stable plus stable equals conspiracy in the minds of the jurors. Now, shush."

"Your honor!" Harpence protested again, annoyed by the delay.

Judge Long hammered with his gavel as he glared at Kent.

Harpence sighed, then said, "Your witness, Mr. Kent." He nodded toward the defense.

Kent was slow to respond. He put his hands on the table and, with effort, pushed himself up, lumbered toward Levinthal, and stared quizzically. "Doctor..." He paused. "Have you ever met Ellen Pitman?"

"No."

"I see." Kent glanced at the jury. "Have you ever had two mental cases exactly alike?"

"Well... no sir, not exactly."

"And doctor, would guilt, no matter how strong, turn a truly stable person insane?" Kent locked his eyes on Levinthal's.

"I... I supposed not."

"In other words, the mind would have to be unstable to be so affected by guilt?"

"Well..."

"Answer yes or no, doctor."

"I'm not sure what you mean by unstable."

"Come now, doctor, you know what I mean." Kent's jowls quaked, revealing his impatience. "The world has millions of guilty people. Our institutions would be deluged if they all went insane."

Dr. Levinthal rubbed his brow. "It's true that some minds would be more affected by guilt than others."

"Thank you, doctor. No more questions." Kent turned and shuffled triumphantly toward Harry. Before sitting, he leaned to the defendant and whispered, "I want a witness who can testify that your wife was strange or unstable long before the kidnapping—maybe even in her youth. I'll have to fight to get 'em on the witness list at this date, but I'll win that one. Think about it, Harry."

The prosecution's next witness was Helen Molinski of Logan Drive, once a Pitman neighbor. Concentrating on Kent, Harry failed to hear the call, but caught sight of the scrawny, hook-nosed woman as she took the stand. A pang pierced his body as he turned a full glare on her. He hadn't seen the neighborhood gossip since the day of rescue operations on the Logan River.

"What the hell's she doing up there?" Harry mumbled as Kent squeezed in beside him. "Is she on the witness list?"

"Molinski," Kent whispered. "Oh, yes, Molinski. Yes, she's on the amended list. Is she trouble?"

Harry simply sighed.

Kent smiled. "I'll do my homework. Don't worry. We'll take care of her."

"Mrs. Molinski, please tell the jury of your conversation with the defendant on the day of the Baker boy's disappearance," Harpence directed.

The woman straightened the collar of her red polka-dot dress, smiled at the jury, cleared her throat, and prepared herself for the biggest performance of her mundane life. "Well, it was quite evident that he had something on his mind. Oh, he was definitely hiding something. When I talked to him, he..."

"Objection." Kent's tone was matter-of-fact.

"Sustained," returned the judge. "The witness will confine her answers to facts, not conjecture. The jury will disregard the last statement, and the stenographer will strike it."

Harry nervously scratched the edge of the table with his fingernails. "That bitch will say anything about anyone," he mumbled.

Kent leaned toward his client. "He's trying to show that you stayed behind and hung around the river in an effort to cover your crime."

"That's crazy."

Harpence lifted his chin. "Mrs. Molinski, just explain what took place between you and the defendant."

"Well, he came running up the street and started questioning me about what was going on—like he didn't know."

"Objection."

Annoyance tightened the judge's neck muscles. "Mrs. Molinski, don't interpret for the court." Again he ordered her statement stricken.

"I'm just trying to tell what I saw."

The judge scowled and hammered twice.

"What did the defendant say to you that day?" Harpence asked.

"Well, that's just it. He didn't say much of anything. He kept glancing at his house, and then walked away. Something was on his mind. He wasn't acting like anyone else."

"Your honor!" Kent boomed in protest. "I ask that this woman be removed from the stand if she persists in this kind of testimony. The prosecutor has presented no evidence that Mrs. Molinski is a crystal-gazing, mind-reading psychic."

"Mr. Harpence, I must insist that the witness confine her remarks to factual answers," the judge instructed. "The jury will disregard the comment that something was on the defendant's mind."

Kent pushed himself up. "Striking words is not enough, your honor. This woman's remarks are surely leaving an impact on the jurors. This is Mr. Harpence's intent, and you and I both know this."

Judge Long nodded, then turned toward the prosecuting attorney. "Proceed with caution, Mr. Harpence."

The prosecutor weighed his words: "What did you say to the defendant, and what did he answer?"

"I said, 'Oh, Mr. Pitman, isn't this a terrible thing? Poor, poor Mrs. Baker—what a sad thing for her, don't you think?'" The witness lowered her brow. "But you know, he didn't even answer. Now don't you think that's..." She caught herself as Kent swelled toward a bellow.

Harpence quickly interjected, "I'm finished, your honor," and spun toward Kent. "Your witness."

Kent sighed and pulled on his lip. He pondered Mrs. Molinski's testimony and concluded that cross-examination would serve little purpose at this time.

Judge Long leaned forward. "Mr. Kent, do you wish to question the witness or not?"

Kent pulled on his lip one more time. "Not now, your honor. But I request permission to recall the witness later if necessary."

"You request is granted." Judge Long tapped once with his gavel. "The court is adjourned until two o'clock this afternoon."

Harry instinctively looked at the jurors, only to be enfeebled by the stares of Narkissian, Dumpty and Watusi.

# Chapter Thirty-Three

The day was still gray when the noon whistle of the rubber mills echoed across town. Streets were shiny wet from light flurries of snow that melted. Puddles lay on the well-worn steps of the courthouse—a concrete rectangle of early 20th century post office vintage, decked with statues of Miss Liberty. Pete's impatience in the slow elevator agitated him to the point where he burst into a splashing run down the steps as he chased Barbara toward the sidewalk.

"Barbara!" he called. "Wait! Come on, now, wait."

Pete reached her as she stepped down from the curb and aimed for her car, parked across the street in front of Smiley's Cafeteria.

"You're acting like an ass," he said, gripping her shoulder and holding firmly. "Give me a few minutes to call in my story. We'll have lunch, okay?"

"I have plans, Pete."

"No you don't. Come on. Stop acting like a spoiled brat. Hell, we can differ, yet still get along. You're the one who spouts all that fancy talk about getting along with anybody. Now stop being a hypocrite."

"I don't want a scene here on the street." She eyed the passers-by who crossed Federal Avenue after the lights changed.

"Have lunch with me, and we'll talk quietly. That's a promise. You do believe in talking things out, don't you? I mean, isn't that your calling?"

"I can't handle it right now, Pete."

"If you can sit down with some pervert to find out why he raped his baby brother, surely you can talk with me."

She tried to pull away.

"Come on, Barb! Have lunch with me." He gripped her more tightly. "Come on, we'll talk about it."

"Let go of me, Pete."

"No."

"Pete, please."

"Don't 'Pete please' me. We've been more than friends for too long a time for that kind of shit."

"You know, you're really turning me off more than ever."

"Well, what do you expect. You've got me so uptight I had my first wet dream since I was seventeen."

"I think you know how to solve that problem."

"I know you want me. You're not fooling me one damn bit."

Barbara's eye's blazed. "You know, Gribbin, you have a monstrous ego." She started to cross the street, but he held her arm. "Let me go or I'll have you locked up for assault."

Pete let go, but Barbara couldn't cross because the lights had changed again.

"I'm sorry. Look at me. Do you want me to get down on my knees right here in the street?"

Barbara sighed and looked him up and down. He was wearing the tan suede jacket she had given him last Christmas. She liked him in it, thinking it gave him a touch of class. "You're going to get watermarks." She brushed wet snow from the shoulders and lapels. "You shouldn't wear suede in this kind of weather. God, you need someone to take care of you."

"Then take care of me."

Again she looked him over, sighed in resignation, and said, "Okay, we'll give it a try. I'll have lunch with you." She stepped up from the gutter.

"Now you're talking." He followed her to the sidewalk.

"Careful. Say the wrong word and I'll change my mind."

"Okay, okay. Let me call in my story, then we'll head for Cooper's."

"Oh no. I'm not sitting at the bar with all your news cronies."

"Then we'll go to the Sherwood. We can sit in a dark corner."

"We don't need a dark corner."

"I want a dark corner."

"Careful."

* * *

The Sherwood Pub, only two blocks from the courthouse, was dark but much too crowded with noon-time lunchers for the likes of Pete. He and Barbara elbowed their way to the rear, but found no tables for two. Lighted by flickering lamps in deep recesses, the Pub was heavy with dark-stained oak beams and thick table tops. A dark oak railing trimmed stairs that led Pete and Barbara to the second level, where they finally found a niche in an alcove. Their faces were turned aglow by a stained-glass window depicting Robin Hood bending his bow.

Barbara settled herself, studied Pete's face, then said, "You know, it's much different dealing with clinic patients than with someone you're involved with emotionally."

"Ahhh, I'm glad you're still emotionally involved with me."

"Play it straight, now, Pete. Okay?"

"Okay." He unfolded his napkin. "You say it's different dealing with me than with a rape victim or a dope addict. I'll buy that. But you haven't even been trying to deal. You've been closing me out."

"Maybe that's because I'm so attracted to you."

"Now that makes a hell of a lot of sense."

"We don't think alike. We don't see the same things. Emotionally, we react differently to other human beings. We have opposite responses to the world outside of ourselves."

"You're overstating."

"No, no. We've avoided... We've overlooked our differences. We've pretended they're not there. Because of this... this physical..."

"Say it. Go on, say it. Because we've got the goddamn hots for each other. We like each other's bodies."

"Pete, listen. We just can't have a bedroom relationship."

"Don't tell me it hasn't been good."

"Of course it has. That's the trouble. And in between we go about our business avoiding our differences. What about the way we perceive things? I want something more." Barbara hesitated, then softly said, "Maybe something permanent. But it wouldn't work if we can't resolve basic differences. We'd be arguing all the time."

"That's the first time you said anything about a permanent relationship."

"And?"

"Well, I don't know."

"Let's get out of here." Barbara started to slide from her seat. "I'm not hungry anyway."

"Wait. Don't go crazy on me, now. Did I say I didn't want a permanent relationship?" Pete reached across the table to take Barbara's hand, but she pulled it away.

"You haven't been listening. I said I'd like one, but we could never have one. Not the way we think."

"It's this damn Pitman case."

"It's not that simple. It's not just the case itself, but the way we react to it. The way we see it. The way we respond to the people involved. The differences—they're symptomatic of much more, something much deeper."

"This is stupid, Barb. Lovers often disagree."

"Lovers? That's the right word, I guess. Lovers. Pete, I want a compatible relationship on many levels, not just in bed."

"You admit you want me. Right?"

"Yes, I want you." Her eyes moistened. "I want you very much."

"I've never seen that before."

"What?"

"Tears in your eyes."

"That's right. I'm Barbara Smedley—quick on her feet, fast with the words, flip as all hell. But cry? Never! Barbara Smedley doesn't cry."

"Hey, what is this? Look, Barb, I do love you. You know that don't you?"

"Well, let's see. You do say it now and then. But always in the heat of passion."

"Hey, I'm that kind of guy. It comes out then. That doesn't

mean..." Pete lowered his voice to a whisper: "Hey, look, Barb, it's just not so easy to say at other times."

Pete kept gazing into Barbara's expressive eyes—eyes that kept asking questions. His arousal was intense, more so than ever, perhaps because he couldn't have her, couldn't even reach out and hold her. The pulsating pressure in the groin weakened his legs and quickened his heart. He could feel his bare feet on the plush carpet in Barbara's bedroom, his body on her bed, under that canopy. Barbara, in a misty cloud of chiffon. Fingers on his chest and thighs.

"Are you okay?"

"Not really. Let's go to your place. Sneak me into your room."

"No."

"I know you want to."

Barbara shook her head. "Besides, you wouldn't make it back by two o'clock."

"Then come to my place."

"Pete, you haven't been listening to me. Or you don't understand."

"I understand that we want each other."

Barbara stood as if to leave.

"Wait." Pete grabbed her hand.

She smiled a crazy, crooked grin, then wrinkled her nose at him while contemplating. "I'll stay. But only if you want to eat with me, not sleep with me."

"Then stay. For God's sakes stay. If that's all I'm going to get, I'll take it, I'll take it. So, come on, sit down." He waited until she was seated again and staring into his eyes, then asked, "What do you want me to do, stop writing about the Pitman case? Is that what you want?"

"That wouldn't change the underlying differences in our thinking, now, would it?"

"I'm not sure they exist. You say we've been blinded by passion. You think we've been going at it so hot and heavy that we never stopped to look at each other. I'm not sure I buy that argument. But I'll play it your way for the sake of discussion. If you're right, then maybe we should take those deep looks. Maybe we'll see something neither of us expected. Hell, if we haven't looked, like you say, then what makes you think we're so different? How would you ever know? Damn it, Barbara, I want you. But I want every part of you. Yes, I'd probably be lost without your stupid old arguments about poor sick rapists and murderers." He smiled at the thought. "Jesus, I never figured I'd hear myself say that." He looked down and toyed with his napkin. "I want you. I need you. Not just in the bedroom, I know that now. Maybe I've always known it." Lifting his eyes and his voice, he said, "Barbara, I've never said I needed anybody in my whole life. Hey, this is hard-nosed Pete Gribbin talking, the loner who thought he didn't need anyone."

Barbara was taken aback. Part of her wanted to reach out to Pete and proclaim some mutual linkage. But the rest of her canceled any attempt, and she continued to dwell on their differences: "When I read your stories, I translate them into values."

"In other words, you read between the lines."

"Not exactly. Your feelings are in your words. I guess I want you to see things the way I see them. Tell me, Pete, what are your feelings about Freddy Pitman?"

"You mean Georgie Baker?"

"If you knew the boy well you'd realize that he'll always be Freddy Pitman. To himself he'll always by Freddy Pitman. I see the boy often, and I know. I'm sort of a go-between. I carry love between father and son."

"Father?"

"Pete, stop it."

"And this go-between stuff—it gives you some kind of satisfaction, right?"

"Shouldn't it?"

"I wish I knew whether you were doing it to help them, or to fill some need of your own."

"Does it really matter?" Barbara studied the colorful image of Robin Hood, then presented a no-nonsense frown as she turned her eyes on Pete. "How well do you really know the boy? If you knew the terrible hurt inside of him you could write with compassion. If you can't write with that kind of understanding, then you're not telling the whole story."

"I'm trying to tell it objectively, without getting involved. If I become too involved, then I might distort, even unknowingly."

"You know damn well no one can be completely objective."

"I can try."

"Subtract feelings and emotion, and you distort the truth. Anyway, you've been deliberately or unknowingly slanting your Pitman pieces."

Pete bristled. He didn't like having to defend his reporting. "My God, Barb, right now it's the prosecution's case. Give it time and it'll balance out. I know your problem. You don't read fairly. Even when you read a two-sided story, only one side pops out at you— the side you don't like."

Barbara looked for the waiter. "Let's not talk about it. We're tying the whole thing to one issue. And that's not fully it. Something far broader pervades our relationship every time we get involved in a case together."

"Case? This didn't start as one of your social-work cases. This has been my investigative news story from the beginning. You jumped into it."

"And it's happened the other way around. In the Martin case you showed no sensitivity whatsoever."

"You know, you're making me out as some sort of superficial idiot. Have you forgotten the time you told me I had a soft side?"

"When was that?"

"You said my childhood hurts gave me sensitivity. I haven't forgotten. Apparently you have."

Barbara said nothing, but her eyes flashed with memory.

"Did you mean it?"

"I suppose."

"You suppose? You know, Barbara, that was the first and only time anyone ever said anything like that to me. No one else has ever seen through my tough hide. I never allowed it. So, did you mean what you said? Or was it all a bad joke. Maybe there was too much moonlight in your eyes that night."

Barbara was moved. It was unlike Pete to admit a soft side. More than that, he had remembered her words.

"So right now it's hard for me to understand your harping on our differences and my lack of understanding and all this crap," Pete said. "Frankly, I think you should reconsider your entire perception of our relationship."

"It's been a man's relationship." Barbara was surprised by her words. They were an attempt to avoid feelings stirring inside of her—feelings from a night of empathy when her insight into Pete's sensitivity pricked a nerve under his elephant's hide.

"And what is that suppose to mean?"

"Men rush into a bedroom relationship, and then maybe it develops into something more. With a woman it's usually the other way around. She wants to feel something first."

"The end result is the same. Right? And now you're confessing that you played the game backwards. Why? Actually I know the answer—or at least part of it. Deep inside you've been troubled by your need to parade me—a guy from outside your world—in front of the Smedley clan, especially Mommy and Daddy. Rebellion is fun, but it has its cost. See? I have insight, too."

Barbara barely heard his words as her thoughts dwelled on that night of empathy. She started to speak, but was interrupted.

"Do you care for a drink?" asked the blond, baby-faced waiter.

"Are you drinking, Barb, or just eating?" Pete asked. "Frankly, I've lost my appetite."

"Nothing to drink." Barbara forced a smile. "I'll have pastrami on rye, and a side of coleslaw."

"I'll have a bottle of stout and a reuben." Pete tossed his words quickly as if they mattered little. His throat was tight, his stomach knotted.

When the waiter was gone, Barbara tried again to pull together her thoughts. Her thinking began to jell. But when she looked at Pete, her crystallizing thoughts were wiped away by his expression. She had never before seen such a look on Peter's face—a blending of abandon, desire, pleading.

"Marry me," he whispered.

Barbara simply stared, certain that she had heard wrong.

"I'm asking you to marry me," he said.

Still no verbal response came from Barbara. She did, however, react with a wide-eyed, wondering gaze—a steady stare that combined shock with confusion. Her lips parted. Her cheeks blushed.

"Marry me," he repeated.

"Oh my God!" Barbara exclaimed. "What have I done to you?" Her words jolted her as much as they did Pete. Suddenly her thoughts galloped. Views of her brief courting days with Pete and the passion that followed crowded her mind. After all, she had been the one who had chased him. Now she had caught him at the very time she had been trying to avoid him. How ironic, she thought.

"Barbara, will you marry me?"

"No. No. Don't ask me now. Please."

The sting was sharp. Barbara saw Peter's eyes die, and she felt his hurt.

# Chapter Thirty-Four

Once again Barbara sat in the rear of the courtroom. She found it difficult to concentrate on the testimony of George Baker, because her thoughts kept drifting to Pete. Her emotions rampaged up and down. Anger battled with delight, and neither was winning.

Harry's head was bowed until Kent whispered, "Stop looking so guilty." In truth, the defendant felt shame and remorse when he looked at Baker.

Harpence was his usual dramatic self—pacing, pausing, thrusting his arms, lifting his chin, popping his eyelids. "After the day of the kidnapping, when did you next see the accused?" he asked.

Baker fished for the answer. Surely his gaunt face drew sympathy from the jury, thought Harry, who by now could picture each juror in his mind's eye. He saw them all staring at him with ill-will.

"I know it was before Christmas—a sad Christmas, I might add." He frowned as he pondered. "Come to think of it, it was before Thanksgiving. Pumpkins. Yes, pumpkins. It was around Halloween. Maybe before. I remember the trees were in color. Dropping their leaves, in fact."

Harry had no doubt about George's appeal to the jury: a slight man with warm blue eyes, a kindly neighbor with receding hair, epitome of the little guy wronged.

"Tell us about that day," Harpence directed.

"As I remember it, Pitman was putting boxes into his car when I came home for lunch. We talked out front, on the lawn. I asked about his vacation."

"And what did he say?"

"He talked about pumpkins, and how nice it was in Oakford in the fall. Said he was going to stay longer than planned."

"In Oakford?"

"Yes."

"He was extending his vacation? Is that what you're saying?" Harpence widened his eyes and smirked at the jurors.

"As it turned out, I never saw him again."

"He never came back?"

"As far as I know. Like I said, I never saw him again. And his house went up for sale before Christmas."

Again Harpence gave a knowing look at the jurors, then stepped close to Baker while pointing at Harry. "On that day—that day around Halloween—did the defendant say anything about the tragedy of your missing baby, your beautiful one-year-old son?"

"Not at first. He seemed anxious to explain his stay in Oakford."

Kent was irked by Baker's attempt to judge Harry's disposition, but he chose not to object, fearing it would simply build more sympathy among the jurors.

"Please go on, Mr. Baker," Harpence instructed.

"Well, then he asked about my wife."

"This man, Harry Pitman..." Harpence pointed again. "...this man who we now know was living with your son—he stood there and asked about your wife?"

"That's right. I remember telling him that she wasn't well, that it would take time for her to recover."

"And how did he react to that?" Presenting a frown, the prosecutor filled his voice with incredulity.

"With sympathy, I believe."

"He expressed his sorrow?"

"Yes."

"All the while knowing exactly where your little boy was?"

"I told him that Elizabeth—that's my wife—that she still hoped little Georgie was alive somewhere."

"And Harry Pitman heard those words, yet gave no indication that he knew the whereabouts of your baby?"

"That's right."

Baker's testimony twisted Harry's entrails, churned his stomach acids, and intensified his feelings of being out of control.

"He was willing to let you continue under a misconception, continue believing that your baby boy had drowned, that his little body had been carried off by the river waters."

Enough is enough, thought Kent. "Objection," he said as gently as possible. "The witness doesn't know the defendant's will and shouldn't be asked to speak on the defendant's intent or willingness."

"Objection sustained."

"Just one more thing," said Harpence, grimacing as if struggling with deep thought. "On the day of the supposed drowning, did you see the defendant, Harry Pitman?"

"I'm not sure. I've tried to remember. It was a difficult day, a nightmare."

"He was avoiding you, perhaps?"

"Objection!" Kent protested, raising his voice louder than he had intended.

Harpence looked at the jury, lifted his eyebrows, and rolled his eyes. "Withdrawn," he said before the judge could sustain Kent's objection.

"Watch yourself, Mr. Harpence," Judge Long warned.

"No more questions. Thank you, Mr. Baker." Without looking at Kent, Harpence added, "Your witness."

"I have no questions," said Kent.

Harry showed surprise and leaned toward his attorney. "Why don't you question him? He made me seem so coldblooded."

"It wouldn't serve our purpose to keep him on the stand," returned Kent in a husky whisper.

"God knows I wanted to tell him about his baby."

"Well, I can't explain your feelings to the jury by questioning Baker. You'll have your turn. I'm not going to play the villain right now."

Harry expected the next witness to be Elizabeth Baker. Instead, it was Peter Gribbin, whose name sent another shiver up the his backbone.

Barbara twitched almost as much as Harry.

"Please tell the court where you are employed, Mr. Gribbin," Harpence said.

"I'm a reporter for the Clarkton Examiner."

"Isn't it true, Mr. Gribbin, that during the months leading to the defendant's arrest you conducted an extensive investigation into the possibility that the Baker baby was kidnapped?"

"Objection." Kent tried to stand, but sank back into his chair. "Testimony may help the jury decide exactly how extensive Mr. Gribbin's so-called investigation was, your honor. But his inquiries cannot be judged as extensive at this time."

"Sustained."

Harpence glanced from Kent to the judge, then rephrased: "Isn't it true, sir, that you conducted an investigation for the purposes of reporting the story in the Examiner?"

"Yes, that's true." Pete made an earnest effort to be expressionless, partly because of Barbara's watchful eye.

Barbara, on the other hand, was angered by Pete's appearance on the stand. Versed in journalistic ethics and attitudes, she knew only too well the reluctance of reporters to testify, reveal their sources, or share their reportorial notes. In her mind, this made Pete a willing witness for the prosecution.

"Do you consider yourself a good reporter, Mr. Gribbin?" Harpence asked.

Kent showed annoyance by puffing air.

"Yes, very good," Pete answered.

"Isn't it true that you broke the Clifton murder case before the police? Same with the Marlene Casino conspiracy?

"Yes. That's true."

"Now, tell me, during all the months of probing in this case— the Baker case—did you ever once find anything that indicated that the defendant was completely ignorant of his wife's actions?"

"No."

"What did you learn of the accused's actions on the day of the baby's disappearance?"

In robot-like staccato, Pete said, "He talked to Helen Molinski on the sidewalk, across from the river, then went into his house, came out again, talked to Police Chief Kirby, then went back into his house."

"Your honor, this is inadmissible hearsay," Kent protested.

"No, your honor," Harpence shot back. "Mr. Gribbin observed the defendant. Isn't that right?"

"Yes, I watched him," Pete testified.

"Proceed," the judge directed.

"How long was he outside?" Harpence asked.

"A matter of minutes, both times."

"As a reporter, you deal with a great many people, right?"

"Yes."

"Would you say that most of them behave in this manner?"

"People are curious. Most would stay along the river."

Barbara's liver was not alone in secreting bile. Her total essence oozed it. "What the hell do you know about human behavior?" she muttered to herself. "Marry you?" Her tongue vibrated to a discreetly hushed Bronx cheer.

"Here was a man," Harpence said, "who lived right across the street from the supposed drowning. And this man—the defendant—went home after a few minutes and stayed there?"

"He did."

"Your honor," interrupted Kent. "I object to these assumptions based on conjecture instead of fact."

Harpence flashed his eyes on Kent. "Are you trying to say that it's not a fact that the defendant went home?"

With effort, Kent pushed himself to his feet and boomed, "I'm saying that it's not factual to assume that all persons remain at the scene of a disaster."

Judge Long hammered with his gavel. "Both of you are out of order. Direct your remarks to the bench, not to each other." He looked from Kent to Harpence. "I know your feelings on generalities, Mr. Harpence. But generalities differ from assumptions, and I think you've crossed the line."

"Your honor," said Harpence, "it's important that the jury realize that the accused did not act normally."

"Normal? Abnormal? Zany, wacky, loony!" Kent's voice reverberated throughout the courtroom. "We've had no expert testimony on normality!"

"You're out of order, Mr. Kent," said the judge. "If you have something to say, direct your words..."

"I apologize, your honor, but..."

"Harry Pitman did not stay along the river because he knew the baby wasn't in the water," Harpence asserted.

"Stop poisoning the minds of the jurors!" Kent shouted. "Your honor, Mr. Harpence's utter disregard for judicial principles is despicable. This calls for a mistrial. If I were you, your honor, I'd charge him with contempt of court."

Judge Long hammered three times. "But you're not me, Mr. Kent." Bristling, he faced the prosecutor. "I must warn you that you cannot use this courtroom as a soapbox. You'll have your chance to summarize."

"I have no further questions," Harpence said, smiling curiously at the jury. "Your witness."

Kent took his time, scribbled notes, then rose slowly and lumbered toward Gribbin. He allowed his piercing stare to penetrate Peter for seconds before he asked, "Did your investigation—excuse me, your extensive investigation—did it disclose Harry Pitman's whereabouts at the exact time the Baker boy was discovered missing?"

Pete thought for a moment. "Well, I'm... I'm not sure."

"You don't know for sure?"

"He was obviously in the neighborhood. He came walking up the street."

"But you're not certain where he was at the exact time?"

"I suppose not."

"Wouldn't this have been vital in an extensive investigation?"

"Maybe."

"Would it surprise you to know that he was in a physician's office at the time?"

Pete looked puzzled. "No," he said softly.

"Speak up, Mr. Gribbin."

"Okay. So, I didn't know he was in a physician's office."

"Maybe there are other things you didn't find out in your extensive investigation. Thank you, Mr. Gribbin. No further questions, your honor."

Pete glanced toward the rear of the courtroom as he stepped down from the witness stand. Barbara glowered at him.

The next witness was a trim, short-haired woman in a black suit, wearing a mannish white collar and a striped necktie. After identifying herself as a supervising operator for the telephone company, she testified that a phone call had been placed from Pitman's Clarkton residence to Oakford on the night of the Baker boy's disappearance. Harpence allowed the jurors to assume the call's purpose, guiding them with a smiling grimace.

Harry had braced himself twice for the testimony of Elizabeth Baker. Now, he braced himself again as the clerk called her name. But to little avail. Suddenly dizzy, he lowered his head and struggled to catch his breath.

Elizabeth wore no makeup. The lights of the courtroom gave a ghostly sheen to her somber face. Her hair was pulled back, aging her slightly. Although pale and drawn, she carried herself well and sat poised and erect, reflecting a righteous and forthright woman. Aware of her faults—compulsiveness, ill temper, nerves that sometimes frayed—she could throttle all and show determination. She lived by the rules set down by her Irish father and followed the wifely ways of her German mother. Women's liberation was not her thing. She preached honesty to her sons and led them to church every Sunday morning. But Teddy and Chuck, damaged by the 12-year tragedy that haunted them, were confounded by an era in which teenagers often disregarded traditional values. Elizabeth answered all with tenacity. Her home, she insisted, was patriarchal in that she deferred to her husband—after letting him know what she wanted.

In spite of her Christian ethics, she hated Harry Pitman and refused to believe that the disappearance of her son was anything but a plotted kidnapping. No man, she believed, could be weak enough to try to appease a neurotic wife who had stolen a child. Her hostility had been inflamed by Peter Gribbin.

Harpence was slow to approach the witness, letting seconds of silence pass before his first question. He was staging again, presenting Elizabeth for close scrutiny by the jury before uncurtaining the drama. When he spoke, his sympathetic tone was saccharine.

"Mrs. Baker, please tell the court, in your own words, about the disappearance of your child."

Elizabeth avoided looking at Harry. She wet her lips. "It was a warm day. Sunny. I had put my baby on the porch in his playpen."

Harry wished he were a tiny mole squeezing through his hole, the warm earth all around him.

"I kept checking on him," said the witness. "But all of a sudden he was gone." Her eyes moistened. "I felt panic. I just knew someone had taken him."

"Why do you say that?" Harpence asked.

"There were two broken slats in the pen, but they were still hanging there. And anyway, the space was so small. I don't believe Georgie squeezed out, crawled down the porch steps, all the way across the street, then across the grass to the river. And with no one seeing him. I just don't believe it."

At that moment a security man in a gray-blue uniform wheeled a white playpen down the center aisle of the courtroom. A murmur spread among the spectators.

"Your honor," said Harpence as he neared the bench and dramatically pointed to the playpen. "I ask that this be marked prosecution exhibit number one."

As the playpen was being tagged and recorded as an item of evidence, Harry's negative feelings about himself slipped him into memories of childhood: Dirty hands. Dirty clothes. Sometimes he'd come home dirty. But he always tried to be good. It never seemed right to be punished when he always tried to be good. Digging tunnels under the back porch. Catching pigeons with a box, a stick and a string. Collecting toadstools in the park. Filling sacks with earthworms. Sometimes he'd get dirty. But he meant to be good.

Harpence stooped near the playpen. His sharp tones cut into Harry's thoughts: "Slat number one is firm. Slat number two is loose at the bottom." He moved his fingers from one to the next. "Slat number three is loose at the bottom. Slat number four is firm." He pulled on it. "The distance between slats is just under four inches, which means that the distance between slat one and slat four is about one foot—a little more since each slat is about a half inch thick." The prosecutor walked toward the jury. "Georgie Baker was one year old. One year old! He would have had to push out those slats and squeeze through a foot-wide space. And let us not forget that his mother found all slats in place after the baby disappeared." Harpence spun and faced the witness. "What did you do, Mrs. Baker, when you found your baby missing?"

"I called my husband."

"And then what?"

"He found one of Georgie's bootees along the river. It was planted there. I'm sure of it."

"Son of a bitch, what is this?" muttered Kent within whisper range of Harry. He struggled to his feet, not wanting to object, but knowing he had little choice. "Your honor. This woman is a mother." His huge chest heaved with each breath. "She has the feelings of a mother, and we can appreciate that. She feels certain things could not have happened. But we're not interested in feelings, as sincere as they might be. So I must object."

Before Judge Long could respond, the witness turned angry eyes on Harry and shouted, "You stole my baby! You and your scheming wife took him right off my porch!"

The bearded Narkissian, the Pentecostal farmer and the big-boned brunette stared at Harry. An instant later the entire jury and most spectators locked eyes on the defendant. The judge hammered and called for order as the courtroom stirred with a rumble of voices.

Seconds later eyes were on Elizabeth as she stood and shouted: "You're a vicious, calculating man!" Her faced flushed. "Your wife couldn't have a baby, so you stole mine!"

Again the jurors and a host of spectators turned their eyes on Harry, who wanted to burrow more deeply than his imagination could take him.

Judge Long was firm yet gentle when he said, "You're out of order, Mrs. Baker. Do you need some time? Perhaps we should break."

Elizabeth fell to her seat and wept hysterically. Harpence tried to comfort her, and then George Baker hurried forward, took her hands in his and said, "Everything's going to be okay. We have Georgie. He's ours now. No matter what happens here, he's ours." At this point, Judge Long declared a short recess and walked to his chambers.

# Chapter Thirty-Five

The December snow had stopped by mid-afternoon, leaving only water on the streets and a scant white trim on trees and shrubs. The sky was gray and a north wind chilled Freddy as he trudged along the choppy waters of the Logan River, carrying his schoolbooks under his arm. His sneakers were soaked from wet snow that covered the soggy grass. The temperature was falling and would soon turn the street water into ice. The boy pulled down the peak of his cap and buttoned his blue-and-white jacket—his Pete's Fish Market baseball jacket. Freddy's Oakford clothes still meant more to him than anything the Bakers could buy him.

He stopped in front of the Baker house and stood there staring, having no desire to cross the street. Mrs. McNally would be there. He didn't like her any more than he liked his brothers, and refused to call her Aunt Vera. The tall, squeaky-mouthed woman with the pink wart under her left eye was Elizabeth Baker's sister, visiting to help keep house during the trial.

Freddy turned, gazed at the river, and thought of his house in Oakford. He ached with homesickness and longed for Harry.

Chuck Baker carried a dark green sack of books over his shoulder as he strolled along the sidewalk across the street. Two years older than Freddy, Chuck was in his first year of high school, was tall for his age, lean and fair-skinned. He had the red hair and long features of his mother.

Stopping in front of his house, Chuck stared across the street at Freddy, who still faced the river and was unaware of his brother.

Gnawing resentment had steadily increased within Chuck, mainly because Freddy had refused all overtures from his family. Now, it tightened his gut. Even the words on Freddy's jacket—Pete's Fish Market—irritated him. Maybe it was because Freddy had ignored the red-and-white jacket the Bakers had bought him. Or maybe it was because any part of Freddy had begun to annoy Chuck.

An impulse sent Chuck sauntering across Logan Drive toward Freddy. As he approached he called, "Whatcha doin' George?"

Freddy was startled from deep thoughts, spun around, glared harshly at his brother, and then declared, "My name is Fred."

"No it isn't," Chuck responded with cool resentment. "Your name's George."

"My name is Fred Pitman! It'll always be Fred Pitman!"

"Like hell!" Chuck sneered and cocked his head.

Freddy's frustration, already extreme before his brother's encroachment, was at the raging point. For the first time in his life he shouted the word he used only in secret, the word so often heard among his peers, the word carved into his beech tree. "Go fuck yourself!"

Chuck's face reddened, and despite Elizabeth's righteous training, he yelled, "You go fuck yourself!"

Muscles tensed in both boys, but Freddy was the first to shove. The bigger boy went sprawling on his buttocks, sliding in the slush and muddy grass, his legs and arms outstretched, his mouth and eyes open with shocked surprise. Chuck's bookbag landed 10 feet away, and Freddy's books scattered, his notebook falling open on the wet snow. Fists clenched and jaw rigid, Freddy spread his feet and locked his wet sneakers in the soggy earth. He punched the peak of his cap, sending the cap flying to the ground, and then looked down on his brother with fire in his eyes. Muddy, wet and hurt, Chuck scrambled awkwardly to his feet and lunged at his brother, huffing with rage. He threw punches wildly, as did Freddy. Neither was a skillful fighter. Blows landed here and there about their bodies while others missed. The boys grabbed each other and scuffled like awkward wrestlers, kicking up slush and mud as they tried to pull one another to the ground. Chuck rammed his knee into Freddy's groin, and the younger boy cried out in pain as he doubled over, giving Chuck a momentary advantage and a chance to pull his opponent to the slushy mud.

As they rolled and tangled, Freddy's fingernails scraped flesh from Chuck's neck, drawing three streaks of blood. Chuck was on top when he grabbed his brother's neck and squeezed. Freddy seized Chuck's wrist, and with a trembling grip, helped by an overflow of adrenaline, he lifted the bigger boy's arm and broke the hold. But seconds later, Chuck smashed a fist into his brother's nose, and blood poured over the younger boy's cheek and into his mouth.

Two doors north of the Bakers, bull-faced Rich Burkhart, broad-shouldered and bulging at the biceps, stood at his living room window in his undershirt watching the boys fight in the mud. "Hey Norma, you should see the Baker kids—Chuck and that new blond kid, the one who was kidnapped. They're going at it something fierce. Punching hell out of each other." The former football lineman grabbed his denim jacket from the newel, stepped outside, and stood watching from the porch.

Freddy dug his fingernails into Chuck's upper lip as he shoved his brother's chin forcefully with the heel of his palm. The severe neck-jerk caused Chuck to loosen his grip as Freddy rammed his knee into Chuck's belly.

Burkhart ran toward them as Mrs. McNally hurried from the Baker house. "You two stop that!" she yelled in a high-pitched squeak. "Stop it this instant!" She was right behind Burkhart as he neared the muddy, blood-splattered boys.

Breathless and grunting, Freddy was on top as Burkhart leaned over and grabbed him with both arms. He had a tight belly-hold on Freddy as he ripped him away from his brother. Both boys were trembling and heaving. Chuck rolled over and vomited.

# Chapter Thirty-Six

Kent had not intended to cross-examine Elizabeth Baker, but changed his mind after hearing her testimony. He approached her slowly, gave a smile of compassion for the jury to observe, and spoke softly.

"Mrs. Baker, please tell the court what kind of neighbors the Pitmans were during the years preceding you child's disappearance."

"In what way?" she asked.

Kent walked to the playpen, and with a touch of tempered drama turned it around so that its broken slats faced the jury. He bent his huge body in an attempt to lean over, changed his mind and tried to squat. Failing, he decided to lean slightly and stretch until he could touch the slats. "I mean, were they friendly? Did you get along with them?"

"They stayed pretty much to themselves. But they were nice. Once we got to know them—yes, I'd say they were good neighbors. That's what made this whole thing such a shock."

Kent pulled on the two broken slats to show that they were detached at the bottom. They swung out easily, dangling from split wood at the top. When he let go, they fell back into place. "And your husband and Harry Pitman? Were they friendly?"

"Yes."

The defense attorney again dislodged the slats and let them fall back into place. He was pleased that his demonstration had shown the free-swinging looseness of the slats, but was disappointed by the width of the space, fearing that the jurors might think it too small for the escape of a one-year-old baby. Feeling an urge to sway the slats one more time, he decided against it, concerned that they might break off altogether.

"Then honestly, Mrs. Baker..." Kent moved toward the witness. "... there was never any reason to suspect that these nice people would conspire against you. Isn't that right?"

"Well, I'll admit that outwardly it seemed that way, but..."

"Mrs. Baker," interrupted Kent, "how did you learn that your boy was living in Oakford?"

"Why, Mr. Gribbin told me."

"That's Peter Gribbin of the Examiner?"

"Yes."

"That's the newspaper reporter who conducted such an extensive investigation?" Aware of his sarcasm, Kent softened his tone as he asked, "How did you find out that Mrs. Pitman was in a mental hospital?"

Elizabeth glanced at the ceiling. "Why, I guess Mr. Gribbin told me."

"Again, it was Peter Gribbin?"

"Yes."

"I see."

Barbara Smedley muttered, "Humph," then stretched her neck in an effort to see Pete who was slouched in his seat on reporters' row.

Kent mused, tipped his head, and kept the court in suspense. Then, in his deepest voice, with directness and the skill of an orator, he asked, "Isn't it true, Mrs. Baker, that the only information you have on the lives of Harry and Ellen Baker, since they left Clarkton a dozen years ago, is from newspaper accounts and reporters such as Pete Gribbin?" He lifted his eyebrows. "Am I correct?"

"Not entirely."

"But to a large degree, right?" Kent intensified his stare. "Thank you, Mrs. Baker." He turned abruptly. "I have no further question for this witness." As he shuffled toward Harry, Harpence rose and announced that the prosecution was resting its case.

Judge Long looked at his watch as Elizabeth Baker stepped down uneasily from the stand. "If there are no more motions," he said, "the defense may proceed with its case. Mr. Kent, you may call your first witness."

Kent had his back to the judge and was leaning slightly, whispering to Harry. He turned and said, "Your honor, several questions have come up, and I need time for homework over the weekend before I proceed. If it pleases the court, I'd like an adjournment until Monday morning."

Again Judge Long glanced at his watch, then looked at Harpence. "If the prosecution has no objections, court is adjourned until 9 o'clock Monday morning." He hammered once with his gavel.

Still standing, Kent stretched and waved in an effort to beckon Barbara before she slipped away from the courtroom. She caught his signal and began to skirt the room, bucking traffic as she made her way forward. The attorney and his client whispered for several minutes before Barbara nudged the fat man with her elbow.

"Oh, Barbara." Kent maneuvered awkwardly to kiss her on the cheek. His peck fell short of its mark. "I want you to find me a one-year-old baby."

"You what?" she asked.

"Find me a one-year-old baby boy. Not chubby. On the thin side, but not obviously skinny."

"You're kidding, aren't you?"

"I'm dead serious. I know you have some babies down there at that clinic of yours. I want one—a boy. A baby boy. If we can prove that the Baker kid wasn't snatched from that pen—or at least show reasonable doubt that he was—I think we can kill the conspiracy theory."

# Chapter Thirty-Seven

Caesar Kent rose slowly and asked that Helen Molinski be recalled to the witness stand. The lanky, hook-nosed gossip was less assured this time, showing none of the cocky confidence that was so evident when Harpence had given her the spotlight. But she was dressed in polka-dots again—this time, yellow on black.

"Mrs. Molinski," began Kent, "you have a neighbor named Banner, is that correct?"

She answered with hesitance: "Yes."

"And did you not accuse Mr. Joseph Banner of having an affair with his neighbor's wife—a Mrs. Loretta Colp—an affair that later turned out to be no more than a meeting to plan a surprise party for Banner's wife? I must warn you, Mrs. Molinski, you're on the witness stand, testifying under oath."

The defense attorney was now at his best, allowing his voice to flow up and down in every pitch and tone imaginable. His inflections excited the curiosity of all. With intonation alone he knew how to fascinate and intrigue.

Outside, Barbara tightened her fur collar around her neck as she raced up the steps of the courthouse. Weekend winds had locked Clarkton in its first freeze of winter. The ground had hardened and puddles had turned to ice. The gray cover of clouds had lingered into this Monday morning. It now darkened the sky and released the last of its flurries to dance and whirl. Barbara slipped on an icy step. She caught herself, pulled open a heavy bronze door and hurried into the building. As before, she slid quietly into a rear seat in the courtroom.

"Your honor," protested Harpence as he leaped to his feet. "I don't see what bearing this has on the case."

"Your honor," said Kent, "I believe the character of the witness is important since the prosecution has used her to question the character of the defendant."

"You may proceed, Mr. Kent," ruled the judge.

Gribbin doodled on his note paper.

"Isn't it true that you told several women in the neighborhood that Joe Banner and Loretta Colp were meeting secretly and carrying on, what you called, 'an affair'?" Kent had obviously done his weekend homework.

"Objection, your honor," Harpence called out. "Heresay."

"I'm asking for a statement of fact, your honor," Kent said. "Did she say it or not? Did she tell these women that, or didn't she."

"I'll allow it," Judge Long said. "The witness will answer."

"Well, I thought they were." Her words were sharp and quick with anxious emotion. "If you had seen them, you would have thought so, too." She looked at the jury. "Anybody would have."

"Isn't it also true that you told Ida Tremmer and Hilda Mitchell that young Jane Colp had to marry the Mason boy because they were intimate night after night in the Colp's garage loft until he finally got her pregnant? A year has passed since the wedding, and it hasn't proven so, has it?"

"Well, they can fix those things, you know."

"And didn't you spread word that Mary Haskins feeds her children nothing but tripe and beans?"

"Well, it's true!"

"How many times have you eaten at the Haskins house?"

Begging to be rescued, Helen Molinski looked at Harpence with frantic distress distorting her expression.

"I object, your honor." The prosecutor was on his feet again, clearly irritated. "Mrs. Molinski is not on trial here."

"I have no further questions," Kent said. He looked at the jury for several seconds and smiled.

Except for cutting stares during his rebukes of the attorneys, Judge Long's expression had changed little since the start of the trial. He was a sober and thoughtful man who possessed a calculating mind, a discerning eye and a dour countenance. Even when reproving witnesses, he did so with modulation. But Helen Molinski's testimony changed that. In a rare slip from the norm, he looked at her with disdain as he quoted historian George Bancroft: "'Truth is not exciting enough to those who depend on the characters and lives of their neighbors for all their amusement.' The witness is excused."

Kent forced control over a moment of levity that shook his jelly-like flesh. He then asked that William Newman be called to the stand. The name alerted Gribbin simply because he had never heard it mentioned in connection with the case. He leaned toward Vince Mazzini, the little, olive-skinned reporter from the Associated Press, and asked, "Who the hell is William Newman?"

"Beats me." Mazzini shrugged his shoulders.

A pang stabbed Harry's heart as he saw Bill Newman for the first time since their college days. The tall, broad-shouldered blond was almost as sprightly and bright-eyed when he took the witness stand as he had been years before at the Sigma Pi Fraternity house. Bill had traded his red-and-white sweater for a business suit, but reflected the same polished image he had displayed years before as a Big-Man-on-Campus. He wore his years better than Harry, who would have recognized him on any street corner as State College's BMOC coed-charmer of days long gone.

Feeling besieged and trampled, Harry felt strangely exposed before Bill and found it a cruel prank of destiny that his classmate-of-old should see him strapped to the rack.

Harry recalled the Sigma Pi parties and the drinking games, the college pathways, Dr. Compton's history class, and the evening lamplights outside Ellen's dormitory. Some images—especially those of good days with Ellen—were painful as they flipped in and out of his memory. His eyes moistened.

Kent paraded his huge body across the front of the courtroom twice, rubbed his neck, frowned, and walked up to Newman. "Please tell the court, Mr. Newman, how you happen to know the defendant."

"We went to college together."

"And what do you do now?

"I'm a partner of Midwestern States Insurance."

"You've had a successful career so far, and I understand that you were successful on campus, too."

"I suppose you might say so."

"As a campus leader, you knew a great many students. And I understand that you knew Ellen Parker, who was later to become Mrs. Harry Pitman. Is that right?"

Newman kept his eyes on Kent. He had yet to look at Harry. "Yes, I knew Ellen."

"Please tell the court, in your own words, your impression of Ellen Parker during those college days."

"I found her fearful and self-conscious. She was easily embarrassed, and awkward in social relationships."

"How do you substantiate such judgments? In other words, Mr. Newman, can you give us specific instances."

"Well..." Newman reflected briefly. "I remember how she would flee from a party, suddenly, unexpectedly."

"You witnessed this?"

"Yes. She would tense up and disappear, pull out of a game or song, and run out of the place. She caused Harry a hell of a lot of grief and embarrassment. I used to wonder why he put up with it."

"Objection."

"Sustained."

"Mr. Newman, just give us factual observations," Kent instructed. "How did the defendant react to Ellen Parker's behavior?"

"He always defended her. He was very protective."

"You say he was protective and defensive?"

"He'd get upset, but the next thing you knew he was making excuses for her."

Kent walked toward the jury, allowing the witness time for thought.

"Another thing," Newman said. "She was always talking about babies. I'm not surprised at what happened." Bill glanced at Harry for the first time. Their eyes met briefly.

Kent spun around quickly for a 300-pound man. "What do you mean?"

"I'm not surprised that she took that baby."

"Objection!" Harpence was livid as he leaped. "Your honor, this is outrageous!" Calming himself, he said, "We're not interested in the opinions of this witness. Besides, it's already established that Ellen Pitman took the child. I suspect Mr. Kent is attempting to prove an impulsive snatch based on conjecture. I ask that this be disallowed."

"Sustained. Strike the last comment."

"I have no more questions." Kent was pleased and showed it as he waddled toward Harry. "Your witness."

Harpence hesitated, then asked, "Don't you agree that many students have self-conscious feelings?"

"But Ellen stood out," Newman asserted. "One time she ran right out of the middle of a circle game."

Harpence wasn't about to ask. He pulled on his ear, pinched his lip, and changed his line of questioning. "You've indicated that Harry Pitman was protective of Ellen Parker. Did he cater to her wishes?"

"He wouldn't help her kidnap a kid, if that's what your asking."

Opinion though it was, Kent had no desire to object. He couldn't contain his smile as he poked Harry with his elbow.

Harpence revealed his frustration by pulling on his ear again. "No more questions, your honor."

As Bill Newman walked from the stand, he took his second look at the defendant, only to find him staring at his hands, apparently in deep thought. What will these fingers be doing? Harry was thinking. What will they be touching? What will they be grasping? Prison bars? What happens to a kidnapper? What happens to a man who shelters a kidnapper? What happens to a man who lives with another man's son? Is he hated by felons and guards? Is he butchered like a child molester? Is he raped?

Such thoughts were usually those of nighttime—exaggerated thoughts that awakened him at ungodly hours before sunrise, disturbing thoughts that often prevented further sleep or tossed him into vexing restlessness.

His painful thinking didn't stop: What will become of Freddy? So keen and seeking. So full of life. Does he finish high school? Does he go to college? Or does he lose his joy? Turn inward? Run?

Rebel? Hate? Mix with wrongdoers?

"No, dear God," Harry muttered. "Surely the roots are too deep."

"What?" Kent asked.

"Nothing."

"I'd like to call Dr. Philip T. Nevins," Kent called out.

"Dr. Philip T. Nevins," the clerk repeated.

# Chapter Thirty-Eight

Freddy was in the woods, far above the bend in the Logan River. He had slipped out of the house at 7 a.m. while George was in the bathroom, Teddy and Chuck were awaiting their turns, and Elizabeth and Vera were colliding in the kitchen. It was unlike Freddy to dress warmly, but on this morning he wore two sweaters under a hooded windbreaker, last year's Christmas gift from Harry. Grim determination locked his jaw.

Having hiked for hours, he was well beyond the hickory trees and huckleberries of Harry's tales. Pushing the hood from his head, he hurried on with the kind of resolve that showed a set purpose, zigzagging around the tall oaks and tulip trees whose naked branches fanned the sky. Inside, he hurt beyond belief. His was a torment that gnawed at the core, giving no surcease.

Now and again he caught sight of the Logan's choppy waters, tossed by the stiffest winds of December. The clouds were in layers—dark, heavy fingers, puffs and streaks blowing at quick-speed under higher, brighter gray. The two-day break-up of the season's first storm was in its final stage—a cold, blustery blast that froze the topsoil. Despite the racing clouds, the winter-bare woodland was far brighter than the summer woods at noonday sun.

Freddy skidded as he leaped over fallen limbs and slipped as he stepped on icy rocks. Frosty dry leaves crunched under his sneakers as he hurried this way and that, avoiding ice-filled hollows.

Although angry with his body for getting tired, he stopped to rest and sat on the solid end of a fallen tree—the remains of a once sturdy maple, its guts now rotted, eaten by insects, gnawed by rodents. He cared little about the discomfort of the frosty wood that chilled and wet his jeans and buttocks. For a moment he toyed with the powdered guts of the decaying tree, letting the heavy dust filter through his fingers, and wondering why it had not frozen. He thought of Harry: Dad would know why. Dad would explain it to me.

Sucking in his lips, he tightened his mouth in an effort to prevent tears. He stood and kicked the rotting tree, hurting his toes, but caring little. The pain made him kick again and again. Physical punishment helped him mask the broader, deeper hurt—the heavy ache inside that made him punish his legs and kept him going. So he hurried on, moving faster than possible in summer when vines would thickly bind the heavy underbrush. He zipped open his windbreaker, for the freezing temperatures failed to keep the sweat from wetting his undershirt.

Far to the northeast, the woods thinned to young saplings fed upon by deer. Freddy stopped, his heart beating rapidly as he watched a doe dart into a thicket. How he wanted to turn to Harry—his father—and point to the deer as it bounded from one thicket to another. Again he drew in his lips, tightened his mouth, bit hard, and trampled on.

Tender trees soon gave way to open fields where last summer's growth stood tall and dry. Grass and weeds rustled and crackled as Freddy cut a path. A ruffed grouse drummed its wings and scampered out of Freddy's way as crows swooped overhead, then flew toward the frozen marshes.

Freddy reached the marshland by noon and found the ice too thin to hold him. He followed the shallow edges, sloshing through the ice and into the mush as he trudged on. The swamp was broken into patches of land, ice-covered water, clumps of tall reeds and dead waterweeds—a haven for ducks and geese. The sun broke through the racing clouds, flashing golden light on Freddy's wind-blown hair as he tramped among tossing tassels and plumes.

The boy fought his anger by shouting inside that he really didn't care: Who gives a fart! Everything's just one big, stupid, jerky pisspot!

Again he held back tears.

The clouds spread wide, and the bright sun warmed the ice, drawing a mist from the marshlands. Brightened by sunlight, patches of fog swirled around the tiny islands.

Freddy's feet caught in a tangle of underwater roots. He fell in the swamp, scraping and slashing himself on broken ice and sword-like reeds, and ripping the hood from his windbreaker. The jolt unlocked his jaw, separating his gritting teeth. It released tension, permitting him to cry. His face red, his cheeks quivering, he picked himself up, then threw himself over a clump of dry grass and sobbed openly.

Later he stood and tightened his muscles again. Roughly and angrily he wiped his tears on his jacket sleeve.

Within 20 minutes of hiking, he caught sight of a highway, elevated on a cinder roadbed that sloped 15 feet from shoulder to marsh. An occasional car or truck marked the horizon as it sped along the curving road. Freddy looked back, then moved on, his sneakers soaked, his feet wet and cold. He reached a strip of frozen earth and stubble that wound its way toward the road. Although his legs ached, he pushed them faster as he climbed the rough terrain.

Freddy used his hands and feet to crawl up the cinder slope, caring little that he scraped his flesh and dirtied his wet and soiled clothes. As he reached the shoulder, a green sedan sped by, followed by nothing—no cars, no trucks, only a single bird swooping overhead and flying into the sun. The boy stood on the edge of the highway, gulping air and heaving his chest. Minutes later he sat cross-legged on the edge of the cold macadam.

Soon a car was visible in the east, making its way toward Freddy around the long curving highway that divided the marshlands. As it neared, the boy stood and put out his thumb. It was nearly upon him before he saw its crooked bumper and bobbling hood, seemingly tied down with a giant rubber band. The 20-year-old Chevy skidded to a screeching halt after passing Freddy. Its dull blue, peeling paint gave way to rust and lead-colored patches here and there. Trinkets and clothing jammed its rear window.

"Get in kid!" yelled a wild-eyed, 25-year-old, grisly male who projected his head from the car as he opened the rear door on Freddy's side.

# Chapter Thirty-Nine

Harry had no negative feelings toward Dr. Nevins. In fact, he regarded the psychiatrist as a sensitive and intuitive man. Yet he felt guilt—the onus of blame—each time he saw the doctor. And this was as true today, with Nevins on the stand, as it had been during face-to-face discussions about Ellen. Now, the feeling tangled itself with images of Northampton State Hospital and his wife's staring into infinity. It emerged from a nagging feeling of fault—a sense that he had not done or said enough. In sessions with Nevins, Harry had talked of the white squirrel, broken zinnias, a sad-eyed puppy, and a host of Ellen's idiosyncrasies. But he had never told the whole truth about Freddie.

"Doctor, please state your employment," Kent directed.

Dr. Nevins was still the skinny, pasty, undernourished man that Harry first met and continued to envision in his dreams. "I'm supervising psychiatrist at Northampton State Hospital," the little man answered in a well-cultivated voice, so deep that it surprised the entire courtroom.

Please explain your relationship with Ellen Pitman." Saving energy, Kent stationed his enormous body in one spot, several feet from the witness.

"She's one of my patients, and a most interesting one. Ellen has repressed much of her life. I might describe her as a woman who has turned inward and pushed conscious thought into her subconscious."

"Dr. Nevins, please explain what might have caused such illness."

"In Ellen's case, I'd say traumatic events in her life, perhaps strong feelings of guilt. She was never stable. We know that. Perhaps that's why she reacted as she did."

"What do you mean?"

"By repressing, as I explained. She simply escaped from things she found painful."

Kent stepped closer to the witness. "Could this guilt have come from the fact that she kidnapped a child?"

"Possibly. Perhaps that's the key that finally locked the door. Time and time again we've found words or phrases that unlocked little portals in her brain. But the key to the big door might be the kidnapping. But we just can't tell her about it. We have to help her remember it. Only then will she accept it. And this can be a long process."

"Will Mrs. Pitman recover?"

"I can't answer that. But from my experience with other cases, I suspect that she may never fully recover."

Harry recalled that snowy day when he and Ellen and Freddy hunted a Christmas tree near the lake.

"She remembers some things?" Kent stepped back, still exerting little energy, saving it for later.

"Oh yes. Let me give you an example. We picked up on Felix, a name she sometimes calls out. It helped us understand her love for soft and cuddly things. Animals. Babies. Felix was a white squirrel—an albino—that Ellen mothered until it met a bloody death at the hands of neighborhood youngsters."

"Doctor, do you see any relationship between the death of this squirrel and the kidnapping?"

"Objection!"

"Your honor," said Kent, who began to shuffle and become more animated, "Dr. Nevins is an expert on functions of the human mind. His testimony about such a connection is appropriate."

"I'll overrule. Proceed with caution, Mr. Kent."

"Is such a connection possible?" Kent's massive chest heaved as he looked at the jury. Within seconds he aimed intense eyes at Nevins. Everyone in the courtroom seemed to sense the importance of the question.

"Ellen's trauma was severe. In my opinion, the killing of the white squirrel could have played a role in her taking the child. Frankly, I have a strong suspicion that, in her mind, Felix and the child are one and the same. The boy is the squirrel. The squirrel is the boy."

Kent had saved his energy for this moment. He strutted in a wide circle, huffed before the jury, and stepped toward Nevins. "As a result of your years of study of Mrs. Pitman..." He paused to add suspense and to pique the attention of the jurors. "This is a vital question, Dr. Nevins, and I hope your years of experience and psychiatric training, coupled with your keen understanding of Ellen Pitman's psychosis will enable you to answer." He paused again. "As a result of your extensive examination of Mrs. Pitman, do you believe that she could have conspired, alone or with her husband, to take the Baker child?"

"Objection!" Harpence called out. "Your honor, I object strenuously! This is way beyond the scope of any psychiatrist. The response of this witness could be nothing other than something plucked from thin air—some sort of guess, for God's sake!"

"Your honor, the jury can make its own judgment about Dr. Nevins and the scope of his knowledge. His expertise has been clearly spelled out."

"I'm going to allow some leeway here," said the judge. "Overruled. The witness may answer."

"My opinion is that Ellen Pitman would not—could not—conspire to do such a thing."

A murmur traveled through the courtroom, and Judge Long hammered for order.

"My studies of her personality lead me to but one conclusion," Nevins continued, "that she would do such a thing only on impulse. Again and again throughout her life she acted on impulse. It's a pattern. I cannot believe she would deviate from this pattern."

"I object!" Moving quickly, Harpence jabbed himself on the corner the table as he stood. "Your honor, this man is simply giving his opinion."

"Your honor," Kent said, "Let me repeat. Dr. Nevins is a highly qualified psychiatrist who has examined Mrs. Pitman for years. He is certainly more qualified than the prosecution's expert witness, who never even examined..."

"Enough! Enough!" Judge Long showed rare impatience. "Objection overruled. Calm yourself, Mr. Harpence. You too, Mr. Kent. The defense may continue."

"Thank you, your honor, but I have no further questions. My worthy opponent may cross-examine if he so wishes."

Harpence was still staring at Judge Long. He gathered his thoughts and then turned toward the witness. "You've never had two cases alike, have you doctor?"

"Not exactly alike."

"And sometimes you're surprised, right?"

"Cases differ, of course. But particular mental disorders reveal specific symptoms. Otherwise we could never diagnose. Naturally we are surprised now and then."

"So, the things you've said about Mrs. Pitman could be wrong?"

"Only a fool would be positive. But I'm confident that I know Ellen Pitman better than anyone. Even better than her husband."

Harpence parted his lips as if to continue, only to hesitate for a few seconds, and then step back. "No further questions."

Kent struggled to his feet. "Your honor, I'd like to recall Alice Gardner."

Harry's squatty, frog-eyed neighbor again stepped to the witness stand.

Judge Long looked at her. "You understand, Mrs. Garner, that you're still under oath?"

"Yes, sir."

"Mrs. Gardner, tell us a little about the Pitmans." Kent's use of Alice as a character witness was part of his all-out effort to soften the jury, a thrust he believed necessary for Harry's survival. "What kind of neighbors were they?"

"Well, believe me, Mr. Kent, they don't come any better than Harry Pitman. A good man, I'll tell you. I felt so sorry for him when his wife got sick. One day I watched her pull up flowers and toss them about the yard. One of the strangest things I ever saw."

"What do you know about the relationship between the defendant and the boy known as Freddy?"

"Finest father there ever was."

"Your honor." Harpence was on his feet again. I object to the use of the word 'father'. The defendant is not the boy's father."

"Your honor," said Kent, "the dictionary gives several definitions of the word 'father', including 'One who cares for as a father might'. Anyway, I'm certain the jury grasps Mrs. Gardner's meaning."

"Objection overruled."

Kent nodded to the witness. "Please go on."

"They did so many things together—like hiking and fishing, making gardens, and, oh, just all sorts of things. And the boy was so proud of his father. Proud as a peacock. He'd talk and talk about him. My dad did this, he'd say, and my dad did that."

"As far as you know, the boy was well educated?"

"They pushed him ahead in school. Up one grade, I think."

"Did you ever hear of the boy getting into any sort of trouble?"

"No, sir. Not as far as I know. Oh, he and Billy Allen got into my grape arbor once, but then so did every kid in the neighborhood."

Kent smiled at the witness, then turned slowly, allowing the jury to see his smile. "The witness is yours, Mr. Harpence."

The prosecutor smirked as he stepped toward the stand. Lifting his chin, he asked, "Do you consider yourself a nosy neighbor?"

"I beg your pardon!" protested the witness, her eyes bulging more than ever.

"You seem to know a lot about your neighbors."

"Our town is small. Most people know each other."

"What is your definition of a fine man, Mrs. Gardner. Do you consider a child-snatcher a fine man?"

"I object, your honor," Kent thundered. "The prosecutor is implying that the defendant is a kidnapper."

"Objection sustained," the judge ruled, his protruding ears flushing slightly. His stare was enough to warn Harpence, who retreated like a scolded puppy.

# Chapter Forty

Freddy ran along the shoulder of the highway, toward the rusty, battered Chevy. As he approached the car, the grisly 25-year-old stepped out and faced him, displaying long and matted hair, an unkempt beard, and a soiled denim jacket, unbuttoned to show his hairy chest. An oversized buckle—a scorpion cast in bronze—pinched his belt together below his navel.

Stopping abruptly, Freddy stood a few yards from the car, hesitant to go on.

"What the hell! You want a ride, or do y'like standin' there freezin' like a dumbass?"

Now Freddy was afraid not to follow through. Attempting to hide his timidity, he walked briskly toward the car.

"What's your handle, kid?"

"What?"

"Your name?"

"Fred."

"Okay, Fred. Now, me, I'm Scorpio. Y'get that? Scorpio." Laughing raucously, he motioned toward the car. "Come on. Get in."

Freddy jumped into the back and soon found himself between Scorpio and a swarthy, pimply faced 19-year-old male who was drinking beer from a can and dribbling it on his grimy T-shirt.

The car was stuffy and hot, despite the December cold, and it reeked of beer, whiskey and pot, among other things. It coughed and spit as it jerked its way back onto the concrete. The driver, wearing a grimy denim vest, gunned it again and again, then raced the motor and sent it roaring down the highway. He was a large, broad-faced 30-year-old with a shaved head, no neck, a gold earring, a butterfly tattoo on his left shoulder and a dirty blue garter around his upper right arm. His eyeglasses were highly reflective mirrors.

Next to the driver sat a skinny 21-year-old dirty blond with ragged bangs and a Fu Manchu mustache. His pale, sunken, naked chest was decked with a shark-tooth necklace. He had shed his denim jacket. It lay wrinkled and bunched at his feet, atop a case of beer. His knees high and wide, he drummed his thighs nervously with his fingers.

Freddy was uncomfortable, to say the least, and not only because of the four men. Sandwiched in the middle of the back seat, he was hot, still wet from the swamp, and sickened by the stench. He wished he had not worn the sweaters. With effort, he struggled out of his jacket and pushed it to the floor between his legs.

"Where y' headed, kid?" asked the driver.

"North, toward Hemlock Valley."

"We ain't goin' that far."

"Have a beer," offered the 19-year-old, bleary-eyed guzzler as he nudged Freddy.

"No thanks."

"Too early for y'? Fuck, man—we ain't been t' bed yet." He bellowed a pot-and-beer-heightened, repetitive guffaw.

The car sped along the highway for several miles before Scorpio yelled, "I gotta pee, man!"

The driver pulled to the side of the road at the next cluster of trees, and the four men burst from the car. Freddy followed. They lined up, Freddy among them, and wet the snow-flecked, dead underbrush. After shaking off his last drop, the pimply faced 19-year-old insisted, in a whiny and sluggish tongue, that it was his turn to "ride shotgun."

"No it ain't!" argued the scrawny front-rider.

"Yeah it is!"

"Like hell, man!"

"Fuck you!"

The hefty driver ended the dispute with a couple shoves, and the two men switched seats. Minutes later, the bushy-haired 19-year-old threw his first beer can at a cow, and Freddy learned the meaning of riding shotgun. The new shotgunner continued to toss cans at anything that moved, and sometimes things that didn't—like an occupied parked car and a dead opossum.

"What do you go for, kid?" asked the skinny, bare-chested 21-year-old who now rubbed shoulders with Freddy.

"What do you mean?"

"I mean, what do you like? What turns y'on?"

# Chapter Forty-One

Each time a friend or neighbor was called to the witness stand, Harry suffered a sinking feeling that made him squirm. When he heard Millie Barnes called, his spirits nose-dived, reaching deep remorse. For years she had filled a warm place in his heart. Now, from the defense table, he watched the farm-woman climb awkwardly into the stand and shift about to find comfort. She wore a homemade dress, a large gray-blue tent sewn especially for the trial. Although her cheeks were as rosy as usual, they failed to puff until after oath-taking when she glanced at Harry and permitted a quick and nervous smile that cut him more deeply.

Kent established Millie as Harry's housekeeper, cook and sitter, then asked her to describe the Pitman home. Tossing adjectives galore, she talked with zeal of "gorgeous" oil paintings, a "terrific" refrigerator, a "glowing" fireplace, a "beautiful" old wisteria vine, and a "humdinger" of a boy's room for Freddy.

"Please tell us about the relationship between the boy and Harry Pitman," said Kent, who again was in his calm but decisive mood, moving little.

Millie rattled on: "They worked together, making things with wood, or digging in the garden. Mr. Pitman taught the boy to grow things. Why, Freddy even learned to graft one kind of fruit tree on another. Fer a young'n, that boy was a hard worker. When he'd come out to the farm, he'd work in the barns till dark. And Mr. Pitman—he'd come out there, and the two of 'em would sit in the field an' talk an' talk. I'd go out lookin' for 'em, and they'd be talking about Vikings or Indians, or that fella who took elephants over the Alps."

Kent infused as much warmth into his expression as possible and stepped back from the witness. "Thank you, Miss Barnes." He glanced toward Harpence. "Your witness, counselor."

The prosecutor saw Millie's testimony as having no direct bearing on the case and, therefore, considered not cross-examining her. But he understood Kent's effort to build a warm image of the defendant, so he changed his mind and decided to damage that portrait.

"Tell me, Miss Barnes, with the defendant working, he didn't always have enough time for the boy, did he?"

"He'd bring him out to the farm."

"And you'd look after him?"

"Yes."

"How much education have you had, Miss Barnes?"

Millie shifted her large buttocks. "Only through sixth grade. But you learn a lot on a farm, believe you me."

"I'm sure that's true." He turned toward the jury as he said, "What you're really saying, Miss Barnes, is that the boy worked in your cattle barns because the defendant didn't have time for him. Isn't that right?"

Millie's face flushed. "Mister—whatever your name is—you couldn't find any father who'd spend more time..."

"Miss Barnes," Harpence interrupted as he stepped toward her. "Isn't it true that the boy shoveled cow manure and cleaned bull pens?"

"Only 'cause he wanted to."

"You're going to tell me that this 13-year-old boy liked to shovel excrement or feces or whatever you want to call it? He actually wanted to pitch bull dung? Come now, Miss Barnes."

"You don't understand."

"I think I do. Your honor, I have no further questions for this witness."

Kent was on his feet. "Your honor, I'd like to re-examine, if the court pleases." He shuffled toward the witness even before the judge's ruling, and then displayed his most compassionate smile.

Harry's mind was doing another run through memories—good memories that hurt. He recalled a breezy October day when the wind howled in the chimney. The porch creaked, calling him to the door where he found smiling Millie with a grinning jack-o'-lantern in one hand, a pumpkin pie in the other.

"The boy liked your farm, didn't he?" Kent asked.

Millie's cheeks puffed out with her first true smile of the day. "Oh, how he loved it, Mr. Kent. He loved the cows. Took special interest in carin' fer 'em. Bein' on the farm was like a vacation for the boy."

"We're talking about summer visits, right?"

"Just when Mr. Pitman didn't have vacation. When he did, the two of 'em would go off somewhere together, happy as a couple of larks."

"Thank you, Miss Barnes. I think we understand." Kent glanced at the jurors, but saw no sign of softening. "You may re-cross, if you wish, Mr. Harpence."

The prosecutor looked up. "I have nothing more."

Harry reacted little when his attorney asked that Dr. James W. Costigan be called to the witness stand. He did not recall the name. But he did recognize the square-jawed physician, despite 12 years of aging. A heavy crop of hair still covered Costigan's ears, but the gray had turned to white.

"Dr. Costigan, please identify yourself by profession and place of business," instructed Kent while pacing before the witness stand, carrying a pink and white document.

"I'm a urologist. My colleagues and I have offices at 312 Elm Avenue, here in Clarkton. We're known as Urology Associates of Logan County."

"Dr. Costigan, have you ever had the defendant, Harry Pitman, as a patient?" Kent pointed and fluttered the document toward Harry.

"Mr. Pitman came to my office once."

"When was that, doctor?"

"Twelve years ago. On an August morning. I checked my records. It was the same day that the Baker baby disappeared and the fire engines raced down my street. I won't forget that day."

"Why did he come to see you?" Kent stopped pacing and stared at the urologist.

"He was concerned about his fertility."

"Can you pinpoint the time of day that you saw him?"

"Yes, about noon. But my receptionist clocked him in at 10:25.

It was a busy day. My records show that Mr. Pitman didn't have an appointment."

"Let me get this straight." Kent swung his girth as quickly as possible and lined his belly with his nose. "Are you saying that the defendant waited an hour and a half before seeing you?"

"Yes, about that."

Harry recalled the sterile walls and vinyl chairs. He saw that tiny room. The bottle. The microscope. A few spermatozoa, moving slowly, this way and that.

"And how long did he consult with you?" Kent asked.

"Thirty to forty minutes."

"Then he left your office after twelve-thirty?"

"Yes. I'd say that's about right."

Gribbin slouched and doodled again. He was annoyed with himself for not having known of Harry's whereabouts at the time of the boy's disappearance.

Vince Mazzini, the AP reporter, nudged Pete and whispered, "No way did Pitman snatch that kid, not if he wanted a doctor to jazz up his juices. If I were out to grab a baby, I sure wouldn't be beating off in some doctor's office."

Pete sank a little lower.

"Thank you, doctor." Kent turned to Judge Long. "I have here official police records indicating the time that George Baker reported his son's disappearance. The telephone call was logged in by Sergeant Robert T. Matthews at 12:17 p.m., your honor, while Harry Pitman was with Dr. Costigan. I should add that Mr. Pitman had been in Dr. Costigan office for almost two hours by that time. Dr. Costigan's testimony leaves no doubt that my client was not near the Baker house or the Logan River at the time of the disappearance of the Baker baby." Kent evinced confidence as he attempted to strut toward Harry. "No further questions, your honor."

Judge Long checked his watch. "Your witness, Mr. Harpence."

"No questions, your honor."

Kent pulled on Harry's sleeve. "We're getting there. But we need just a little more to show the unlikelihood of your suggesting anything to Ellen, or conspiring with her. I don't want one member of that jury to think that you told her to grab the baby."

Judge Long took another look at his watch and adjourned for the day.

"I'm going to put Freddy on the stand after you," Kent whispered to Harry.

"No." Harry's alarm was obvious. He grabbed Kent by the lapel as they rose from their seats.

"I have to."

"No. Absolutely not. That kid's been through enough."

Kent struggled to keep his voice down. "Goddamnit, Harry, don't you realize that putting Freddy up there would be the greatest gift you could ever give him? Think about it. More than anything, he wants to help you. Tell me, what more could he give you?"

"No. It would hurt."

"Who? Him or you?"

"No. I don't want him up there."

"Don't be a shithead, Harry."

# Chapter Forty-Two

Harry was on the witness stand when Barbara arrived in the courtroom on Tuesday morning. As usual, she stretched her neck to see Pete and was surprised to find him next to Joe Noski.

Elizabeth Baker sat alone, stirring whispers about her husband's whereabouts.

Trying to contain himself, Harry spoke softly as he described Ellen's compulsive need to mother. But the sound of his own voice—seemingly detached from him—disrupted his thinking. He stammered now and again.

By the time testimony turned to the white squirrel, he had gained more control and raised his voice. "I can still see her hovering over the dead squirrel. I wish... I wish I could describe the look on her face."

"I object, your honor," Harpence said. "We've heard enough about this squirrel. It has little if anything to do with the case at hand."

"Your honor," Kent said. "The defense is attempting to show Ellen Pitman's frame of mind at the time the child was saved from the river and taken away."

"It has never been established that the baby was 'saved from the river'."

"I'll rephrase that, your honor. The defense is trying to show Mrs. Pitman's disposition at the time the child was taken."

Judge Long glanced from attorney to attorney. "You may continue, Mr. Pitman."

Harry proceeded to explain how the squirrel's death had led to two puppies—one stolen and returned, the other a surprise gift from him. "She loved Harvey. Bought him all sorts of gifts. She even made him a red coat for Christmas. But Harvey went blind and had to be put down. Ellen got strange. Really strange. She did all kinds of odd..." Harry lost his train of thought. He simply stared into the courtroom. The silence seemed unending. Judge Long was about to interject, when Harry said, "Anyway... Anyway, we hadn't been married that long. Five or six years, I guess. We had time to have a baby. Time, that's all we needed. I don't know why she didn't give me time."

Kent prodded him: "Why did you tell your wife to go off to the Oakford house?"

"She was upset. I thought she could think things out."

"How upset was she?"

"She was distraught. I couldn't talk to her."

"And why did you go to Dr. Costigan?"

"For the same reason. She was so upset. I wanted to find out if I was responsible for us not having a baby." Harry felt shame, but managed to look at the jurors. He seemed to ask them to understand. Speaking directly to them, he said, "I'm pretty much sterile, I guess."

Kent planted his massive self near the defendant, yet at an angle permitting the jury to see his and Harry's faces. "What happened after you left Dr. Costigan's office?"

"I saw the fire engines and emergency trucks, and all the people and commotion at the river. But I also saw that my car was gone."

"Your car?"

"Yes, my car. It was gone. That's why I went into the house. That's why I didn't stay at the river. I was worried. I was surprised Ellen had left."

"Even though you had told her to go?"

"Yes. I really didn't think she would. I telephoned her that night to see if she was okay."

"Did she tell you about the baby?"

"No. No, she didn't. I had no idea." Harry's voice seemed to shift into overdrive. "It wasn't until weeks later. When I went to Oakford. First I heard the baby cry, then saw him, and I got all sick inside." The images nearly panicked Harry. Tremors disrupted his words. "I yelled at Ellen, and I remember kicking this gift... this gift that I brought for her. My God, there was my wife with the one thing I couldn't give her—a baby."

Kent sought a way to calm Harry. He waited, then quietly asked, "Why didn't you return the baby?"

"I was going to. That very day I was going to. But she pled with me to wait until morning. The next day I was going to, and every day thereafter. And then it was too late. I guess I took the easy way. I was so afraid of losing everything—my wife, my job, my respect. I was wrong. But somehow I just didn't know how to take Freddy from her."

Harry wiped his brow. He was hot, yet his hands were cold and wet. No one could fully understand, he told himself. No one could feel what he felt. Unsure of what he had said, he was wounded by some of the words that kept swimming around in his head. He was certain that he had said the wrong things and made an emotional fool of himself.

Kent glanced at the jury. Narkissian's eyes were cold, his expression somber. The others seemed just as grim. All eyes were on the defendant, except those of the wispy-haired secretary. She looked down at her hands and picked at her cuticle.

"Please explain, as best you can, your relationship with the boy," Kent said.

"I grew to love him. I suppose I could have fought it. But when Ellen started to change, I grasped onto him. I guess I needed him. He became everything to me." Harry wanted to wipe his eyes, but couldn't bring himself to do it before the staring eyes of the court. He sat still. The courtroom was quiet.

Finally Harpence spoke: "Your honor, I don't understand the delay?"

Judge Long looked at the defense attorney. "Mr. Kent, have you completed your examination?"

Kent sighed to himself. He was uncertain. He was not pleased, but tried not to show it. "Your honor, I realize that it's not even noon yet, but I would like to appeal to the court's good nature and ask for an adjournment until tomorrow."

"For what reason?"

"There are certain things I want to look into before I continue."

"Can't these things be done after today's sessions?" Judge Long showed his rare annoyance.

"Frankly, your honor, I'm not certain whether to continue my examination of the defendant at this time. I need a chance to look into other matters before I make that decision."

Elizabeth Baker looked askance. But Harpence was pleased, not only because he saw Kent's uncertainty, but because a delay would enable him to review the morning's testimony before cross-examination of the defendant.

"Your honor," Harpence said, "if Mr. Kent needs more time, we have no objections."

"How much time do you need, Mr. Kent?" asked the judge.

# Chapter Forty-Three

Caesar Kent was a caged beast. He was a snorting hippopotamus, thumping from one wall to the other in his oak-paneled office—huffing, grunting, puffing after every belch. He had yet to sit behind his desk. And he had poor Miss Brett in a dither since his arrival at noon. The spoon-nosed brunette nervously tugged on her left ear. She had given up any hope of going to lunch. But her stomach growled more from jumpy nerves than from hunger.

Kent pushed his intercom button for the seventh time. "Try Barbara Smedley again, and tell her to get over here. We don't have much time. And get Joe Finny on the line. Right away."

"Yes, Mr. Kent. Oh, Mr. Kent—the man's here with the playpen."

"Have him bring it in." Kent took another pinch of snuff and pushed it under his lip.

Miss Brett led the way as a dark, curly-haired delivery boy tipped a playpen on its side and carried it into the office.

"Where do you want it," asked the 18-year-old.

"Goddamnit, I asked for a white playpen. This one's blue!"

The young man dropped the playpen near the massive desk, and just stood gaping at the blubbery attorney.

"It'll have to do," Kent mumbled. "Get your ass out of here."

Miss Brett waved the youth out of the office with three flutters of her hand.

"Get me a saw," Kent demanded.

"A saw, Mr. Kent?" Miss Brett wasn't sure where she would find a saw.

"A saw! Yes, a saw! Also a hammer, a screwdriver, two inch-long hinges and six screws."

"Yes, sir." She hurried toward the door, then turned. "Do you want these items first, or do you want me to call Miss Smedley or Mr. Finny?"

"That order will do just fine, Eleanor—one, two, three." He pushed the playpen with his foot, centering it in front of his desk.

"Yes, Mr. Kent." Under her breath she repeated: "A saw, a hammer, a screwdriver, two inch-long hinges and six screws." After a moment of quandary, she decided to call 7979, the Building Maintenance Office.

"And tell Humphrey to come in here," the attorney bellowed. "I can use his help." Humphrey was the janitor and handyman assigned to floors five, six, seven and eight.

"Yes, sir." She flitted away quickly.

Kent fumed his way toward his law books on the west wall, then toward the windows in the east wall. His thoughts raced: If Plan B works—no need to keep Harry on the stand. Maybe set him up for recall, just in case. Make arrangements for Freddy to testify. Right away. Then hope. The boy's testimony might soften that goddamn jury. Or it might burst the whole the fuckin' balloon.

Miss Brett buzzed.

"Yes?"

"Miss Smedley on line two."

"Barbara, where the hell are you?"

"I'm on my way. It took a little doing, but I have what you want."

"Well, get over here with it."

"But I couldn't get a blue-eyed blond. You'll have to settled for Baby Hernandez—dark hair, dark eyes."

"Hernandez! Christ almighty!"

"Best I could do."

"Well, hurry the hell up."

Kent circled his desk mumbling to himself, then bent his immense body and gripped a couple playpen slats with both hands. They were firm. He pondered the question: Go with Plan B first?—Baby

Hernandez? Or with Freddy? Both chancy. A gamble either way.

Barbara arrived to find Kent and Humphrey hovering over the playpen, putting finishing touches on the swinging slats. Humphrey, a slight, bent, 62-year-old Rumpelstiltskin in coveralls, was inserting the last screw as Kent turned to see Barbara holding a round-face Baby Hernandez. The year-old boy was bundled in a yellow snowsuit.

"Best you could do, huh?"

"He's just the right size, and his weight nearly fits your specification. We don't get many blond babies at the clinic." Barbara tossed a paper bag of toys, rattles and Pampers onto Kent's desk, then shifted the baby's weight from right to left arm. "Look at him. Isn't he cute?" The baby's hair was thick and straight, his eyes big, his cheeks puffy.

"Cute doesn't count as much as creating the right image in the minds of those jurors. I wanted it as close as possible. But we have to go with what we've got."

"You can have him for the afternoon. Mrs. Hernandez works. I had to hunt her down in the mill district. She's a nice woman. She trusts me. So, I'm going to stay with you." She kissed his cheek. "But you like my company, don't you, Caesar?"

"What the hell. I guess I'll have to put up with you." Kent struggled to bend. "Actually, I'll need you, sweetheart." He flipped the slats out, and they fell back into place. "Nice job, Humph. Thanks. Here." He slipped Humphrey a ten-dollar bill.

"Glad t' help, Mr. Kent. Thanks much." Humphrey looked as puzzled now as he did when he had entered the office. He took one last quizzical glance at the playpen, then hobbled away as Miss Brett buzzed.

"Yes, Eleanor?"

"I have Mr. Finny on line three."

"Hello, Joe. I have another fast order. A platform—like a Christmas tree platform, only heavier and higher. Wider than a baby's playpen. About thirty inches high. And four steps leading up to it. Like porch steps. Get what I mean?"

As Kent continued talking to Finny, Barbara kept moving about and bouncing Baby Hernandez. She wiped slobber from his chin.

The little boy responded with "Googybabagoo-ga."

"You don't think he'll react differently to blue than to white, do you?" Kent asked after hanging up the phone.

Barbara simply shook her head in disbelief as she took a close look at the playpen. "Hinges?"

"The two vertical slats in the Baker's pen aren't really broken at the top. They move because of a split in the top horizontal piece, swinging almost as if they were hinged. It's the best I could do at simulating."

Barbara lowered the baby into the playpen. He began to cry, so she picked him up and walked about the room, bouncing him again.

"Let's start," Kent said, sighing as if disturbed by the thought.

"You'll never do it in one afternoon." Barbara said while removing the baby's snowsuit. "You are a nice little fellow. Yes, you are." She placed him in the playpen, and he began to cry again.

Kent pulled a blue rattle from the bag and stared to shake it, but the baby kept crying while crawling on all-fours toward the slats. "Does this kid walk?"

"A little, but then he falls over. He even says a few words, like 'mama' and 'dada.' Here, give me that." Barbara took the rattle from Kent, held it in the playpen, and shook it with steady, quick jerks. The big-eyed baby stopped crying and watched the rattle.

"All right, now, outside," Kent said. "Hold the rattle outside the pen. Here, let me." The fat attorney grabbed the rattle and tried to squat, but lost his balance. He fell to his knees with a thud, but kept shaking the rattle. "Prop the kid up, damn it. Get him to lean on those hinged slats. Go on, Barb. He's got to learn he can get out."

"Let him explore on his own."

"Get more toys out of that bag."

"You know, Caesar, your big idea might not work."

"Oh, it'll work. It's got to work. We'll just keep at it until it does. If you think this is rough, wait'll we try to teach him to crawl down steps."

"You can't do it."

"We have to. We don't have a choice."

Barbara shook her head. "Come one, come all! Welcome to Caesar's loony farm. We train baby's to break out of pens and fall down steps!"

"Get serious!"

Barbara pulled a teddy bear from the bag.

"Grab a bunch of those toys," Kent demanded impatiently as the pain in his knees became unbearable. The attorney put his hands on the floor and assumed an all-four position like the baby. "Spread them around on the floor." He began to make funny faces, ridiculous distortions that were all the more grotesque on a big-headed hippopotamus. "What's the kid's name?"

"Just Baby. I wasn't kidding. They call him Baby. Baby Hernandez."

"Baby?"

"Baby."

"Here Baby. Come on Baby. Here Baby."

"Caesar, you're not calling a dog!"

Barbara held the teddy bear in one hand and a double-knobbed, pink-and-blue rattle in the other. Kent struggled to rise, but ended up sitting on the floor, his immense thighs spread wide. He shook the blue rattle frantically.

"Easy Caesar! You're scaring him."

It was mid-afternoon before Baby Hernandez left the playpen. Kent pushed him, and not too gently. "He fits, at least! See that? He fits?"

"You know, Caesar dear, this is a bit unreal. Even if you get him to push his way out of there, it's through conditioning. It's not natural."

"I just want to show that he fits. That's all. But he's got to do it on his own. I can't push or pull, or that goddamn, stupid-ass jury will think I'm squeezing him."

Baby Hernandez began to cry again.

"Oh, God, I guess I scared the poor kid," Kent bemoaned.

"No. I think he needs changing. Let me take care of that."

Kent maneuvered to his feet with the aid of his desk while Barbara lifted the crying baby and put him bottom-down on that same desk. She pulled a pack of Pampers and a roll of tissue from the bag.

Miss Brett buzzed.

"Yes?" responded Kent, who couldn't shake a kink out of his left knee.

"Mr. Harpence is on line one, and Mr. Finny is on line two."

"Ask Finny to hold, or tell him I'll call back." Looking at Barbara, Kent questioned, "What the hell does Harpence want?" He lifted the telephone and stepped away from Barbara.

"Caesar, we've got problems," said the prosecutor.

"What's up, Karl?"

"It's the Baker kid. He's missing."

Barbara could see alarm on Kent's face.

"Which of the Baker kids are you talking about?" Kent ask, even though he knew the answer.

"George—or Freddy—or whatever the hell his name is."

"You've got to be kidding." Kent could feel his case being sucked down the sewer.

"I'm not. They think he ran away. He's been gone since yesterday. They didn't call the cops until this morning."

"Yesterday? What the hell do you mean, yesterday?"

"He didn't come home from school yesterday afternoon. The Bakers didn't tell anybody. They were afraid it would mess up the trial in some way. I guess they thought they might lose the kid, or something. Anyway, George Baker went out looking on his own."

"What a fuckin' idiot. No wonder he wasn't in court this morning."

Seized by apprehension, Barbara stopped wiping Baby Hernandez's bare bottom and stared at Kent.

Chapter Forty-Four

# Baker Boy Missing Again, Police Suspect Runaway

## Pitman Testifies on 'Love' As Kidnap Trial Continues

### Police Find Hood On Marshland Ice

**By Peter Gribbin**

George Baker, Jr., also known as Frederick Pitman, key figure in the Pitman kidnapping trial, has disappeared for the second time in 12 years.

The 13-year-old boy never showed up Monday morning at Logan Valley Middle School, but was not discovered missing until late that day when he failed to return home. His disappearance was not reported to police until yesterday.

The Baker boy has been living with his natural parents, George and Elizabeth Baker of 707 Logan Drive, since a custody hearing following the arrest more than three months ago of Harry K. Pitman of Oakford for his alleged part in the kidnapping 12 years ago.

Young George, who prefers to be called Frederick, the name given to him by Pitman and his wife, Ellen, is believed to have walked through the Sweetmeadow Marshlands. The hood of his windbreaker was found by police on the icy edge of the swamp late yesterday.

Elizabeth Baker told police that her son had been distraught over his separation from Pitman, the man he calls his "father." Released on $100,000 bail, Pitman has been in seclusion and was unavailable for comment at press time.His attorney, Caesar Kent, told reporters today that his client is "seriously depressed."

In an unexpected development, the Bakers have appealed to Pitman to help find their son. "My wife Elizabeth and I have asked his attorney to urge Mr. Pitman to help us locate the boy," said Baker Sr. "We are well aware of Mr. Pitman's love for our son, and we know that he, better than anyone, might know where to look for the boy. Also, we believe young George would listen to Pitman—perhaps only to him." Judge Victor B. Long, the presiding judge in the case, must rule on Pitman's participation in the search.

The boy was wearing a blue windbreaker when he left home at about 7 a.m. Monday. Clarkton police have urged anyone seeing a blond, blue-eyed youngster, especially in the vicinity of the Route 17 Marshland Bypass, to report their sighting to any police department or the FBI. Westhampton Township Police and federal agents have been searching the Oakford area of Hemlock Valley, including the streams, caves and gorges around Lake Mohawk where the boy and Pitman often hiked and fished.

The disappearance of "Freddy," as he is often called by defense witnesses in the kidnap trial, came as Pitman was about to take the witness stand in his own defense. The scene in court yesterday was an emotional one as the defendant told of his love for the boy and the need that love filled in his life after his wife became "strange" and was finally committed to Northampton State Hospital, where she remains today.

Pitman's eyes moistened as he said, "...I grasped onto him... Soon he was everything to me." The strong bond between the defendant and "Freddy" has become increasingly apparent as the trial has proceeded.

Earlier, Pitman told of his visit to the office of Dr. James Costigan, Clarkton urologist, during the actual moments when his wife supposedly picked up "Freddy," then only a year old, and took him to Oakford. Obviously shaken, he stammered, "I'm pretty much sterile, I guess."

The defendant testified that he did not know his wife took the baby until weeks later when...

# Chapter Forty-Five

The disappearance of Freddy provoked more interest in the trial. Gribbin's story in the Examiner, Noski's front page piece in the Courier, and television, radio and national wire service coverage drew large crowds to the courthouse where reporters and cameramen clustered outside the building. Knowing the courtroom would be filled, Barbara arrived earlier than usual and was lucky to find a seat in the left-rear corner, thanks to a slender woman who made room by shoving the man next to her.

Harpence was at his peak of motion—gesturing and thrashing about, thrusting his arms, shaking his finger under Harry's nose. Up and down went his voice inflections, punctuating his movements.

"Holy shit, he's going to pop a blood vessel," mumbled Kent.

"You don't mean to tell me—to tell this court—to tell these intelligent jurors, that just like that—all of a sudden—you sent your wife off on a seventy-mile journey to Hemlock Valley— alone?" Harpence stared incredulously at the jury, then turned back to Harry. "And at that very moment a little baby miraculously hopped out of a playpen and dashed across the street, without getting hit by a car or being seen by anyone, and deposited a bootee on the river bank? And at the same time you just happen to be in a doctor's office?"

"I wouldn't put emphasis where you do. But, yes, I believe the baby did crawl away from its pen."

"You believe it! You believe it!"

"And I've never denied that my wife picked him up and took him away."

"Of course you wouldn't emphasize what I emphasize. Of course you wouldn't." Harpence lifted his chin and gave the jury a look at his profile. "You've admitted being nearly sterile. It seems to me that sterility might be motivation for stealing a child."

"Not when there are ways to correct infertility. Besides, I didn't know about my problem until I saw Dr. Costigan."

Kent was pleased, and he smiled inside. He liked his client's answers, even though he sensed that the defendant was blurting impulsively. There was little question in his mind that Harry's thoughts were on Freddy. The truth was, Harry's I-don't-care-what-happens-to-me attitude, worked to the defense's advantage. It was a stance that permitted Harry to freely retort with little fear of reprisal. At this juncture, his life meant nothing to him. Again and again he told God that he would gladly forfeit it for the boy's safe return. At the same time he damned destiny for putting him on the stand to be cross-examined at a time when tormenting images plagued him—images of Freddy alone somewhere, in trouble, cold, hurt, agonizing, misused.

Focusing on the witness, Harpence steadied his stare and said, "Strange that a man should find his wife harboring someone else's baby, yet do nothing about it. Don't you think?"

The words "someone else's baby" impelled Harry to flash his eyes on the Bakers' seats. Elizabeth wasn't there. Her husband sat alone. Harry's thoughts were momentarily deflected.

"Did you hear, me, Mr. Pitman?" Harpence asked.

"I told my story. I told it the best way I know how."

"The witness will answer the question," Judge Long directed.

"That's all right, your honor," Harpence said. "I'll withdraw the question." He pranced about in heavy thought and decided to bombard the defendant with a barrage of questions in an effort to unnerve him. "Did you see the baby that day?"

Harry was about to say no, but hesitated. "Yes—yes, I did."

"Oh, you did? How come you didn't tell the court?"

"I was never asked. I didn't think of it."

"You didn't think of it? You saw the baby the day he was

kidnapped, and you didn't think of it?"

"I was on my way to Dr. Costigan's. I remember glancing toward the Bakers' porch. The baby was in his playpen."

"What thoughts went through your mind then?"

"No thoughts. What do you mean?"

"You know very well what I mean."

Judge Long felt the tension and tightened his hold on his gavel.

"No particular thoughts entered my head."

"Come on, now, Mr. Pitman. Why don't you tell us the rest? And don't look at your counsel for help."

"I'm not!" shouted Harry. His exploding point was barely held in check by glances from the defense attorney.

Kent slapped his table, pushed up his body, grunted loudly, and charged, "Your honor, the prosecutor is harassing the witness. I strongly object."

Judge Long hammered twice and shot stares of warning at both attorneys. "In the interest of a fair trial I must ask that tempers be calmed."

Harpence took several deep breaths, then asked, "Is it true that you placed a telephone call to your wife on the day of the baby's disappearance?"

Harry pictured Freddy's wind-blown hair. He saw him walking on some lonely road.

"Mr. Pitman? That phone call?"

"Yes, I called my wife."

"Why?"

"To see if she arrived safely. Isn't that a normal thing to do?"

"Just answer the question." Harpence shook his head, feigning disbelief. "I have another theory, Mr. Pitman. Isn't it true that you had no interest in the rescue operations because you knew all along that the baby wasn't in the river? Isn't it true that you called your wife to check on the success of the kidnapping?"

"No! That's not true!"

Harpence spun quickly and headed for his seat. "I have no further questions."

Kent relaxed. "You did just fine," he whispered to Harry as the defendant took his seat. Rising slowly, he said, "Your honor, since my next witness was to have been the boy, George Baker, also know as Frederick Pitman, and since that boy is missing, I can do nothing else at this time but request postponement until, hopefully, we learn the whereabouts of that boy."

"Have you no other witnesses at this time?"

"No, your honor."

After the session, Barbara waited outside on the crowded steps for Pete. She was jostled again and again by spectators who pushed their way down while TV cameramen forced their way up. Minutes passed before Pete elbowed his way through the crowd and started down the steps.

"Pete!" she yelled. "Pete, wait!" She caught up with him quickly. "I liked your story."

"Really?"

"Yes. I took it as your mea culpa—your confession that I was right."

"Damn you! What a backhanded compliment."

Barbara slipped her arm around his. "Come on." She pulled him down the steps and away from the crowd. "Don't be a poor sport, now."

"You never gave me a chance. I would have written the story that way regardless of you or your feelings. I told you things would balance out as the pieces fell together."

"You can't give an inch, can you?" She kicked his foot, then presented a silly smirk as she kissed him on the cheek.

"I guess I'm dense as hell, but I'm not reading your signals."

"Tell you what. Why don't you call me tonight. Or better yet, come see me."

"Come see you?"

"The usual time. Late. After Daddy retires."

Pete's juices began to flow. He could barely tolerate the feelings as he tried to read the teasing grin on Barbara's face. Glancing at his watch, he damned the hours that stretched between now and then.

# Chapter Forty-Six

Barbara answered the door of the main portico only minutes before midnight and greeted Pete with a kiss on the lips—a long, moist kiss. She was dressed in black silk oriental pajamas—soft, flowing, and decorated with a red dragon over one breast. He held tightly. She could feel the passionate pumping of his blood. Offering no hello—in fact, no verbal greeting at all—he hurried her into the entrance hall, tossed his jacket onto the tile floor, and held her firmly again. Aroused even before his arrival, he was now lustfully out of control as he felt her breasts against his chest and tasted her neck, her lips, her ear lobe. He broke away and impatiently pulled her toward the stairs.

"No, we're going this way, Barbara said as she freed herself and began to walk toward her father's library.

"What?" His tone was desperate.

"We're going this way."

"No. No tea party, please. I don't need any clams or oysters."

Barbara didn't look back. She simply slipped away quickly, the black silk giving an illusion of her drifting off and vanishing. Pete stood at the foot of the stairs, gaping and trying to gather his wits—not an easy task considering his pumping libido.

"What the hell," he muttered before calling, "Barbara!" Letting but a few seconds escape, he took off after her, hurrying across the broad entrance hall.

"You can have Daddy's chair," Barbara said as Pete entered the library. "Go on. Sit."

"What is this?" Pete glanced about, but saw no food or drink.

"We're going to talk." She seated herself in a ladder back and faced her father's chair.

"Jesus, I don't believe this." Pete reluctantly slide into the big leather chair, slouching as much as possible. "You better not tell your old man about this. He'll burn the goddamn chair."

"Kent's great, isn't he?"

"Is that what you want to talk about? The trial? Yeah, he's doing all right."

"He's great. That's because of his bottled up energy. It just explodes."

"You mean because he's sexually frustrated? Hell, if that's what it takes to be great, I ought to be the greatest of all reporters. I should be a Pulitzer Prize winner, at least!"

"What do you know about the boy? Anything new?"

"So, that's what this is all about."

"Please."

"Well, I know they're taking Pitman to Oakford tomorrow."

"He wants to help. He's really hurting."

"There's a good chance they'll find the kid. Runaways are a dime a dozen. They find a lot of them."

"And many end up with their pictures on milk cartoons."

"You really care, don't you?"

"Don't you?"

"Yeah, I guess so." He looked into her imploring eyes. "Yes, of course I care."

After a lengthy pause, Barbara began, "Peter..."

"Yeah?"

"I really called you in here to ask you something about us. Something important."

"What?"

"Does your marriage proposal still hold?"

Pete was taken aback. He sat up straight. "You're kidding."

"No."

"Well, sure."

"That doesn't sound very convincing."

"No, no, no. I mean it. I'm just surprised."

"So?"

"So, what do you want? Do you want me to say it all over again? Are you accepting?"

"Maybe?"

"Oh my God, you're accepting?"

"Maybe I want you to say it all over again."

"Okay, okay. On my knees, is that what you want?"

"Just say it."

"Marry me."

"Why?"

"Why should you marry me?" Pete stood, scratched his head, and began to pace around the room. "I know what you are. You'll never give me peace. You'll be interfering with every story I write. You'll be fighting with lawyers, politicians, reporters and the system. You'll keep me up night after night telling me pathetic tales about people at your freakin' clinic. And I'll hear about every goddamn social problem plaguing the goddamn world. But I don't care. I want to marry you. We'll fight. It'll be chaos sometimes. But I don't give a hoot. I want you for what you are. You'll be you. I'll be me. And we'll have one hell of a marriage."

Barbara leaped at him when he made his next pass by her chair. She tossed her arms around him, kissed him, then took him by the arm and led him out of the library and up the stairs.

The sight of the plush furnishing in Barbara's bedroom had always been Pete's aphrodisiac. But he needed no turn-on tonight. "Don't bother," he said when she suggested her "misty blue negligee." As they pulled each other onto the canopied bed, he said, "Those Chinese jammies are doing just fine." He slipped his hands under the red dragon and toyed with her breasts as he looked into her eyes and said, "You're beautiful."

"Ah, how rare! A compliment from Pete Gribbin."

"Hey, I'm learning."

"You better mean it."

"I do, I do. Honest."

Pete flipped over and struggled to undress, yanking with impatience, and tossing his clothes this way and that. Rolling back, he held himself above her and gazed into her eyes.

"You're quite a hunk yourself," Barbara said. "Not like any of those pasty-white blue-bloods of my past."

He laughed and then nuzzled. He kissed her about the neck and ears before slowly removing her pajama top while caressing her torso, breasts and shoulders.

Later that night as they lay next to each other, depleted of energy, Barbara whispered, "Does your marriage proposal still hold?"

"Oh, God, I was hoping you had forgotten that."

"You what?" Barbara sprang up.

"Hell, I was desperate then. I wanted a little action. What the hell did you expect me to say?"

"You bastard, you!" She grabbed a pillow and hit him with it three times on the chest, once across the face, and once on his shriveled penis.

"Hey, cut that out!" He pulled the pillow from her and tossed it to the floor. Then he grasped both of her arms as she was about to pound him with her fists. He held tightly and laughed. "Of course I'll marry you. Hell, I couldn't live without you."

# Chapter Forty-Seven

Alice Gardner looked out her front window and saw a big, shiny, black sedan and a police car pull up in front of the Pitman's house. She shifted to get a better look through the hemlocks and laurels, then hurried onto her porch in time to see two men in dark suits and George Baker get out of the sedan. Seconds later, Harry Pitman and two uniformed officers stepped from the squad car. Alice dashed into the house to tell Wayne.

"Let me go alone," Harry said. "Please. I've got to go alone. It's the only way."

Agent Koop shook his head and took Harry by the elbow.

"Let him go alone," Baker insisted. "The boy is my son, and I say let him go alone. You don't really think he's going to run?"

Agent Johnson looked at Koop, who nodded and flicked his hand.

"Please stay here, all of you," Harry pled. He looked haggard, but edgy with anxiety.

The men watched as Harry walked along the south side of the house and ducked under low limbs. As he hurried through the backyard, only the garden rocks that Freddy had collected diverted his thoughts for an instant. He quickened his pace across the frozen, snow-flecked ground, hoping that he was right, pleading with God to make him right.

Harry pushed through the brittle thicket of dry grasses and weeds behind the garage, and then quick-stepped into the woods. Thinned of summer growth, the heavy stand of trees was open to patches of sunlight. Its pathways were wider and easier to navigate.

A thick bed of brown and rotted leaves lay frozen to the earth. Yet Harry could not see the tree hut because of pines and hemlocks. He crackled and snapped his way toward the old beech tree, suddenly wondering if the hut were there at all. He was upon it before he began to understand. What he saw almost made him cry with pride and heartache. The tree held what appeared to be a giant ball of evergreens. The entire hut was wrapped in a thick, bushy mass. Pliable hemlock boughs were intertwined with branches of pine that hung from the roof. Bushy sprays of spruce jutted from the woven mat to give the covering a rough and shaggy look. Even the bottom of the hut had been concealed by bending limbs to the trunk and knotting them.

"Hey, up there!" Harry called.

No answer. Harry knew that he must have been sighted long before he reached the tree. At least he must have been heard as he crunched over twigs and dry, frosted leaves.

"Freddy, it's me."

No reply.

"Please."

"I'm here." The boy's answer was soft and sad.

"May I come up?"

"Suppose so."

Harry tossed his topcoat and suitcoat over a low limb and shivered as he struggled to climb toward the hut. Awkward, weakened by events, he pulled and pushed with never-say-die effort that pulsated through his muscles and bulged his blood vessels. Gulping air, he struggled to find his way through the prickly evergreens. He scratched his face and poked an eye as he felt for the entrance. One last heave lifted him through the greens and into the hut.

"Some camouflage." Harry stayed crouched inside the entrance, waiting for his eyes to adjust to the darkness.

"Mainly to keep warm," answered Freddy, who wanted to grab Harry and hug him, but stayed huddled in a back corner.

The sound of the boy's voice gave Harry relief from the heaviest burden of his life. He didn't move as the image of Freddy gradually sharpened. Within a moment he saw sad eyes, a sullen expression, a hunched posture, a soiled and ripped windbreaker zipped to the neck, a shiver. Freddy was cold despite old newspapers from the garage, stuffed into every crack and corner of the hut. Windows had been closed with cardboard, and a paint-splattered tarpaulin covered the floor. An empty cracker box lay next to the boy.

"Are you okay?" Harry asked.

"Yeah."

"Freddy, you're not okay, and we both know it. I'm not okay either." Harry was almost afraid to reach out and take his son in his arms. Maybe because the desire was so strong. He waited.

"Who's with you?" the boy asked.

"Cops. I would have come alone if I could have. They wouldn't let me."

"I don't want to go back there. You can't make me."

"Freddy, you can't stay here. You're cold. You must be starving. What have you been eating?"

Freddy didn't answer.

"Crackers? Where did you get the crackers?" Harry was annoyed with himself for even asking.

No answer.

"How did you get here?"

"I hitchhiked. Some guys drove me most of the way. Then I got into this farmer's truck. I jumped out at Woodbine and followed the railroad tracks." The thoughts nearly traumatized Freddy as they had again and again since his living nightmare ended. He remembered Harry's warning about creeps who buggered young guys. Never would he tell everything that happened. He couldn't.

Suddenly Harry reached for Freddy and smothered him in his arms. The boy gave himself completely, squeezed with desperation, and cried with heavy sobs.

"I love you, Freddy. I love you so much."

"I love you, Dad. Please stay with me. I don't want to go back there."

"I need your help, Freddy. I really need it." Harry broke his tight hold, moved back, but kept his hands on Freddy's shoulders. His eyes pleaded. "You know I'm on trial. Mr. Kent, my lawyer—he says you can help me more than anyone. He wants you to testify in court. He wants you to tell about us—about you and me."

"But do I have to live with the Bakers?"

Harry sat next to Freddy and put his arm around him. "They're your real parents. You know that. They love you. And besides, I just can't get by unless I know you're safe somewhere. You see, I'll probably have to go away—maybe for a long time."

"You mean prison?"

"Maybe. And I'll have to know where you are. I'll have to know you're safe with someone who loves you. Otherwise you'll put me through the worst kind of hell a man could suffer. I just couldn't go on. I love you too much."

Freddy sniffled. Harry pulled a handkerchief from his pocket and wiped the boy's nose.

"You'll be a man someday," Harry said. "Gosh, you're almost that now. You'll be fourteen in a couple months. Another few years and you'll be on your own. And we'll see each other sometimes. You just wait and see."

Harry could feel Freddy's tears.

"I'm just thankful I've been privileged to know you," Harry said. He was glad the hut was dark, because he could feel his eyes well. "Through a crazy trick of fate we were brought together. And it's been great, huh? Just think of all the wonderful things we have to remember." He put his wet cheek against Freddy's wet cheek as he held the boy tightly. "It was wrong the way it happened, and it hurt other people. But damn, I'm so glad I had a chance to get to know you. You're the greatest thing that ever happened to me. You're a fine, courageous young man. And you'll grow to be a strong and good person. I know. I just know it."

"I'll testify for you, Dad."

# Chapter Forty-Eight

Kent wanted the jurors to feel that an attack on the "father" was an attack on the "son." Empathy was the key. His intent? Make them live Freddy's love for Harry.

The handsome, blond, blue-eyed boy was dressed in a blue suit and tie and a pale yellow shirt—shades selected to bring out the youngster's natural colors. His hair was meticulously combed and parted. It glistened under the courtroom lights.

All eyes were on Freddy as Kent allowed him to talk on and on about his life in Oakford, about fishing and hiking, sandlot baseball, his tree hut, Billy Allen, his rock garden, and Harry, Harry, Harry and Harry—his dad.

"I want to stay with him, but he told me I can't. If I can't, then at least I don't want anything to happen to him."

"Your honor," Harpence protested. "This isn't testimony. It's a deliberate, well-planned emotional scene to gain sympathy." The prosecutor stepped toward the judge, then looked at Freddy. "This boy has been through a lot. He's a nice young man, and we all feel for him." Again Harpence focused on Judge Long. "But he's obviously been coached by the defense attorney."

"Your honor, the boy has not been coached," Kent said. "Mr. Harpence will have his chance to cross-examine. Since this court will establish more than guilt or innocence, I think an understanding of the boy's feelings are in order."

"Are you objecting, Mr. Harpence?" the judge asked.

"Yes, I object. The questions and answers are irrelevant."

"Overruled."

Kent tried to read the faces of the jurors. He thought he saw a touch of compassion in the eyes of the two secretaries, the big-boned brunette, and the shoemaker. Turning to Freddy, he asked, "Was the defendant—this man you call your father—was he honest about where you came from?"

"Objection. The defense attorney is asking the boy to judge falsehoods from truths."

"I'll rephrase, your honor. Freddy, did the defendant, Harry Pitman, tell you where you came from?" Kent knew the question was a gamble, since he hadn't had sufficient time to explore the point thoroughly before putting the boy on the witness stand.

"We talked about it a little. But I knew some things anyway."

Harry was tense. He kept his eyes on Freddy as he had from the start. A sense of pride mixed with his pain.

"Freddy, do you think you could explain what you mean by 'things'?"

"I knew that I was found by my mother."

"By mother you mean your father's... Excuse me, the defendant's wife, Ellen Pitman. Right?"

George Baker put his arm around Elizabeth and gently tapped her shoulder.

"She's in the hospital. She wanted to believe I was really her son. Sometimes Mom and Dad would talk about it, and I'd listen from upstairs. Dad would get upset because of what she did, but he didn't want to make her sicker."

Kent could not have been more pleased. He decided to probe more. "And what did Harry Pitman—your father—what did he tell you?"

Baker lowered his eyes and tightened his hold on his wife.

"That she found me and took me. That it was wrong, but he didn't want to make her sicker." Freddy's voice quivered slightly, but he sat upright, kept his eyes on Kent, and spoke with pure, youthful sincerity.

Kent struggled to contain the pleasure that bubbled inside of him. He was well aware that the forthright words of innocent youth had given substance to Harry's testimony. "No more questions, your honor." Scanning the jury, he caught the shoemaker smiling at Freddy. Even Narkissian had softened his look.

Harpence was slow to approach the witness, and even slower to ask his first question. "Young man, you understand right from wrong, don't you?"

"Yes sir." The boy second-guessed Harpence. "My dad knows it was wrong for my mother to take me away from the Bakers. He told me it was wrong. But he loved me so much he couldn't take me back."

"Tell me..."

Freddy interrupted: "And he told me I should go back and live with them."

Harry could not hold back his tears.

"Tell me, Georgie, were you told how..."

"My name's not Georgie. It's Fred Pitman."

Harpence was taken aback. He pinched his lip, then began again. "Young man, were you instructed on how to behave on the witness stand."

"What do you mean?"

"That big man over there—Mr. Kent—didn't he tell you what to say?"

"He told me to tell the truth."

Harpence was stopped, and his expression showed it. He stood still for a moment, then turned from the witness. Not until he reached his seat did he quietly say, "No more questions."

Freddy made a move toward the defendant as a court attendant, a dark-haired woman in blue, escorted him from the witness stand. Harry shook his head emphatically, and the boy snapped forward and walked from the courtroom, yearning to know if he had said the right things and fearing that he would not see his father again—a fear that Harry sensed.

After Judge Long asked Kent if he had more witnesses, the defense attorney requested permission to use the playpen and other props for a demonstration. The judge asked both attorneys to approach the bench. After a lengthy discussion, Harpence objected.

"Overruled. Proceed, Mr. Kent."

As Freddy was taken from the courtroom, Kent moved his

massive frame into the aisle, looked toward the rear, and signaled dramatically by waving both hands high in the air. Whatever was about to happen, he wanted everyone to know. Head up and belly bulging, he strutted with exaggerated gestures—the kind of theatrics he relished—to the left of the judge where he seized the prosecution's exhibit number one, the playpen, and lifted it high.

"Mr. Kent, we don't need the dramatics," the judge said. "I'm warning you. Watch yourself."

In the rear, the courtroom doors swung open and in came two men in carpenter's overalls. All eyes were on them as they carried a 10-by-10 foot platform, lifted it above the heads of the spectators, and paraded down the aisle. Painted gray, the platform appeared to be a section of a porch, with steps at one side, and even a short strip of railing. It was as if someone had actually cut out a square piece of front porch.

Following a few feet behind the platform was Barbara Smedley, carrying Baby Hernandez in her arms. Pete Gribbin's eyes bulged, his mouth fell open, and he dropped his wad of paper. Seconds later he smiled to himself. In fact, he could hardly hold back a laugh. She'll never change, he thought.

The platform was positioned on the floor in front of the judge. Kent placed the playpen on it, with the broken slats facing the steps and the jury. Judge Long leaned forward and tipped his beak to take a look as a murmur in the courtroom grew to a noisy surge of voices. He hammered loud and long with his gavel.

Barbara stood in the aisle, bouncing Baby Hernandez.

"You said playpen and props, Mr. Kent." Judge Long said. "Is the baby a prop?"

"I guess you could say that, your honor." Kent approached the bench, yet spoke loud enough for the jury to hear. "I intend to demonstrate that a baby of the same age and size as the Baker boy—at the time of his disappearance—can easily escape from this playpen."

"Your honor." Harpence rose, again jabbing himself on the table in his haste. "Your honor," he repeated, "I must object again. This... this kind of staging... this, this, this theatrical farce... it makes a mockery of the court!"

"I'm simply trying to show that a year-old child can fit through that hole," Kent said with little emotion. "May I proceed, your honor?"

Judge Long stared at Kent, putting him on notice. "You may."

As he sat, Harpence tossed his hands in disgust.

Kent nodded to Barbara, who then leaned over the platform and lowered the baby into the playpen. She stepped aside as Kent began to waddle backwards toward the jury, keeping his eyes on the baby, who sat in the center of the pen, smiling and uttering gibberish. Suddenly the corpulent attorney flapped his arms and clucked like a chicken.

Gribbin found the sight so amusing that he couldn't control his laughter. He put his hands over his mouth as his face flushed, and struggled to contain himself. His entire body shook and his eyes teared. Vince Mazzini, the AP reporter, poked him in the ribs, while Noski kicked him in the leg. When Pete started to gasp for breath, Noski pounded him of the back until he began to recover.

Tension mounted in Barbara as she watched the baby. She feared the worst. "Come on now," she mumbled to herself. "Please. Do it, boy, do it."

Baby Hernandez smiled broadly, crawled to the broken slats, pushed them, and continued right out onto the "porch." He started down the steps head first, then suddenly tumbled and fell to the floor with a thud. Gasps and murmurs rippled through the courtroom. The baby's wailing cries resounded, and Kent immediately went into high gear, flapping his "wings" faster and clucking louder. The little boy stopped crying, picked himself up, smiled, and crawled across the floor toward Kent, who waddled backward all the way to the jury box. Baby Hernandez didn't stop until he tugged on Kent's trouser leg.

The courtroom was in an uproar. Judge Long hammered for order as Harpence leaped to his feet. Barbara rushed to Baby Hernandez and lifted him into her arms.

"I'll have to clear the courtroom if we can't have order," the judge shouted.

"Your honor, obviously this baby was trained," Harpence protested as frustration twitch his facial muscles.

"Your honor," Kent said. "I don't deny practicing with the baby. I simply wanted to show that he fits through that hole."

# Chapter Forty-Nine

We have shown, without question, that the defendant was not near the Baker boy at the time of the child's disappearance," said Caesar Kent as he began his closing argument. He paced before the jurors, looking at them one by one. "Harry Pitman was at a doctor's office trying to find out if he were to blame for his childless marriage, hoping that something could be done to give a son or daughter to the woman he loved." Kent was at his peak of eloquence. "The defendant didn't even know of his infertility at that time, but was awaiting the doctor's verdict. He had no reason to kidnap a baby."

Kent gave the jurors time for thought. He leaned against the railing and mused, then began anew, using his eyes to strengthen his words.

"Ellen Parker Pitman was a sensitive woman who craved love and protection, and the defendant loved her all the more because she needed him. He loved her so much that he overlooked her weaknesses from the very start."

Kent moved his eyes from Martucci, the old shoemaker, to Wilcox, the Pentecostal farmer, to Rebecca Greenberg, the salesgirl. "There's no question that Ellen Pitman took the baby on impulse. We can't feel as she felt. We don't know how strong, how tragically compelling her kind of mother love was, because she was sick with it. When she picked up that baby boy, saving him—saving his life—saving him from the rushing waters of the Logan River, and then held him to her breasts, she was blinded by all but the desire for that baby. Kidnapping wasn't a thought here."

Again George Baker put his arm around his wife to comfort her.

Kent paced, then looked directly into the eyes of Narkissian. "Try to understand what it was like for Harry Pitman when he arrived in Oakford and found this baby with his wife." The defense attorney moved his big body again, fixing his eyes on Dumpty. "Realize that he had just learned that he was almost sterile." Back to Narkissian with a hard stare. "Think of the terrifying reactions he had seen in his wife when Felix, the white squirrel, was brutally killed." Again he moved his eyes from juror to juror, aiming them at the big-boned brunette when he said, "He didn't know how to take this beautiful child from her—this beautiful blond boy, who Dr. Nevins sees as the second coming of the white squirrel, a reincarnation in the form of a perfect and handsome human being that was the dream of Ellen Pitman's life.

"We have shown without question that Harry Pitman was an exceptional father." Kent moved along the railing of the jury box. "He educated the boy, taught him a love of nature and a zest for life, helped him to understand the strengths and frailties of the human species. The prosecutor will tell you that this should have nothing to do with the case, that you are here solely to determine guilt or innocence. But is life ever like that? Don't we use good to balance the bad? How can we dismiss the years of Harry Pitman's good deeds? How can we dismiss his efforts to mold the handsome young man you saw on the witness stand this morning?" Kent moved his eyes from Watusi to the Kabuki secretary. "What you saw and heard tells the real truth about this man."

Moving toward his windup, Kent paused for dramatic effect, leaned on the railing, and again stared at juror after juror. Having toyed with their emotions, he was ready for his final assault on their heartstrings.

"As the defendant's wife became sicker and sicker and sicker, what did Harry Pitman have but the boy he loved? So he did a most human thing. He held more tightly."

Kent loosened his necktie and collar, shuffled up and down before the jurors, then turned his back to them and stepped away. Seconds later he spun around as suddenly as he could. He stared at the 12 men and women with a beseeching look on his face, and called out, "Don't destroy this man!"

He had set the stage for his final appeal—something he hoped would haunt the jurors as they deliberated. Gathering all the intensity he could muster, and adding just a touch of quiver, he spoke with emotion and force: "Remember, what you do to the father, you do to the son. Every blow you strike against this man will land harder on the boy. You saw the love. You felt it in your hearts. In making your decision, weigh carefully its effect on that innocent 13-year-old boy. Don't crush him. Don't destroy his hopes and prayers, his very life."

"I don't believe this," Harpence mumbled. "The final act of the fatman's goddamn sideshow. What a disgrace."

Kent let his hands fall to his sides, stood silently, and looked into the faces of the jury. He allowed seconds to pass before turning and walking slowly toward Harry.

Harpence shuffled some papers and took time adjusting his thoughts. He had prepared well, but shifted ideas after hearing Kent's appeal. He was somewhat rattled by his own aggravation as he began his summation.

"Harry Pitman is guilty whether he was an accomplice from the start, or whether he protected and harbored the guilty. Therefore, guilty is the only verdict you can reach. Mr. Kent has put up a smoke screen. He's tried to cloud the issue, hoping for a mercy plea."

Harpence struck one of his poses—chin high, a frown of deep thought. "The defense must think you are very gullible indeed. How strange, how weird the tales we are told." He looked at Narkissian, but kept moving. "Ellen Pitman is sent off alone because her actions are erratic. It seems to me that's exactly when you would not send a woman off alone. And then the defendant is terribly shocked to find his wife with the Baker baby. But he doesn't do anything about it. Months go by. Years go by." The prosecutor threw his hands up in a gesture of disbelief.

"Ladies and gentlemen, I think the facts are clear. A man and a woman couldn't have a child of their own, so they took someone else's. It's as simple as that. Fancy talk by my worthy opponent can't change that." Harpence stopped moving and looked at the foreman again. "It really doesn't matter whether the baby was taken from the porch or the river bank, so Mr. Kent's stunt with the playpen was a dramatic bit of nothing. The defense attorney has appealed to your emotions because he has no case. But we must rule by laws, not by our hearts alone. How many more criminals would be roaming our streets if we succumbed to every sad story, to every case presented in a sympathetic way by a skilled lawyer?"

Pacing and gesturing again, Harpence sharpened his tongue: "You heard the words of Elizabeth Baker, the boy's real mother. You saw her grief. This woman—this mother—she sensed the truth from the very start. She had the instincts and intuition of a mother. She knew."

Kent scoffed. "And he talks about my theatrics."

"But let me make something very clear," said Harpence as he prepared to emphasize his backup argument. "The defendant is just as guilty if he participated by harboring, protecting, failing to report this heinous crime. I'm sure Judge Long will explain the precedents established in the case of Manning versus the State of Ohio in August, 1919." The prosecutor glanced from face to face. "You're intelligent men and women. Don't be taken in by melodramatic stunts and emotional appeals." He paused, deliberately counting the seconds. "Again, I say, there's only one verdict. And that's guilty."

## Chapter Fifty

# Pitman Guilty in Kidnap Case
## Stolen Baker Youngster Calls Defendant 'Father'
### Emotional Session Leads to Mercy Plea

**By Peter Gribbin**

Harry K. Pitman was found guilty here today for his part in the kidnapping, 12 years ago, of George Baker Jr., who disappeared at the age of one from the playpen on the porch of his parents' home on Logan Drive.

The trial, one of the most publicized in Clarkton history, came to an end this afternoon when the jury of six men and six women asked clemency for the 43-year-old advertising artist, whose wife remains ill in Northampton State Hospital.

Today's testimony and verdict climaxed an investigation and trial sparked by this newspaper when the Baker boy was found living with Pitman in the Hemlock Valley hamlet of Oakford. Judge Victor B. Long, the presiding judge in the case, is expected to pronounce sentence tomorrow.

The defendant lowered his eyes as the verdict was read. George and Elizabeth Baker, parents of the kidnapped boy, embraced each other. Later, they expressed relief to reporters that the trial was over.

The decision was announced only hours after the kidnap victim, also know as Frederick Pitman, looked out over the crowded courtroom and claimed Harry Pitman as his father. He knew he was not born of the defendant, but to him this was not a prerequisite for fatherhood. The man who had reared him, taught him, sent him to school, fished and hiked with him and loved him was his father. "I want to stay with him," cried the youngster.

The courtroom remained hushed as the boy walked from the witness stand, tears streaming from his eyes. Jurors and spectators alike were well aware that he was being separated from the father he loved.

The jury foreman, Shant Narkissian, began reading the verdict and clemency appeal at 2:45 p.m., right after the jury filed back into the courtroom following only two hours of deliberation. Clemency was asked on three grounds: (1) "Because we believe the defendant did not actually take the child." (2) "Because we believe the distressed nature of the defendant's wife impeded his return of the child." (3) "Because we believe the manner in which the defendant reared the boy was commendable."

The jury's clemency appeal gave credence to the growing feeling among court observers that the kidnapped boy, now 13 years old, was in every way but birth the son of Harry Pitman.

"Pitman's actions cannot be condoned," said Narkissian after the trial. "But at least now we can understand them."

Caesar Kent, defense attorney, said he was pleased despite the guilty verdict, but would withhold further comment until after sentencing by Judge Long. Karl Harpence, prosecuting attorney, said he expected the guilty verdict since it was "the only possible outcome."

The scene in the courtroom was emotional from start to finish today. After the boy revealed that he had long known that Pitman's wife had "found me and took me," the defense placed a year-old baby into a playpen and turned the courtroom drama into an uproar as...

# Epilogue

Harry Pitman was sentenced to nine years in the state prison at Hollingsdale.

He was released on parole in five years, and on a snowy day in December walked through the prison gates.

Waiting outside the stone walls was a handsome, 18-year-old freshman from Colgate University. His name was Fred Pitman.